GOLDHORN

A DYSTOPIAN NOVEL

S.A. BROWN

Author: S.A. Brown
www.sabrown.net

ISBN 9798533295192 (Paperback)

For Mum and Dad

Goldhorn [definition]: A financial term for a company valued at $500 trillion. It was coined in the year 2056, when the West's seven major technological companies merged to form a conglomerate, called Sunnyvale.

The term comes from the name of a mythical creature, following from the fact that the first $1 billion private companies were called 'unicorns'.

'Our own information, from the everyday to the deeply personal, is being weaponized against us with military efficiency... These scraps of data, each one harmless enough on its own, are carefully assembled, synthesized, traded and sold. Taken to its extreme, this process creates an enduring digital profile and lets companies know you better than you may know yourself... We shouldn't sugarcoat the consequences. This is surveillance.'
Tim Cook (CEO of Apple)

'When a society or a civilization perishes, one condition may always be found. They forgot where they came from. They lost sight of what brought them along.'
Carl Sandburg

'The silicon chip will transform everything, except everything that matters, and the rest will still be up to us.'
Bernard Levin

Part One

1

Guy Smith was ninety years old. He was sat in the corner of a spotless coffee shop – so clean, white and sterile that it resembled a hospital waiting room – sipping an iced tea. It was solely machine-made: as soon as he entered through the glass-panelled door, the shop's sensors connected with the miniscule microchip in the rim of his spectacles and automatically began preparing his favourite drink.

A simple verbal command would have overridden the process and allowed him to select a different beverage – there were a great deal to choose from – but he was becoming passive in his old age. It was ready and waiting in twenty-eight seconds, in a logoed biodegradable cup, and exactly seventy-two Sunnyvale points (SVPs) were deducted from his account (with a surcharge included).

Long ago, he had logged into his account to try to remove the automatic surcharge on all purchases, but it had resulted in a penalty of a thousand SVPs.

He was also sharply reprimanded and denounced by his daughter, who told him she was mortified at the public shame of his cheapness. Only an ingrate or idiot would decide not to include the tip, she said. Didn't he know how important coffee shops were in the running of Sunnyvale? Their profits are reinvested into the organisation and, therefore, the West. *Every coffee makes the world a better place*, is their mantra.

'But they're *voluntary* tips, aren't they?' Guy had asked.

'Yes. But if you decide not to volunteer, there are repercussions,' she said.

She had cut him off afterwards, saying that her career was too important to be jeopardised by such an out-of-touch and ill-natured father. This incident was the final straw. She was the Regional Director of Progress and Happiness for Sunnyvale in the north-east of England, whose headquarters were based in York. She couldn't afford any scandals.

He was only called Guy Smith inside his own head – it was a self-created pseudonym. He could remember that the name had great significance – the first name was from something important, and the second name from something else that was important – but he couldn't precisely pinpoint what they were.

A deep-rooted instinct told him they were chosen to suit his rebellious and freedom-loving nature, and it gave him a little kick of pride. *They haven't quite got me yet.* But then the thought would wither, and disappear.

His real birth name was lost to the fog of memory, and as he hadn't spoken to another human being in several months he was unlikely to be reminded by anyone. Despite his lack of human contact, he was a lucky man. He was fortunate to be free at all. There were enough blots on his record to last several lifetimes, but the authorities had decided to show leniency. He was a harmless recalcitrant who would die soon anyway, they reasoned.

According to the old Gregorian calendar, this was the year 2083. But comprehensive plans were in place to overhaul such an antiquated system. 2084 would be known as Year 1 in the Sunnyvale Era.

*

Outside, it was a glorious April afternoon. The sun had broken through the morning cloud cover, bathing the cobbled streets in light and forcing Guy to squint from his vantage point in the windowed corner of the coffee shop on Coney Street.

In the long-forgotten Victorian era – as distant in society's memory as when Vikings roamed the land – this street had bustled with commerce and activity. The pillar-fronted George Hotel welcomed weary horse-drawn travellers from afar; greengrocers, tailors, gunsmiths and pawnbrokers vied for customer's hard-earned shillings, pounds and pence; and St Martin le Grand church, with its gold-bracketed, double-sided clock overhanging the street, served as a refuge of quiet and solitude to those in need.

Guy was looking exactly at where the clock used to be, high in the air. He was still squinting from the sun, but he was also now squinting with focus. His clouded mind was playing tricks. He was sure he could remember a real clock from his youth, when he would walk into town hand-in-hand with his mum. It had a Little Admiral figure on top – a small statue – that would revolve on the hour. Or was he just imagining it? Had the 'clock' always been a circular telescreen instead?

The image on the screen was a simple one – an orange background, with three words emblazoned in black capital letters: SUNNYVALE IS PROGRESS. The words dissolved and were replaced by the phrase: PROGRESS IS FREEDOM. It then flicked to a picture of a brightly-burning sun, with the word VALE underneath it. The individual letters separated to reveal four words:

Virtuous
Altruistic
Liberal
Ethical

The building it was attached to was no longer a church, as enlightened civilisation had long outgrown religion. The ancient stonework was completely draped in huge polyester sheets, like the material flags are made from. They were perfectly straight, crisp and unruffled, as if they had been ironed.

An electronic ticker, like the famous ones in Times Square in New York, was attached all the way around the building's perimeter. Its red text scrolled constantly across the long, rectangular screen. 'Sunnyvale is Progress. Progress is Freedom. Sunnyvale – Virtuous, Altruistic, Liberal, Ethical,' followed by various commercials and promotions.

The polyester sheets were adorned with Sunnyvale's logo, exactly the same as the one on Guy's cup of iced tea. It was an image of a bright orange sun shining over a narrow blue stream running through a lush green valley, with a small rainbow on the horizon. It was ubiquitous around the city and beyond.

The logo had once reminded Guy of the film *How Green was My Valley*, which he could vaguely recall watching one rainy Sunday afternoon as a child. He had been enraptured by the singing of "Bread of Heaven" by the Welsh miners, in deep baritone. It was just one small snippet of memory that used to warm him inside, but it came to sicken him that it could become linked in his mind with the company's shameless logo. It tried to insinuate: *Buy Sunnyvale for sunlit uplands! Buy Sunnyvale for a better world! Sunnyvale will feed you till you want no more!*

Inside the building, no visitors were allowed. Sunnyvale had largely subsumed the properties and assets owned by the Church of England (and, indeed, most other independent entities and organisations in the West). The former church was now a back-up, overflow warehouse for their services and stock in the region.

The main warehouse and office HQ – where Guy's estranged daughter worked – was the building formerly known as York Minster, just half a kilometre away (metric measurements were now compulsory in all areas of life – any mention of inches, feet, yards, chains, furlongs and miles would be met with bemusement).

York Minster was one of the largest cathedrals in Europe in its heyday, so it made the ideal storage space for Sunnyvale's extensive range of items and goods, predominantly the latest *must-have* technological devices. They could be delivered to anywhere within a fifty-kilometre radius in a matter of minutes, primarily by drone.

Sunnyvale were constantly looking at ways to improve their delivery times, and it was possible for someone living within a few kilometres of the warehouse to receive their package just moments after ordering. The all-time record for this branch was forty-four seconds, when an employee at another of Sunnyvale's coffee shops – this one located directly opposite HQ – ordered a new protective case for her Sunnyvale Smart E-Reader. A drone wasn't even needed – one of the warehouse staff just strolled across the street and delivered it by hand, in a perverse moment of backward progress.

As Guy continued to squint at the circular telescreen, his attention was caught by a tall, twenty-something, red-haired lady walking hurriedly underneath it (everyone seemed to hurry about nowadays, he thought). She was deep in conversation through her headset and mask. It was a strange contraption: the mask was made of cotton, covering the nose and mouth, and the attached earphones were clipped onto each ear.

It therefore doubled up as a protective mask and a means

of communication, connected wirelessly to the sensor in her wrist. It was called a Sunnyvale Smart Shroud (though Guy couldn't recall this). He could remember, however, the huge marketing campaign when it was first released: there was a billboard-sized advert on the side of Sunnyvale's HQ, and many of the West's famous sights and monuments were adorned with the Smart Shroud. The Statue of Liberty in New York, for instance, and all the figures on Mount Rushmore in South Dakota, as well as Christ the Redeemer in Rio de Janeiro. It was an evocative and effective marketing tool.

Guy was one of the few people around who didn't wear one (in the coffee shop, for instance, each of the seven other customers were doing so). It often earned him suspicious glares, as did his microchipped glasses, which were called Sunnyvale Smart Spectacles. They were once the height of sophisticated technology, about twenty years ago, but now almost everybody else had the chip installed in their wrists, so it couldn't be mislaid. These implants were called Sunnyvale Smart Sensors.

Guy finished the last dregs of his iced tea and unwittingly earned ten SVPs for throwing his cup in the correct recycling bin. Thirteen minutes later, he was dead.

*

Guy's death was sudden and innocent – today was just his day to go. After leaving the coffee shop, he began one of his listless walks around the city, with no purpose or destination. The roaming somehow gave him a sense of freedom, even if he could no longer articulate why.

As he ambled up Stonegate, and turned left onto High Petergate, he felt a stabbing pain in his chest. His breath shortened. He stumbled to an unoccupied wooden bench opposite Sunnyvale's HQ – known only to him and a handful of others as the former Minster – and slumped onto it.

His eyes were drooping, and the last remnants of fight were draining from his body. His last view of this world was of the ubiquitous logo – that damn, bloody, interminable logo – with the sun, the valley, and the rainbow on the horizon. With his last breath, he spat sardonically: 'Sunny*vile*... Sunny*vile*,' in a final act of obstinacy.

He was an old man, and then he was a dead man. He slipped from life to death as easily as one drops off to sleep at night. His threadbare grey hair glistened with grease and sweat, and his blue eyes – which once shimmered with life and mischief – were closed forevermore. The Sunnyvale Smart Spectacles had fallen from his face and lay, cracked, on the floor by his feet.

He looked like he was sleeping, so dozens of passers-by – all wearing their mask-headphones, in a variety of different colours – barely gave him a second glance.

It wasn't until night came, when the city's police force spotted him through their night-vision drone, that his death was discovered. The Sunnyvale Smart Drone was one of dozens that patrolled the city at all hours of day and night, constantly monitoring York's inhabitants from a height of around thirty metres (and delivering countless packages).

They emitted an incessant buzzing sound, like there was a bee or wasp flying overhead. It earned them the nickname 'Stingers'. It was shortly before midnight when a Stinger locked on to Guy's lifeless body, and immediately alerted the small team of police officers back at the station that something was afoot. On a good night they could get through a full shift without having to leave the warmth of their control room, so a collective sigh greeted the video live-stream on their computer screens.

Half an hour later, Guy's body was in the morgue. Another half an hour later, he was cremated.

2

Harrison Snow was twenty years old. He was sat on a custom-made gaming chair in the corner of his bedroom, sipping a soda. He was chatting virtually to six friends at once through his Sunnyvale Smart Sensor – they were joshing about the e-sports football World Cup that was taking place the coming summer.

The most popular pastime in the West was watching people play sport-based video games. The best players were superstars, and the World Cup was the most prestigious event in the e-sports calendar. It had long superseded the actual football World Cup for intrigue and drama.

'Listen, listen,' Harrison said. 'I bet you a hundred SVPs that the main man JT wins this Saturday. He's unbelievable. His win ratio is the highest out of everyone, I don't think he's lost a game in over six months. The numbers don't lie.'

One of the voices replied, and their face was projected from Harrison's Smart Sensor when he did so – a hologram of a full-sized human head.

'You've got it all wrong, Harrison,' the voice said. 'He's over-rated. He hasn't had to come from behind once all season – how do you know how he'll react when he's under pressure? Anyone can play well when they're in the lead and in their comfort zone. I'll take you up on your bet.'

'Deal,' Harrison said assuredly, running a hand through his wavy brown hair. He had a floppy fringe permanently hanging over his forehead. A notification popped up on his Smart Sensor. 'Got to go everyone,' he said. 'I've got another call.'

A hologram of his mum's face was then projected into the room. She looked as impatient and business-like as ever. 'I've had some news, Harrison,' she said. 'Your grandfather died last night. Good riddance to him. But as we're his only family in York his bungalow has been left to us, and we have to deal with all the stuff left there. Can you sort it out? You remember where he lived, don't you? I don't have the time or the energy to do it myself.'

'OK, Mum,' Harrison replied. Death was an alien concept to him, and he didn't know how to compute the information. 'I think I remember which one was his bungalow, but I was only a little kid the last time I was there. Can I keep the SVPs if I sell any of his stuff?'

'Do what you want with it,' she said. 'I don't even want to think about him or his possessions. He was a bad man. He was dangerous. Just sort it out. I have to go – I'm presenting in a meeting soon.'

The Smart Sensor made a little *blip* noise and her hologram face disappeared. Harrison stared mutely into the distance, his blue eyes looking vacant and confused.

*

The following morning, Harrison gingerly made his way to his grandfather's bungalow. It was a couple of kilometres from the city centre, and he summoned a self-driven, electric car to take him there (the cost was automatically deducted from his account through his Smart Sensor).

He hadn't been to his grandfather's place in years – ever since his mum fell out with him – and he was filled with trepidation. He'd been warned regularly by his mum about the old man's senility and decrepitude, though this didn't tally with the figure Harrison could remember from his early childhood. He recalled a bright-eyed, broad-shouldered and energetic man.

He'd given Harrison piggybacks in the garden, and encouraged him to kick a real football, rather than playing on the latest video simulation (or, indeed, watching others play on the simulation). He could still recall the thrill of charging around the grass as an infant with his grandfather in pursuit, playing these old-fashioned sounding games like 'hide and seek' and 'hop scotch'.

He struggled with the word 'Grandad' as a toddler, so he always referred to him as 'Pop'. Pop was (or, rather, had been) his and mum's only relative in the area. The rest of the family were dispersed throughout the West and had largely lost contact, aside from the annual 'Happy Birthday' notification on his Smart Sensor.

Harrison had never met his dad. His mum had arranged for a donor through an app called 'Elite Sperm', pitched at high-flying professionals without the time or inclination to form a relationship with a male partner. Secrecy was enshrined in the app's terms and conditions, so Harrison wouldn't be able to track the donor down, even if he wanted to. His mum didn't know, either. She had only an anonymous profile to go by, which listed his key features: height, weight, hair colour, eye colour, profession, a history of diseases in his family, and his IQ score.

The better the features, as determined by the app's algorithm, the steeper the cost. Harrison's mum was ambitious and on the rise when she made her selection – and she was in her mid-thirties and reckoned one child would be enough – so she had forked out for a donor in the higher echelons.

Sperm donors were nothing new, of course, but because of her status she was able to trial a revolutionary technology called a 'foetus incubator', later marketed as a Sunnyvale Smart Baby Pod. It meant that, rather than being artificially impregnated, her eggs were fertilised with the sperm in a test tube. The foetus then spent nine months in the sophisticated incubator, or pod, completely separate from the womb. It received all required nutrients in perfect measure, and the risk of a miscarriage was extremely low.

It was an ingenious invention: women would no longer be shackled with the unfair burden of childbirth, and their careers would no longer be unjustly jeopardised. All female staff at Sunnyvale were encouraged to take advantage, and Harrison's mum was an eager participant.

Years later, the product of this transaction would occasionally enquire about his father, but she quickly shut down the topic if it ever came up (as if she regretted the whole episode) and he had learned not to bother mentioning it. Still, Harrison often tried to envisage his dad in his head, but he could never form an image beyond a shadowy outline. Pop was the only older male figure he had ever connected with.

Harrison arrived at the detached bungalow, which was at the very end of a quiet cul-de-sac. There was a small half-metre-high brick wall in front of the empty tarmac drive, and he could tell the bungalow was still and vacant. Either side of the burgundy front door were five medium-sized bay windows – one set of five fronted the lounge, the other set fronted Pop's bedroom.

He had a sudden jolt of panic when he realised he didn't know the four-digit entry code to get through the front door, nor would he be able to use the voice recognition software. But the entrance panel looked dusty and unused. He tried the handle and the door opened with ease. *Was it always left unlocked?* Harrison thought. *Maybe Pop had gone senile.*

As he stepped into the carpeted hallway, Harrison called 'Hello' into the emptiness, and immediately felt silly for doing so. He was hit with another surging jolt of panic, however, when he was greeted with a reply.

*

'Meow,' came the reply. A fluffy white cat came walking through from the kitchen at the back of the house. Harrison smiled in relief and bent down to stroke the wispy fur at the top of its head. The cat purred in delight, clearly happy to have company again, and no doubt hoping it would be fed as soon as possible.

'I never knew Pop had a cat,' Harrison said to himself, as he inspected the thin, belt-like collar around its neck. It was also white in colour, and there was a small, circular metal disc attached to it. It read: 'Aslan'.

'Aslan sounds like a boy's name,' Harrison said. 'So you must be a he. How you doing, Aslan? Let's get you some food, you must be starving.' Aslan seemed to understand what he was saying – he raced excitedly back to the kitchen, tail in the air, and waited eagerly by the ceramic feeding bowl near the back door.

Harrison walked through the hallway. On his right was a lounge and then a spare bedroom; on his left was Pop's bedroom, then a closet, and then a bathroom. At the end, a long rectangular kitchen, encompassing the full width of the house, completed a modest, understated and unspectacular abode. It had seemed much bigger when he was a child.

The kitchen was rustic and basic – a wooden table, an oven, a toaster and other bits and pieces – and there was a refrigerator in the corner. It was no Sunnyvale Smart Fridge, however. These clever devices measured the shelf life and nutritional value of their contents, and automatically ordered food in when it was needed – from Sunnyvale, of course.

The old supermarket brand names still existed, but the businesses had all been taken over, behind the scenes, several years ago by Sunnyvale. With such cheap supply chains and near-instant delivery, they had driven out all competitors from the market: smaller grocery stores, fruit and veg stalls, corner shops and farmer's markets were non-existent. They hadn't been *banned*, as such. They were just economically unviable.

Harrison tried a few cupboards until he found a packet of cat food, which he opened and poured into the bowl. It was an overcast April day – thus slightly chilly in the kitchen – and the only sound was Aslan purring contentedly as he ate.

Out of curiosity, Harrison opened the door of the old-fashioned, white-fronted fridge in the corner. It certainly wasn't a smart one – it seemed like all it was designed to do was to keep food cool. It wasn't connected wirelessly to any network, nor was it linked to any handheld device or Smart Sensor. *Pop really was a dinosaur*, he thought. *He must have had to physically go out in person to get his shopping!*

The shelves were completely empty, but there was a small compartment at the top of the fridge, which looked like the freezer. Harrison had to pull hard to open the little rectangular door, which was almost jammed shut because of the ice, and was rewarded with the sight of something he had never before seen in the flesh.

Meat. A solid lump of beef, to be precise, according to the label. From a cow. Harrison's initial instinct was to recoil – Sunnyvale had imposed veganism on its citizens for many years, as a key tenet of its 'Ethical' philosophy – but his curiosity once again took over.

He leant in and poked at it with his index finger – it was surprisingly tough and sinewy. Pop must have bought it on the black market. *Perhaps he was a little dangerous.*

He was about to take the beef out of the freezer for closer inspection, when Aslan startled him by brushing against his legs and meowing for more food. He sighed, closed the freezer door and refilled the ceramic bowl, and then remembered that he had a job to do.

*

He was there to suss out exactly what he could sell, but the early indications were unpromising. The fridge may interest some kind of antique dealer, at best, but there were no other items in the kitchen that would be worth even a token fee.

He walked back through the hallway and into Pop's bedroom. Again, it was sparse: a double bed with bland, brown sheets, an old pine wardrobe, a tall lamp, a pair of tartan slippers, a walking stick, and a small bedside table with a half-empty glass of water on it. He opened the wardrobe for a cursory glance and found nothing but plain, brown clothes made from corduroy and cotton, and a standard, old man's selection of shoes, underwear and socks.

The spare bedroom was even more underwhelming. There was just a mishmash of everyday, old-fashioned items, worth nothing on the open market or the black market, except perhaps to an eccentric collector of some sort. Harrison was growing frustrated, and he shooed Aslan away when he meandered over to greedily request a third helping.

The lounge contained a modest sofa, a rug, a small table and nothing else. The mantelpiece was empty, and there wasn't even a Sunnyvale Smart TV. Come to think of it, there was barely anything electronic in the whole house. *Perhaps he's been burgled*, Harrison thought. But it didn't look that way. It was simply the most boring house Harrison had ever seen, and he was beginning to understand why his mum regarded Pop with such suspicion. How could anyone live like this?

Harrison hadn't bothered to take his shoes off, so he was ready for an immediate departure. He would tell his mum there was nothing of note at the bungalow, apart from a cat and some beef, and it should be put on the market as soon as possible. The whole process would be swift and smooth: Sunnyvale would advertise the bungalow on their behalf, as well as handling all the legal and technical elements of the sale. Estate agents and expensive, meddlesome middlemen were redundant.

As he made his way to the front door, something made Harrison pause. He felt a twinge of guilt. *What's going to happen to Aslan?* The new owners could move in as early as next week, and there's no guarantee they would want to keep a cat. He weighed up whether he could take Aslan with him, but his mum detested animals and had forbidden him from ever having a pet.

Harrison was stumped, but then an idea struck. Could he take Aslan and keep him safe in his bedroom until he could find a new home for him? His mum was at work so often that she may not even notice.

With a sudden resolve, he decided this was the best course of action. All he needed was a box or cage of some sort to ensure Aslan wouldn't escape on the journey. He couldn't remember seeing one on his uneventful tour, but Pop must have one stored away somewhere.

The closet. He had neglected it earlier, but it was his best chance of success. He strode over and opened the closet door with gusto, but his optimism was mistaken. It was equally as spartan and uncluttered as the rest of the house, containing just a mop and bucket, an ancient vacuum cleaner, a step ladder and an old electric fan.

Aslan would have to be carried by hand. If he didn't like it, he would be left to the mercy of the next owners. 'Aslan,' Harrison shouted, but this time he received no reply. He ventured back into the kitchen and sighed with frustration, as there was no sign of the cat. 'Where the hell is he?' he whispered to himself.

A movement in the back garden caught his eye, and he craned his neck to look out of the window. Aslan had exited the house – presumably through the cat flap on the back door – and he was currently sat on top of the large shed at the bottom of the garden.

It was made out of brick, rather than wood, with a tall black door and a sloping tiled roof. Aslan was looking straight at Harrison through the window and meowing. Harrison shook his head with impatience and walked out the back door (which was also unlocked). It was a dull and cold morning, with no breeze or rain.

'Come on Aslan,' he said. 'It's time to go. Come on.' The cat stayed stubbornly on the roof. His bushy tail flickered and his languid, intelligent eyes looked directly at Harrison's.

Harrison edged closer with his arms outstretched, trying to signal to Aslan that he wanted to hold him, but the cat remained unmoved. If only he had the cat box with him, he could pick Aslan up and sweep him into the box in one swift movement. *Could it be in the shed?*

It was the decision to act on this thought that altered Harrison's life forever. On such trivial happenstance can one's whole fate take a different trajectory.

3

The shed – strangely – was harder to get into than the house. This time it *was* locked, and the numbered keypad by the door had clearly been in regular use. Harrison now faced the challenge of working out the four-digit entrance code. It seemed like a lot of effort for a cat box, but the fact the shed was locked had piqued his curiosity as to whether there was anything more valuable inside.

He cast his mind back to his time with Pop. Were there any clues, buried in the recesses of his memory, which he could unearth? He knew that Pop was in his late seventies when he saw him last, which would mean he was around ninety when he died. His date of birth would, therefore, be in the region of 1993.

He tried 1992, 1993 and 1994, but to no avail. How many more guesses would he be allowed before it deactivated and locked him out permanently? Harrison racked his brain for more ideas. Pop was a history buff, which had always displeased Harrison's mum. 'He's more bothered about the past than the future,' she would say. 'Don't let him poison your brain. Life is all about progress and moving forward. Those silly fairytales and bedtime stories he reads to you are bad for your development.'

Harrison searched his memory for a significant historical date that Pop may have used, but nothing was forthcoming. He let out a little grunt of frustration, and tried 1234, then 9999, in the hope that Pop had chosen an easy, meaningless, generic combination. But he knew it wouldn't be the case. Pop loved numbers, puzzles and games, and there's no way he would have picked the code on a whim.

Aslan was watching Harrison's struggle with indifference. 'This is all for your benefit, Aslan,' Harrison said. 'I should just leave you to the next owners. I'm too nice.' Aslan continued to look down from his perch on the sloped roof, and the metal disc on his collar was slowly rocking back and forth.

'Hold on a second,' Harrison said. He stood on his tiptoes – he was already above average height while flat-footed – and managed to gently grab hold of Aslan, who wasn't entirely comfortable but also didn't resist. He held him up so they were face to face and eye to eye.

The metal disc was now slowly rotating from the movement. On one side it said 'Aslan', and Harrison realised there was something etched on the other side too. It read: '1811'. He half-smiled and half-frowned, while placing Aslan on the floor and stroking his head. 'Let's see if this works then, Aslan. Did Pop make his little kitty the secret holder?'

He typed 1811 into the keypad and heard the mechanism react immediately. The lock clicked open and he turned the handle on the thick black door. He was in.

*

After such an effort to gain entrance, his disappointment was acute when he was greeted with the sight of a dusty, unkempt and – much in keeping with the rest of the property – underwhelming shed.

Despite the windowless brick exterior, the interior was primarily made of wood, including the floor. There were some pieces of gardening equipment lying about, as well as an old, deflated football that Harrison recognised from years ago, as well as a steel toolbox and a dusty First Aid kit. Other than that, it looked like nothing more than a homely space for spiders to weave their webs.

None of it made sense. Why would a man – especially one quite possibly in the throes of senility – take such care in locking his empty shed, but not his house? And why would he go to the effort of putting the entrance code on his cat's collar? Had he just gone insane? Was there no explanation other than his old age and eccentricity?

Aslan meowed and trotted into the shed. It was a large rectangular space, roughly the same size and shape as the kitchen in the bungalow. Aslan meowed again and moved into the back corner of the shed, next to a rusty rake and green watering can. Soggy, brown leaves were dotted around nearby.

Aslan began scraping his claws on the wooden floor, in a typical feline stretch-scratch posture. As he did so, one of the planks seemed to move slightly. Harrison moved closer, his eyes focusing intently on the floor. Nothing surprised him about this cat now – was he, once again, trying to tell him something?

About two dozen planks ran across the base width of the shed, all nondescript and identical. Or so it seemed on first impression. Now he was squatting down next to Aslan, Harrison could see that there was an ever-so-slight alteration in this section of the floor. The top halves of four planks were a lighter shade of brown, well disguised by the leaves and the miscellaneous equipment.

Harrison moved the rake and the watering can aside, as Aslan stopped scratching. It revealed a stainless steel hinge bracket and a small, metal handle. It was a trap door, and it would be almost impossible to find unless you were looking for it. Harrison yanked on the handle and the door opened up towards him. There was a wooden ladder to climb down, and a cavernous space below.

Harrison stroked Aslan vigorously on the head. 'You're the cleverest cat I've ever seen!'

He walked back over to close the thick shed door, heard the lock click into place, and then began his ascent down the trap door and the wooden ladder.

*

A couple of kilometres away, back at Sunnyvale's HQ in the city centre, Harrison's mum – Alexa – was scouring through a report at work. It outlined Sunnyvale's plans for a Great Leap Forward in the coming decade.

It would build on an era of technological explosion. As early as the 1960s, experts had predicted that the growth of microprocessors would be exponential – more specifically, they observed that the number of transistors on a microchip was doubling about every two years, and they expected this trend to continue. Concurrently, costs would fall sharply.

They were right. A personal computer, a PC, in the 2020s cost about a sixth of the amount it did in the 1980s, but it was five hundred times more powerful. Some refrigerators, microwaves and calculators in the same decade possessed more computing power than the Apollo 11 module which landed on the moon in 1969. There are countless similar examples.

The growth and pace of change fluctuated somewhat throughout the rest of the century, but the general trend remained relentlessly upward. Digital technology – in all forms conceivable to the human imagination – crept inexorably into people's daily lives, increasingly shaping and defining their experiences, thoughts, memories and interactions. With the development of the Sunnyvale Smart Sensor, it had been literally *implanted* into their bodies. Human and artificial intelligence were becoming synonymous.

There were glorious triumphs, especially in the field of medicine. Near-miracles were performed. The boundaries of scientific exploration were constantly being pushed and challenged. To say the sky was the limit would be to declare yourself a miserable pessimist – the observable universe was now the limit, and it was there to be analysed and understood.

Nation states had essentially dissolved. There had been no dramatic coup d'état, nor had there been a democratic vote to this end. It just *happened*. Each country still had all the baubles and badges of sovereignty. In England (now separate from Scotland, Wales and a unified Ireland) there was still the royal family, the BBC and the Houses of Parliament. But they were hollow husks. They were like penny farthings – amusing to have around and to look at in museums, but long ago overtaken by the forces of modernity.

Ultimate power now rested with multinational technological corporations, led by self-proclaimed 'digital utopians'. The growth of these organisations was extraordinary: by the mid-decades of the century, their combined value on the stock market was unprecedentedly dominant.

The merging of the Big Seven in 2056 solidified their status as chief power-players in the West. Sunnyvale's tentacles spread into every area of finance and business, politics, media, sport, the arts, medicine, education and everyday life.

The West was a clunky and Manichean term that referred to the USA and its allies, while the East described China and its allies. Many countries escaped easy placement in either category, but it was generally accepted as broadly useful shorthand for the new Cold War. The East was equally influenced by its own digital utopians. The greatest weapon on either side was a keyboard, and the most fearsome and valuable soldiers were hackers. They were trained and drilled like the Marines and Navy SEALs of old. The best of the best.

Those who were wealthy and talented revelled in the opportunity to make the most of a small, intimately connected world (even if it was, rather roughly, divided into two blocs). They were the handful of winners in this system. There were many more losers. Jobs and livelihoods which had sustained human prosperity for centuries had disappeared. Economic inequality had widened dramatically.

AI hadn't taken over the world in the form of human-killing cyborgs, but there had been a significant shift in the balance of power. After all, several decades had passed since computers were capable of beating the very best humans at chess, Go or *Jeopardy*. Now, human beings were assisted, regulated, tracked and surveilled by technology from dawn to dusk, from cradle to grave.

Progress only travelled in one direction. To those at the top, of course, this was a wonderful thing. Alexa Snow was one of those at the zenith, and her commitment to her role was being noticed at Sunnyvale. She was ready for another promotion.

*

Harrison stepped off the bottom rung of the ladder and spun around. His mouth literally opened in surprise and wonder. The room was exactly the same size as the shed above it, but – in great contrast – it was full of things. *Things* was the only word Harrison could think of to describe them, as there was too much for him to take in at once.

An automatic light had come on overhead as soon as the trap door opened, and the ceiling was surprisingly high – Harrison would have to stand on his tiptoes and stretch to touch it. He was standing on a thick, cream carpet, which reminded him of Aslan's fur, and he felt compelled to remove his trainers, which he left by the base of the ladder.

The room was cosy, but also deceptively spacious. In the centre, drawing the eye, was a comfortable-looking leather armchair. It was blue, and Harrison's first instinct was to jump on it and sink into its softness. It rotated three hundred and sixty degrees, so he spun around like an unsupervised child. There was a small, square oak table next to it, holding a glass decanter and tumbler, three-quarters full with whisky.

To Harrison's left, once he had finished spinning, a full wall of the room was taken up by the largest multi-tiered bookshelf he had ever seen. He'd heard that there used to be these buildings called 'libraries', which stored physical books, but they'd disappeared before he was born. Perhaps this is what they used to look like.

Mounted on the wall at the far end of the room was a large television, which the armchair was initially facing. It didn't look like a Sunnyvale Smart TV, however. There was no webcam facing the viewer at the top, and (much like the fridge upstairs) it seemingly had no outside connection. It probably meant there was no multi-dimensional facility, nor would it be able to stream Sunnyvale's vast directory of films and TV programmes. What on earth could you watch on it?

The right-hand wall had a long, marble mantelpiece attached to it. It was full, from end to end, of wooden-framed photographs. Again, Harrison was unused to seeing them in physical form – all of his family photos were stored in the Sunnyvale Smart Cloud. He could access them whenever he needed through his Smart Sensor, but he could now understand the appeal of holding them in your hand.

He picked up the one nearest to him, which showed Pop in his prime. He was wearing a tuxedo at some kind of formal event, and his brown, gelled hair was swept perfectly to one side. He was broad and lean in his immaculate suit, and his eyes were fresh and full of life. He must have been in his late twenties or early thirties, and he could easily have passed as Harrison's older brother.

The photograph next along showed Pop at an even younger age. This time, he was wearing a black leather jacket and he had a cigarette in his mouth. He was stood in the middle of a group of six – five men and one woman – with one hand in his jeans pocket and the other holding a beer bottle. The young woman, stood the closest to Pop, had a tomboyish look, and the other young men were dressed similarly. All cool and edgy, but a little self-conscious, as if they were bluffing a little. Harrison guessed that they were all around sixteen, and had snuck into a gig underage.

They were in a bar or pub of some sort, and there was a live band playing in the background. Harrison could recall Pop mentioning his favourite music bar by the river in York, and it was probably this one. 'It's now another bloody soulless coffee shop,' he would say, if they ever walked past it. 'We had some good nights in there.'

Harrison scanned up and down the mantelpiece, smiling. One of the framed photographs at the far end drew him in, as he recognised a much younger version of himself. He was a toddler, with ruddy cheeks and a wavy mess of brown hair, sitting on Pop's shoulders. The picture had been taken as him and Pop were laughing about something, and the view in the background was idyllic. Acres of greenery, beneath a crisp, clear sky. Harrison held the frame in his hand and looked at the photo for over a minute.

The wall to Harrison's right had some kind of four-legged device resting against it, as well as some boxes stacked in the corner. They looked like old games of some sort, and the top one had the word 'Monopoly' written on it in red letters. It rang a small bell in Harrison's sub-conscious. Had he played it a couple of times as a youngster? Wasn't there something about Pass and Go, and a jail, and an old boot? And wasn't there money involved too? Notes of different colours and denominations?

The four-legged device was waist-high, and it had a square, red lid which was open. There was a black disc inside, about the size of a large dinner plate, and there was a red, smaller circle in the middle of the disc. It had the words 'The Rolling

Stones' written on it in an elaborate yellow font.

A small flicker of recognition registered in Harrison's mind, again. He was feeling increasingly bold and giddy with the discovery of Pop's secret lair, and he decided to see if he could get the device to work. There was a thin plastic lever attached to the side, with a small silver needle protruding from it, which looked like it should interact with the disc in some way.

He randomly pressed a couple of buttons at the front of the device and, to his surprise, the disc started spinning. No sound was forthcoming, however. He looked for a second, and then gently moved the plastic lever over the disc with his forefinger. Its small silver needle settled into one of the disc's grooves. Suddenly, a melodious sound filled the room, and a raspy male voice began to sing. It was like nothing Harrison had heard before, and he was instantly beguiled.

Harrison listened to the whole song while gently tapping a foot to the rhythm. He remembered where he'd heard of the Rolling Stones before: at school, he had occasionally learnt of the many authors, artists and musicians whose works were forbidden in these more enlightened times. 'Their messages are offensive and corrosive, and they have no place in a free society,' the teacher had said.

This band had written a song called 'Brown Sugar', which contained outdated language and cultural references. The only logical and moral consequence was to completely ban their music from consumption – anybody who tried to download their songs would receive a severe fine, as well as public denunciation. Pop, evidently, had managed to find a way around the regulations.

There were three wooden shelves attached to the wall next to the music-playing device, holding dozens – if not hundreds – of square cardboard sleeves, each containing a black disc. Harrison flicked through them, and saw that most of them had intricate, eye-catching artwork on the front.

A couple of the names he recognised, most of them he didn't: Bob Dylan, Kris Kristofferson, Aretha Franklin, Queen, Oasis, The Stone Roses, Nirvana, The Beatles, Sam Cooke, The Who, Elvis, ACDC, Chuck Berry, The Eagles, Fleetwood Mac, Tina Turner, Louis Armstrong. On a shelf labelled 'Classical' there was Beethoven, Mozart, Britten, Bach, Brahms, Wagner and more.

Harrison wanted to listen to them all. He was starting to feel a newfound appreciation for Pop. *He wasn't insane, he was cool!*

4

Alexa received the good news in her usual phlegmatic and professional manner. It was a significant promotion: she had risen from Regional Director of Progress and Happiness (one of five throughout England) to National Director in the same department. Essentially, her peers were now her subordinates. She was another notch up the chain of command, and she intended to keep climbing.

She lived with Harrison a five-minute walk away from Sunnyvale HQ, which was one of the reasons for her success. With such an easy commute, she could be in the office for long stretches of time without feeling too jaded. It meant Harrison was more self-sufficient than most young men his age, as he had largely been left alone throughout his teens. They shared a large, ornate townhouse overlooking the river and could go days without seeing each other.

This evening, however, their paths did cross. Alexa arrived home in her grey pant suit, dropped her designer handbag on the marble kitchen top, took off her Sunnyvale Smart Shroud and verbally commanded the Sunnyvale Smart Kettle to start boiling. As she did so, Harrison walked through from the lounge. 'Make that two cups of tea,' he said to the kettle.

'How did it go at the bungalow?' Alexa asked.

'It was fine,' Harrison replied.

'What does that mean? Is there a lot for us to sort out before we can put it on the market?'

'Yeah, there is actually. It'll take me quite a while to get through it all. There's all sorts of junk in the lounge and his bedroom. He must have been a hoarder.'

'Well, that doesn't surprise me,' Alexa said. 'We could

send a cleaning team round if you need, get it done ASAP.'

'No, no,' Harrison said. 'It's all under control. I don't mind doing it.'

'If you insist,' she said. She paused a moment, and added: 'I got a promotion today. It'll mean a lot more travelling to other Sunnyvale sites around the country, but I'll still be based in York. We have a big visit from the Great Liberator to HQ this summer, and I'll be co-ordinating the whole thing.'

'Congratulations, Mum,' Harrison said matter-of-factly. 'You deserve it. Who's the Great Liberator?'

Her slate-blue eyes flashed with anger, a rare sign of stress when she was usually as unflappable as an automaton. 'Don't you pay attention to anything, Harrison?' she scowled. 'We made an announcement last week.'

Her dark hair, in a short bob, remained perfectly sprayed and groomed, and her face was remarkably unlined for a lady in her mid-fifties. The secret, perhaps, lay in Sunnyvale's extensive investment in anti-ageing products.

'The Great Liberator was known until recently as the CEO, the Chief Executive Officer,' she said. 'The new name is much more accurate and helpful. Sunnyvale is Progress. Progress is Freedom. The CEO – or Great Liberator – is in charge of facilitating that freedom. I wonder where all those private school fees went, sometimes.'

'Oh yeah, I thought it sounded familiar.'

The conversation was over, as if it had been a meeting at work. All logical points had been discussed, conclusions had been reached, and the minutes had been drawn up. They collected their cups of tea in silence and retreated to their respective bedrooms.

As soon as Harrison closed the bedroom door behind him, he felt relief wash over him. Had his lie been convincing enough? Was there a chance his mum would visit the bungalow herself and realise it was practically empty? He reassured himself that she would be much too busy to go out of her way, especially with the new promotion. She had no emotional investment in Pop or the bungalow – she just wanted someone else to deal with it.

He was still assimilating what he had seen earlier today. Clearly, there was more to Pop than had met the eye. He must have been something of a maverick or rebel to go to the extreme lengths of building an underground bunker so he could enjoy forbidden books, films and music. It gave Harrison a kick of pride to know one of his relatives could be so industrious and brave. And foolhardy.

The memory that stood out most was the *smell* of the room. Maybe it was the old books, or the music-playing device, or the tangible photographs. It was a smell of history, of nostalgia, of something he instinctively understood but couldn't explain.

He had to visit the bunker again, but he knew his time was limited. He could put his mum off for a while, but eventually she wouldn't tolerate any more delays in selling the bungalow, and then the treasure trove would be lost forever (or, worse, it would be discovered by the authorities).

He stewed on the problem for a while, but it was getting late. Shortly, he was falling asleep. At some point during the night – when the sub-conscious deals with the day's problems in a more convincing manner – an idea emerged in Harrison's head. It was risky, but it would be worth the reward.

*

Alexa was up and away so early the next morning that the plan would have to wait until the evening. Harrison spent the morning in his bedroom watching e-sports – tracking the relentless feed of comments, reactions and memes about the ongoing action – in anticipation of the upcoming World Cup, but something was niggling him. He could remember Pop encouraging him to *play* sport, rather than watching other people 'play' it online.

'Come on, Harrison,' he would say. 'Instead of watching someone on the other side of the world click some buttons in a simulation, why not go outside and try the real thing? When I was a young lad, we still liked to actually meet our friends in person to have a kick around. Don't get sucked into that virtual world, lad. You'll end up half-human, half-computer.'

Was there some truth to what Pop had said? It had been so easy to dismiss him a few days ago, when he was just a distant part of his childhood, and a senile old man who he never saw. Out of sight, out of mind and out of memory. But his words now carried a certain resonance.

Harrison's bedroom was large, light and high-ceilinged. He had every digital item he could possibly wish for, including some Sunnyvale prototypes that weren't even on the open market yet. They were scattered around the room: on his desk, his bedside table, and even on the floor.

He was watching the e-sports on an enormous Sunnyvale Smart TV, mounted on the wall opposite his bed, which simultaneously projected his face to the world through the webcam above the screen. He switched it into interactive, multidimensional, multisensory mode, virtually transporting himself into the thick of the action.

The graphics were so realistic that it really did feel like he was in the middle of a dewy-grassed pitch, in front of a baying crowd, admiring the best players in the world from up close. He was in 'fan mode', so he couldn't actually influence the action (and the other e-players couldn't see him on their screens) but he could get so close to the ball, and he could feel the elements on his face, it felt like he really was *in* the game.

It was intoxicating, but it was all fake. A mirage. He could normally lose himself for hours doing this, but it suddenly felt dissatisfying. It was as if Pop was stood next to the bed and pouring a jug of ice-cold water on the top of his head, drenching him and shivering his spine. He turned the Smart TV off and lay staring at the ceiling, unable to ascertain whether he was drowning, or whether he felt refreshed.

He jumped up with vigour. He was surprisingly strong considering his near-sedentary lifestyle, with well-built thighs and calves. It was about time he tested them out a bit. He scrambled in the back of the wardrobe for a suitable pair of trainers, threw on an old T-shirt and some shorts, and five minutes later he was jogging down the street for the first time in years.

He'd forgotten his Smart Shroud, which earned him several funny looks, and he was soon gulping in air from the exertion. His muscles were burning, and his legs felt like two bags of wet cement. Sweat poured from his forehead, even though it was another cool April day, and his lower back threatened to seize up. He was going at a pace only marginally quicker than walking, and he felt like an old man struggling up the stairs with a walking stick.

But he was determined to persevere. He had no particular direction, and he struggled down a dozen stone steps to find himself alongside the River Ouse, one of the city's two main rivers. Much had altered in York in recent decades: most statues and monuments had been removed or replaced; high-street shops were derelict and decaying; gardens and parks were largely empty and neglected, as there was no need to venture outdoors (and even those who did invariably wore a Smart Shroud).

Despite this maelstrom of change, the River Ouse remained constant. It was a timeless waterway through the city's past. Harrison was blowing and struggling, but it helped to follow the path alongside the river as it snaked its way through and beyond the city.

He ran past the grassy, tree-lined spot where Pop had once tried to teach him how to fish (Harrison had found it excruciatingly boring and had given up after an hour), and when he felt like his legs could go no further, he spotted a bench in the distance and burst into a sprint for the home straight.

He strained and pushed and ploughed on as quickly as he could, before slumping onto the bench with exhaustion. He planned to sit until he regained his breath, and then he would walk back.

As he leaned his elbows on his knees and drew deep, rapid breaths, a low buzzing sound caught his attention. A Stinger was overhead, seemingly monitoring him. Or was he just being paranoid? His brain had been working overtime ever since his brief visit to Pop's bunker – he was making connections and assertions that his previously tired and saturated mind would never have made before. It was like he was waking from a slumber.

He looked up at the Stinger, blocking the sun behind it with the palm of his hand. It had already used its facial recognition software to cross-check him with a database of wanted criminals, for which he was clean. However, he was listed as a relative and possible associate of the late Joseph Snow, otherwise known by the pseudonym Guy Smith.

Smith was well known to the authorities, but the likelihood of Harrison being involved with him was rated as 'Low Risk' due to Smith's poor relations with his family. Nonetheless, a line was automatically added to Harrison's profile: 'Possibly suspicious behaviour, jogging with no Smart Shroud. 12:16pm, April 4. Further observation needed.'

The Stinger hovered overhead for another thirty seconds, and then buzzed off into the distance.

*

Harrison arrived home, showered and waited for his mum to return. He was nervous about his plan, as he rarely – if ever – directly confronted her with ideas or suggestions about anything. On the few occasions he had summoned the courage, it had been quickly quashed with a withering put-down.

Eventually, she came through the front door, looking characteristically neat and professional. The promotion may have meant longer hours, but it also meant greater authority and confidence. She felt and looked the part.

'Evening, Mum,' Harrison said, as she went through the usual routine of removing her Smart Shroud and commanding the kettle to make a cup of tea.

'Hello Harrison,' she replied neutrally.

'I know you've just got back from work but I have an idea to run by you, if you have time,' he said.

'Go on then,' she said. 'Make it quick.'

She was leaning on the marble breakfast bar, waiting for Harrison to pitch his idea like a prospective client at work.

'Well,' he said. 'I'm no longer a teenager and I think it's about time I had some independence and responsibility. I can't live with you forever. How would you feel about me moving into Pop's old bungalow?

'Before you answer,' he continued, 'I know you'd be missing out on the SVPs from selling it. But it's a family asset, and we can always sell it in the future if things don't work out. It would be good for me, and think of the space you'd have here with me out the way.'

She thought for a few moments, her face betraying nothing.

'I think it's a good idea,' she said. 'As you say, you can't live here forever. I'd rather just sell it and forget all about that ghastly man, but I have no problem with you moving there.'

Harrison smiled broadly, with surprise as much as joy.

'I didn't expect you to agree so easily,' he said. 'I had a longer spiel planned.'

'Save it,' she said. 'It makes sense. You can move in there if you want, but with one proviso.'

'What's that?'

'You need to get a job,' she said sharply. 'The timing works well, actually, because I've been meaning to talk to you about this for a while. I've indulged your laziness for too long, ever since you finished school with distinct mediocrity. I can arrange for you to start at Sunnyvale HQ next week, which is an opportunity most young men would give anything for. HQ is where the best of the best work, so be grateful for the chance and make sure you don't show me up.'

Harrison began to stutter a reply, but he was cut off.

'I'm not standing here all night discussing it,' she said, as she took her cup of tea. 'It's a generous compromise – the bungalow for the job. It's more than you deserve, frankly.'

Harrison was still pleasantly surprised at the swiftness with which she had agreed to his initial idea, even accounting for the caveat. A job wouldn't be so bad, he reasoned. He didn't have anything else lined up, and he had to admit he was lucky to have a mum so high up at Sunnyvale HQ. The alternative would be some generic work that would barely pay enough to make it worthwhile.

'Straight to the point, as always,' he said. 'It's a deal.' He held out his hand in a half-joking way, and she seemed to take it seriously. Mother and son shook hands on the impromptu agreement, and the conversation was over.

5

The following week, Harrison's new life was underway. He had spent the weekend moving all of his items into Pop's bungalow and removing anything that he definitely wouldn't need, such as Pop's old clothes. Before long, it began to feel like his place, as it had been so sparse initially.

He had greeted Aslan with delight (and fed him multiple times) but had resisted the temptation to venture to the shed and through the trap door – he was worried about the possibility of his mum calling in without notice. It was unlikely, but not impossible, that she would want to explore the new family asset.

He spent his first full night in the bungalow on Sunday, and was woken early on Monday morning by the alarm in his Smart Sensor. The world of work beckoned. He groaned, forced down some breakfast and buttoned up his suit jacket for the first time in many months. Sunnyvale HQ was his destination, and he suddenly regretted moving somewhere further away from his new workplace.

He hadn't given the job much thought until now, as he had been focusing excitedly on the idea of moving to the bungalow, complete with its treasure-filled bunker. But now the whole thing felt rather silly. Why had he sacrificed such a comfortable set-up for a smaller place, and with the added price of a job with his mum? He would probably end up seeing a lot more of her now than when he lived with her. How could he be so foolish?

Before he could wallow in self-pity, he realised he was pushing it for time. It wouldn't be wise to turn up late on his first day, even if he was generally unenthusiastic about the whole enterprise.

His mum had said to meet her outside HQ's south entrance at eight, and he arrived with only a few seconds to spare. She was ready and waiting in another of her pant suits, with a matching pair of kitten heels and a Smart Shroud. Calm, collected and co-ordinated. Harrison towered over her in his smart pinstripe suit, but he still felt like he was participating in a 'bring your child to work' day. Even though he was twenty, he often felt twelve in her presence.

The grand west entrance to HQ, with the original arched cathedral doors, was only used for special visitors and ceremonies. Instead, Alexa and Harrison entered through an inconspicuous side door by the south entrance into a small, but very plush, lobby.

It had a shiny porcelain floor, freshly cleaned and varnished overnight, and it was decorated like the interior of an expensive hotel: plants, chairs, sofas and an air of comfortable efficiency. The ceiling was vast and extravagant, with painted beams, hinting that this had once been a building of great renown.

'There was a fire in this part, caused by lightning, about a hundred years ago,' Alexa said, as she noticed Harrison staring upwards in awe. 'This part of the roof was rebuilt. You can still see the bosses that were added by a children's television show. Blue Peter, or something like that.'

She laughed at the quaintness of the name. Sunnyvale, of course, now controlled all forms of children's broadcasting and entertainment through the Smart Sensors and Smart TVs.

'Overall, we haven't had to make too many alterations to the building,' she continued. 'You know this used to be a religious place, don't you?'

Harrison nodded, but offered no further explanation. He only knew because he could remember Pop grumbling whenever they walked past it. 'They have no respect for anything,' he would lament, shaking his head at the logoed polyester sheets and the cinema-sized screens on each wall, playing glitzy commercials and public announcements all day long. (Right now, it was showing an advert for the Smart Shroud: 'Safety, Serenity, Style.')

'We added that wall straight ahead, to seal off this lobby,' Alexa said. 'Other than that, it was just a case of clearing out some of the clutter. Tombs, organs, stuff like that. The huge stone pillars get in the way a bit, but obviously we can't remove them. It's not the most practical space in the world, but we wanted something spectacular. And we needed something that was large.

'Ultimately, this is a warehouse, more than an office,' she continued. 'It's billed as HQ for the region, but many managerial staff work remotely. You'll be joining the office-based workers in another space outside, which I'll show you in a minute. And my office is at the north end of the building, in what they used to call the Chapter House.

'Other than that, beyond that wall, the space is simply used to house tens of thousands of Sunnyvale items. We call it stock. From there, the stock can be transported to anywhere in the region, in lightning-quick time. It's managed mainly by AI, but we still need dozens of warehouse workers to keep things ticking over.'

A trio of smiling security guards were manning a full-body scanner at the front of the lobby, which they both had to pass through. 'Morning ma'am,' one of them said to Alexa, which she acknowledged with a nod.

'Security is very important here, as you can imagine,' she said to Harrison. 'These scanners are not only checking for any weapons or items that could be smuggled in, they're also checking your body temperature, your medical history and your digital profile. We can't be too careful. Terrorism and industrial espionage are constant threats, and this site could very well be targeted by the East. To get you this job, I had to undergo a lie detector test and swear an affidavit that you were clean.'

Harrison was slightly taken aback by all this information. He had never really tried to picture his mum at work before, and he was beginning to understand why she was so at home here. She strode through the lobby with purpose, and was greeted deferentially by passers-by as she did so.

Just a short walk later, they were at the far-end of the lobby. On the white wall in front of them – beyond which was the main bulk of the ancient building – was a large, oil-paint portrait in a polished wooden frame, overlooking the room.

It was of a man, about forty years old, with piercing green eyes behind sleek, horn-rimmed spectacles, which sat on a small, feminine nose. He had a close-lipped smile, with a little upturn on his left cheek, and he was gazing directly out of the portrait. He looked to be balding, but he was wearing a black beret so it was difficult to tell.

Alexa stopped in front of the portrait, raised her right hand across her heart, and said: 'Sunnyvale is Progress. Progress is Freedom.' She looked at Harrison pointedly, and he meekly followed suit.

'This is the Great Liberator,' she said. 'His name is Edward Allen, as you should know. He's a great man. He hasn't been at the top for long, but he's already taking Sunnyvale to new heights. Isn't it a beautiful portrait?'

Harrison mumbled in agreement and fiddled with his starchy collar. It was going to take some time to get used to wearing formal clothes every day. He felt stifled and restricted.

'He's making a point of visiting as many strategically important Sunnyvale centres in the West as he can,' she said. 'Which is why he'll be gracing us with his presence this summer. What makes it even more special is his visit here will be on the date of Sunnyvale's anniversary: August the eighteenth. It'll be an honour, and I'm making sure everything is perfect for his arrival.'

They turned back on themselves, past a desk with a smiling receptionist, and then past the top of some stone steps.

'We originally planned for the office to be down there in the old undercroft,' Alexa said. 'But this building is archaic. There are layers and layers of different architecture, over centuries, and it's often too complex to fiddle with. We quickly realised it wouldn't be the most functional office space, even with our capabilities. Some things, unfortunately, are just easier to leave alone.'

'So technology isn't always progress, then?' Harrison said light-heartedly.

'Harrison,' Alexa said, in a venomous whisper. 'Stop it. Don't undermine me on your first day here. Any problems you cause will be a reflection on me.'

Harrison rolled his eyes and followed her back outside into the bracing morning air, catching the smell of her expensive perfume. They walked across the road and round to the entrance of another old church. It was a majestic building in its own right – with three spectacular arched windows at its front – but it was dwarfed by HQ.

'Welcome to our on-site control room,' she said, as they stepped through its heavy wooden doors and passed some more security scanners.

It had been stripped and remodelled to look like a typical office, except for several stone pillars. It was cool and still, and mostly unoccupied at this time in the morning. It had a dark carpet, so Alexa's heels made little sound as she walked, and the only natural light came through the surrounding stained-glass windows.

Dozens of evenly-spaced computer monitors formed an open plan semi-circle at the far end. In the left-hand corner there was a glass-panelled office containing a large laminate table, where the control room manager presumably worked, and there was a larger room, with an even larger table, conjoined to it. Harrison guessed that would be for meetings and presentations.

It was calm, quiet and secluded. It felt like another world – a secret lair – much like the bunker at Pop's bungalow.

'It's normally busier than this, of course,' Alexa said. 'But I thought it would be easier to show you around before most people arrive. As I said, plenty of managerial staff work remotely, but this can also be used as their base. We're an agile and adaptable workforce, with experts in every field.'

'Speaking of experts,' she said, with a rare smile, 'I'll introduce you soon to Elliot Patrick, who you'll be working with closely over the coming weeks. He'll be teaching you the basics of your job, and he's your assigned mentor during your induction period.'

She waved over to a lone figure at the computer monitors, and a thin, pale, mousy-haired man waved back. 'He's one of the best,' she said quietly. 'So make sure you listen to what he has to say. Now, I'll briefly run through some health and safety procedures, and then I'll leave you in Elliot's trusty hands.'

'Quick question,' Harrison said. 'Do we have to wear Smart Shrouds all day inside?'

'No,' Alexa replied. 'Some people like to, but we don't make it compulsory. We do, however, expect our employees to be brand ambassadors outside of the workplace. So make sure yours is always readily available. You should wear it as often as possible when you're out and about.'

*

Elliot Patrick was good at his job, and he knew it. He was sat casually in a leather computer chair, set at a small incline, and he radiated confidence as he explained what his duties were. Unlike Harrison, he was wearing casual clothes: jeans, a T-shirt and white trainers, and although he must have been nearly twice Harrison's age, he still looked like an overgrown schoolchild.

'My job is to oversee Sunnyvale's online presence,' he said. 'I'm based in York because I like it here, but I could be working in London if I wanted, or back in America. You may have noticed from my accent that I'm from across the pond. My family roots are Irish and German, but we're now stateside.'

Harrison couldn't have cared less about his family origins, but he nodded along.

'My job title has changed a few times,' Elliot continued. 'I think it's currently Chief of Truth.' He laughed, in a faux self-deprecatory way. 'Don't ask me who comes up with these things.'

Harrison smiled weakly.

'Anyway,' Elliot said. 'I manage a very important team throughout the West whose job is to ensure Sunnyvale's online presence and profile is accurate at all times. I think they used to call it 'public relations'. We have sophisticated AI to help us, of course, and I actually helped design and create a lot of it.

'Specifically, we have algorithms that can automatically detect dissent and falsehood, and delete them at source. But, alas, it isn't yet perfect. We still have untruths slipping through the net, and it's our duty to prevent them spreading. We'll start you off with something straightforward and, over time, we'll introduce you to the bigger parts of the job. Do you have any questions?'

Harrison thought for a moment. 'Please can you show me an example of what you mean?'

'Sure,' Elliot replied. He enjoyed any opportunity to demonstrate his work. He turned on the monitor in front of him, and the large screen showed eight columns of fast-scrolling text.

It was scrolling so quickly that it was impossible to make out what any of it said.

'This screen is showing us every mention of the word 'Sunnyvale' in the West so far today, and bear in mind it's not yet nine o'clock here, and it's the middle of the night across the Atlantic. In a few hours' time this will be scrolling at five times the speed.'

'What do you mean it captures every mention of the word?' Harrison said. 'Do you mean in people's social media posts?'

'Yeah, it includes that,' Elliot said. 'And also people's emails, messages, video calls and spoken conversations. The Smart Sensors have voice recognition. Of course, no human being could ever track even a millionth of one per cent of these hits, but our AI can.

'It automatically sorts these mentions into three categories: Harmless, Unknown and Immediate Threat. The overwhelming majority fall into the former, and only a tiny handful into the latter. Naturally, we're well prepared for them. But a fair few end up in the middle category – they can be too abstract or unclear for the AI to decipher, and that's where my team come in handy. We're more than handy, actually. We're essential.'

'OK,' Harrison said. 'But who's to presume every direct threat to Sunnyvale will actually include the use of the word? Surely people could use codewords.'

'That's a very good point,' Elliot said, relishing the chance to show off Sunnyvale's prowess. 'What I've described to you is only the tip of the iceberg. We have much more extensive AI in place across the West to identify anyone who is even just a *potential* threat. That's left to a more specialist team, and a lot of what they do requires top-level clearance.

'I've worked with some of them in the past, and what they can do is mightily impressive. I'm a computer science specialist, and they make me look like a monkey with a typewriter. For the purposes of your induction and your role here, don't worry about the bigger picture. Our job is just to focus on the direct mentions of Sunnyvale and to ensure only the truth remains. Some people call us 'Sweepers', as we're cleaning up the organisation's reputation.'

Harrison nodded, for what felt like the hundredth time already.

'Welcome to your first day as a Sunnyvale Sweeper,' Elliot said, with a smile. 'It may be a silly title, but it's noble work. We help keep the organisation and, by extension, the West safe from misinformation and mistruths.'

6

Harrison was so tired every night after his first week of work that he completely neglected the bunker in the shed. Alexa hadn't visited the bungalow once, and he now trusted that he was safe from a sudden imposition from her. But it was draining, non-stop work being trained as a Sweeper, and by the time he had returned home, eaten dinner and fed Aslan, he was invariably ready to slump into bed.

Saturday morning came to his immense relief. He enjoyed a lie in, with Aslan purring and sleeping on the bed by his feet, and vowed to make the most of a free day. He could finally explore the bunker at leisure, which he was tremendously excited about. It was the only reason he had made the effort of moving there, after all.

After a shower and some breakfast, he made his way to the shed and typed 1811 into the keypad. He instinctively looked left and right to make sure nobody was watching him. He only had a neighbour on one side and the garden fence was way above head height, so he felt secure.

He stepped into the shed and locked the door behind him, and a minute later he was standing with bare feet on the cream carpet. He smiled at the feeling of playful freedom, like a child who has made a den or a fort, and pressed the two buttons at the front of the music-playing device.

The disc started spinning, and he moved the lever over and onto it. A catchy drum-and-guitar melody started. It was by the Rolling Stones again, he realised, but it was different to the one that had played before – clearly the song was determined by which groove the silver needle settled into.

Harrison couldn't quite make out all the words – it was something about 'honky tonks' – but he liked what he was hearing. The music was over a hundred years old, but there was something about it that stirred him inside. More than anything else, it was *fun*. Everything else in his world right now seemed to be so serious, especially at work.

He jumped into the blue leather armchair and closed his eyes, jiggling his foot to the beat, until it moved automatically on to the next song. He turned the volume down so it was just background music, and spun around to see the room in its entirety.

It looked even better than during his first visit. He was drawn immediately towards the bookshelves, packed from end to end with paperbacks and hardbacks of every shape, size and thickness. They didn't appear to be in any particular order.

He picked a chunky, orange-bound book from the third shelf down, which was roughly level with his eyes. The front cover, with a small tear in its bottom right corner, read: *Shakespeare – The Complete Works*.

One of the old, worn pages inside, about three-quarters of the way through the book, was folded in the top right corner, marked for easy access. Harrison gently flicked to it. The text was miniscule. About halfway down the page, a short passage was underlined in green ink:

> *Cowards die many times before their deaths;*
> *The valiant never taste of death but once.*

Harrison read it aloud over the background music, and then he read it aloud again. It must have meant something to Pop, and he was determined to memorise it out of respect. He rifled through the pages with his thumb, and held them up to his nose – it was definitely the books that gave this room such a unique smell. He returned Shakespeare to the shelf and continued browsing.

A book of similar chunkiness caught his eye, and it also had an orange cover. The spine was so faded, however, that it was almost white. The title was *Grimm's Complete Fairy Tales*. Harrison smiled childishly, and his imagination was cast back about fifteen years. Whenever he used to visit Pop, before the ex-communication, he would beg to be read a fairytale.

Pop would place a finger on his lips and shush Harrison. 'I will do if we get chance,' he would say. 'But your mother doesn't like me doing so. It'll have to be our secret.'

Harrison would nod conspiratorially, and often he would have to leave disappointed if the opportunity never arose. But, now and again, his mother would be distracted, or she would nip out to run an errand, or to deal with something at work, and Pop would produce *Grimm's Complete Fairy Tales* from nowhere.

The names of the stories were like something from a mystical age, and Harrison pored through the contents page to see how many he could remember. 'The Frog Prince', 'The Gallant Tailor', 'The Little Farmer', 'The Golden Key' – he laughed as he realised he could, at least vaguely, recall them all. 'The Robber Bridegroom', 'The Mouse, The Bird, and The Sausage', 'The Peasant's Wise Daughter'. He worked through the full list with a melancholic smile.

He spent the rest of his Saturday in the bunker, exploring the bookshelves and the music collection, and tasting the whisky in the glass decanter (it was sharp and warmed his whole body up). He got the non-smart TV to work, and discovered that it played these ancient discs called DVDs, dozens of which were lined up on the bottom-right bookshelf.

After a late night and a long, peaceful sleep in the blue armchair, he did exactly the same again on Sunday.

*

Monday morning thus came as a shock to the system. Sunnyvale HQ was no match for the bunker in the shed. Harrison had, in fact, decided that 'bunker' was an insufficiently descriptive term for his newfound sanctuary. With the help of an old Oxford English dictionary on the shelf, he had settled on calling it his 'haven'.

He thought 'Harrison's Haven' had a cool ring to it, and he mockingly recalled Elliot Patrick when he read of the word's associative roots with the German word 'Hafen', meaning harbour. *My family roots are Irish and German,* he imitated in a nasally voice.

After just one week he was sick of Elliot Patrick and his mentorship. The prospect of a second week was bleak, but he had to get on with it. He couldn't afford an argument with his mum, as a fall-out with her could mean losing the job, the bungalow and the haven in one fell swoop.

He arrived at work in good time, as he was well rested from his weekend of leisure. He went through the security scanner, making eye contact with the portrait of the Great Liberator. He was expected to parrot the line 'Sunnyvale is Progress. Progress is Freedom,' in front of the painting every morning, but he tried to avoid doing so if nobody was close by.

He crossed back to the control room and to his usual seat in the semi-circle of computers. Employees were supposed to constantly 'hot desk', meaning they never had a fixed station, but most people had a favourite spot and used it whenever possible.

Harrison's place was at the very edge of the semi-circle, which he felt gave him at least a smidgeon of breathing space. It meant he could only have a neighbour to one side. Mercifully, there was no sign yet of Elliot Patrick, who often filled that seat to pass on his wisdom to Harrison.

There were only a couple of other people filling the semi-circle, both sat towards the other end. He waved across to them:

they were brother-and-sister twins, with strikingly similar black hair and round, brown eyes. They always seemed to be the first to arrive and the last to leave, and on Harrison's first day they had introduced themselves as the Lamb twins (he never caught their first names). They each smiled back.

Harrison took his seat at the end and enjoyed a few moments of serenity. He even braved closing his eyes for a moment, but his peace was short-lived as Alexa soon came bounding over in her colour co-ordinated pant suit and heels.

'Morning, Harrison,' she said, from behind the computer desk.

'Morning,' he replied. He never knew how he was supposed to address her at work. Mum? Alexa? Mrs Snow? Ma'am?

'How did your first week go?' she asked. 'I was away most of last week and haven't had chance to speak to Elliot yet.'

'Yeah, it was really interesting,' he lied. 'It's great to learn from someone as experienced and enthusiastic as Elliot.'

'Has he explained what your job will entail?'

'Of course,' he said. 'I'm a Sweeper, and he's given me a good grounding in the main duties. He also said he would show me how to edit Sunnypedia articles, which is something I could be doing long-term. He said it would be helpful to get a grasp of it now.'

'Very good,' she said. 'Keep it up.' She departed with a curt nod and a brief smile, which was as close to maternal affection as he had ever received.

*

His hopes of a day without supervision steadily grew throughout the morning, until they were dashed just before noon. Elliot Patrick sauntered down the staircase – wearing scruffy jeans, a casual, checked shirt and a logoed Sunnyvale beanie – and set himself up in the glass-panelled office in the corner. Harrison had learnt that it was officially a free space for anybody to use, but there was an unofficial rule that only senior employees could actually do so.

Ten minutes later, Elliot strolled over to Harrison's station and took the seat next to him. He had a steaming coffee in his hand, in a logoed cup.

'How's it gone this morning?' he asked. 'I thought I'd leave you to it to see if you'd use your own initiative.'

'I'm still getting to grips with it all, but it's been OK,' Harrison said. 'I came across one example in the Unknown pile which I wasn't sure what to do with. I've passed on the details to you in an email.'

'Show me on here,' Elliot said.

Harrison clicked on a different tab, which brought up his email to Elliot.

'I know that I'm supposed to react to any threats immediately,' Harrison said. 'But I just wanted to double check this one with you first.'

'Understandable,' Elliot said. 'You're learning quickly but these things take time, and there's never any harm in double checking.'

Elliot pulled his wheeled chair closer to Harrison's monitor and adjusted his glasses. The email read:

Hi Elliot,

The AI identified this as Unknown this morning, and I thought I should run it by you before I act on it. It's from a verbal conversation between two people in London, recorded by their Smart Sensors:

Person 1:
Steve, listen to this one, mate. I heard it the other day:
There once was a Great Liberator,
More like a Great Dictator,
He was bald as a coot,
Slimy as a newt,
And as ugly as the Terminator.

Person 2:
[Laughs] Not the best, Jim, but also not the worst. What about this one?
How many Great Liberators does it take to change a light bulb? None. There's enough light shining out of his arsehole already.

Person 1: [Laughs]
[Conversation continues for six minutes]

Regards,
Harrison

'I have their names and details recorded, of course,' Harrison said. 'I just called them Person 1 and Person 2 for convenience.'

'Good work,' Elliot said. 'The AI is incredibly sophisticated but it can struggle with the nuances of humour. Or, in this case, attempted humour. If in doubt it places it in Unknown and then we can have a look.'

'What happens now?' Harrison said.

'Well, this is clearly a threat to Sunnyvale. It's a vicious slur on the Great Liberator. Who knows what other dark opinions they have? We'll do a thorough search of their digital profiles. There's rarely smoke without fire, and I'd bet many SVPs that they're involved in suspicious activities. At the very least, they'll both need to spend time at a re-education camp.'

'What exactly is on their digital profiles?' Harrison said.

'Everything,' Elliot replied simply. 'We have a good fish through and, nine times out of ten, we find more incriminating evidence. No doubt that'll be the case with these two gentlemen. There's no place for their vile insults and threats in our society.'

'So there's nothing more I need to do?' Harrison said.

'No, you can pat yourself on the back for a job well done. In future, rather than emailing me directly you can upload a report into our special incident database. I showed you how to do this on Friday morning, I think.'

'OK,' Harrison said.

'Either me or one of my team working elsewhere will see it, almost immediately,' Elliot said. 'Our shift patterns are flexible but we ensure that several of us are *always* monitoring the incident database, for things like this. We can act on it ourselves, or pass it elsewhere, depending on the threat level.'

'How many Sweepers are there out there, like me?' Harrison said.

'Hundreds, sometimes thousands, at any one time,' Elliot replied. 'But as soon as you clicked on this threat it became specifically yours to deal with, and the other Sweepers were locked out. It means we don't waste resources by having several people working on the same incident from the Unknown pile. You did the right thing checking with me, and don't be afraid to do the same in future.'

'Thanks,' Harrison said. 'Please can you show me the incident database again? I remember you showing me before but it hasn't all sunk in yet.'

'Sure. And later this afternoon I'll show you how to edit Sunnypedia articles.'

*

Sunnypedia was the world's largest online encyclopaedia. Harrison had grown up with it, and was familiar with how to use it. What he hadn't appreciated was how vast the network of Sunnyvale employees was to maintain, monitor and edit the site. It was a prodigious task.

'Over the pond, we have dozens of offices, each the size of the warehouse upstairs, filled with Sunnypedia specialists,' Elliot said. 'But we also like to show Sweepers some of the basic tasks, so they can chip in when they're having a quiet day. Every little helps.'

'How many articles are there in total?' Harrison asked.

'Oh, several hundred million. Most of them are in English, but there are some in other western languages too.'

'How is it possible to manage that, even with the warehouses full of employees?'

'It used to be a publicly-curated resource,' Elliot said. 'Just about anybody could log on and create or edit an article, hence the sheer volume of content. Now, we control all of it. I'm sure you can understand why that was necessary.'

Harrison nodded, as he felt like he had to.

'Of course, there are many people, topics or themes which are out-of-bounds,' Elliot said. 'But our policy is that to completely remove them would increase their allure. We often leave their pages up on Sunnypedia, with a clear warning about their wrongdoing. Let's think of something to look up, as an example.'

'Try the Rolling Stones,' Harrison said boldly. 'I remember being warned about them at school.'

Elliot looked sideways at Harrison and typed 'Rolling Stones' into the search bar.

A page loaded immediately, but the title had a line through it, so it read ~~'The Rolling Stones.~~' The text underneath was short and succinct:

The Rolling Stones were an English rock band formed in 1962. The private or commercial consumption and/or distribution of their music has been prohibited. Anyone in breach of this ban will be charged under the Sunnyvale Terrorism Act of 2057.

Elliot waited until Harrison had read the paragraph, and typed 'Mark Twain' into the search bar.

'He was a very famous author in the USA,' Elliot said. 'But his works have rightly been liquidated.'

Samuel Langhorne Clemens, known by his pen name Mark Twain, (1835-1910) was an American writer. The private or commercial consumption and/or distribution of his work has been prohibited. Anyone in breach of this ban will be charged under the Sunnyvale Terrorism Act of 2057.

'So will my job involve maintaining articles like this?' Harrison said.

'Not really, I was just showing you these as an example. Generally speaking, these are dead pages and require no upkeep, unless there's some kind of hack or error. Your main job will be amending and updating the live pages – those with actual content.'

'Like what?'

'Take your pick. Just about anyone famous has a Sunnypedia page.'

'OK. How about the Prime Minister?'

'Good choice,' Elliot said. 'High-profile political figures are top of our priority list. Their pages are often targeted by hackers and they require constant vigilance.'

The Prime Minister's page included a small, square photograph at the top, complete with the obligatory statesmanlike smile. His biography was long and broken up into different categories: 'Early Life', 'Career', 'Personal Life' and so on. Harrison had read or heard most of it before.

'It's more difficult with living people,' Elliot said. 'As their reputation is constantly fluctuating. Right now, your ennobled Prime Minister is a good partner of Sunnyvale. His party accept our considerable funding with open arms – as do the opposition, by the way. He understands the agreement nicely.

'As such, his Sunnypedia page is warm and generous, if a little dry in places. If, hypothetically, his party were to reject our funding, we possess the capability of – shall we say – *correcting* the biography. There's no mention of the sexual harassment case that was hushed up when he was at university. Or the fact his mistress had a miscarriage two years ago.'

'Would you be able to add that to the page right now?' Harrison said.

'Pretty much. I could make the edit here and submit it, and it would then be passed on to one of the Sunnypedia managers for approval. A few clicks of the button later, and it would be live.'

'For the whole world to read,' Harrison said.

'Exactly,' Elliot said. 'There was an American writer called H. L. Mencken, who said: "When I hear a man applauded by the mob I always feel a pang of pity for him. All he has to do to be hissed is to live long enough."

'Well, we control that mob,' Elliot said. 'They applaud when we want them to applaud, and they hiss when we want them to hiss. Pretty cool, isn't it?'

7

Harrison's life continued in this pattern for several weeks. From Monday to Friday, he worked as an increasingly proficient Sweeper at Sunnyvale HQ, and at the weekend he would enjoy as much time as possible in his haven.

It was something of a double life. He knew he was risking his healthy income and future by indulging in Pop's old books, films and music (and, occasionally, whisky) but he couldn't resist their lure. Everybody has hobbies, he reasoned. And how could he be perceived as a threat to Sunnyvale when he was doing so much to keep it safe? He was reporting directly to the Chief of Truth and he was doing a good job, even if he wasn't especially enthusiastic about his work.

His competence was rewarded with the news that he had passed his probationary period. It came with a contract of employment, a small pay rise, and a pep talk from Elliot Patrick.

'Congratulations Harrison,' he said. 'I look forward to seeing you progress. If you increase your focus and commitment, you could go far.'

He added: 'All contracted employees here at HQ take an additional one-on-one seminar with me, where I go over the confidentiality agreement you've just signed, and help you map out a career plan with Sunnyvale. I'll also be going over our illustrious history, and our future. We want every employee to feel like they're part of the same exciting journey.'

*

The seminar took place the following morning in the large meeting room. It was a warm June day outside, with a light breeze blissfully blowing, but in the control room it was the same as ever. Still. Sedate. Clinical.

'As you are, of course, already aware of my role and standing in Sunnyvale, I'll dispense with the formal introductions,' Elliot said. 'Not everyone is lucky enough to have me as their mentor, so these seminars are often the first time I meet a new employee.'

Harrison considered cracking a joke, but it would only have fallen on deaf ears.

'And I should also dispense with the history lesson,' Elliot continued. 'Seeing as you are the son of Alexa Snow. I'm sure you've heard it all a thousand times. But rules are rules, and I can't tick this box in front of me until every element of the seminar is completed in full.'

A hologram TV screen was projecting from the centre of the table, and it provided the visual cues for Elliot's presentation. The screen simply showed the word Sunnyvale, with the famous logo underneath. Elliot was standing by the screen, and Harrison was sat at the end of the table with a glass of water in front of him. A captive audience of one. The cushioned chair was comfortable, and Harrison forced himself to sit upright. It would be a bad idea to slip off to sleep.

'Firstly, a simple pop quiz,' Elliot said. 'What do the letters V, A, L and E stand for in our mission statement?'

Harrison momentarily panicked, but then realised it was an easy question. You'd have to have been living under a rock for many years to be uncertain. The message was everywhere.

'Virtuous, Altruistic, Liberal and Ethical,' Harrison said. The four letters separated on the screen, and spelt out the words Harrison had spoken.

'That was a straight-forward one to warm us up,' Elliot said. 'Just to make sure you were paying attention.' Elliot smiled, but only with his mouth. His thin, brown eyes were unmoved.

'Sunnyvale was born twenty-seven years ago,' Elliot said. 'When the seven leading companies in Silicon Valley merged to form a conglomerate. It was by far the biggest event in the history of business and capitalism. Talks behind the scenes took several years to complete, until the deal was finally announced on the eighteenth of August, 2056. Hence why this date is celebrated every year.

'We were the first 'Goldhorn', a new term coined to describe an organisation valued at five hundred trillion dollars. It brought the cumulative reach and power of the Big Seven under one umbrella. It was unprecedented. Historic. Momentous. Choose any superlative you want, and it wouldn't quite capture the magnitude of this event.

'No organisation in the history of the world has ever had such an impact on people's everyday life and work. If you want to talk to a friend, you do it with our help. If you want to go out for a meal, you do it with our help. If you have to do a spreadsheet for work, you do it with our help. If you want to buy a new pair of shoes, you do it with our help. If you want to take a pill for your headache, you do it with our help. If you find yourself in a court of law, our technology decides your fate. So on and so forth, ad infinitum.

'It's a tremendous privilege, but also a tremendous responsibility. I mentioned a moment ago that the deal was the biggest in the history of capitalism – I don't just mean because of the scale of the finances involved, but because it has fundamentally altered the landscape forever. Thanks to Sunnyvale, we now live in a *post*-capitalist society. This was no accident. It was the very intention of the architects of the merger from the beginning. The only way to beat capitalism was to overwhelm it, using its own system and its own rules. We're no longer just a *company*. We've transcended such outdated concepts.'

Harrison nodded and took a sip of his glass of water. He wondered how many times Elliot had regurgitated this script.

'A vast restructuring was badly needed,' Elliot said. 'The first half of the twenty-first century – just like the whole of the twentieth – was racked with instability. Economic depression. Civil unrest. Violence and division. Dictators and despots. History was repeating itself.

'But the Big Seven thrived amidst the chaos. They were well placed to cope in a changing world, where most businesses weren't. Their profits and control grew as each year passed. People realised they couldn't live without them. Western society had broken down. Its pillars had crumbled into dust. It needed a saviour. From the ashes, Sunnyvale rose like a phoenix.'

As he said this, video clips of rioting were showing on the hologram screen. Flames. Overturned cars. Smashed windows. Mass panic and hysteria. When he said 'rose like a phoenix', the chaos stopped. It was replaced by a tranquil soundtrack (Harrison's indulgence in Pop's collection of classical music led him to believe it may have been some kind of piano sonata by Beethoven). The Sunnyvale logo also appeared, as the music continued. The brightly-burning sun. The narrow blue stream. The lush green valley. The small rainbow on the horizon.

'A post-capitalist world,' Elliot continued, 'with Sunnyvale at its helm, is more virtuous, more altruistic, more liberal and more ethical than anything that came before. We are the drivers and facilitators of a better world. We are at the vanguard of a new world order.'

Elliot's voice was soft and nasally, but he was gathering momentum and speaking with fervour.

'It is crucial that everyone fortunate enough to work here understands this. This is no normal job. This isn't about collecting your SVPs each month for doing the bare minimum. We're brothers-and-sisters-in-arms. We're comrades.'

Elliot thumped his chest as he said this, which took Harrison by surprise.

'We're comrades,' Elliot repeated. 'Sunnyvale is Progress. Progress is Freedom.'

The slogan – the mantra – flashed up on the screen, together with a triumphant, orchestral tune. *Beethoven again*, Harrison thought.

Elliot's thin eyes arrowed in on Harrison's. 'Repeat after me, Harrison,' he said. 'Sunnyvale is Progress. Progress is Freedom.'

Harrison paused a second, and said quietly: 'Sunnyvale is Progress. Progress is Freedom.'

'Louder,' Elliot demanded. 'And with real meaning.'

This time Harrison repeated it with as much forced gusto as he could. The orchestral tune continued in the background. 'Sunnyvale is Progress! Progress is Freedom!'

'Good,' Elliot said. 'Never forget how fortunate you are to be part of this journey. Every day our tireless work makes the world a better place.'

8

That afternoon, Harrison's Sunnyvale education continued apace. He was making his way to his first Monthly Meeting (it was something only fully-fledged members of staff, rather than newbies on probation, could attend). It would be an exaggeration to say he was excited, but he was certainly curious. Another rabble-rousing team talk from Elliot Patrick would be quite amusing.

It was being held in Alexa's office, at the north end of the building, in what used to be known as the Chapter House. It meant a welcome change to his usual scenery and routine, which consisted solely of checking in with the main security through the south door and then heading straight back across the road to the control room. This would involve an adventurous walk from south to north, cutting through the main body of the building, where the warehouse was located.

He was walking through the lobby when he bumped into the Lamb twins, who smiled in unison when Harrison asked if they were also going to the meeting.

'Of course we are,' the brother said. 'It's the highlight of the month.'

'Mhmm,' the sister agreed. 'There's chatter, comradeship and vegan cake. What's not to like?'

Their symmetrical smiles held for a second longer than was comfortable, and Harrison returned with a weak grimace.

'Sorry, Harrison. We have to ask,' the brother said, as they stopped in front of the portrait of the Great Liberator. 'What's it like being the son of Alexa Snow? She's a wonderful woman. We don't mean to be sycophantic, but we really are great admirers.'

'She's an inspiration,' the sister added enthusiastically.

Harrison stopped himself from rolling his eyes. 'I don't like to talk about her at work, really,' he said. 'I'd rather just be treated like anyone else. But yeah, she's very good at her job. It's inspiring. Yeah.'

The Lamb twins were too polite to say so, but they were clearly disappointed by the lack of colour he had provided. It was awkwardly silent for a moment, until the brother said: 'Have you been through the warehouse before?'

'I haven't,' Harrison said. 'I was kind of expecting a grand tour in my first few days, but it never happened. I've just been going straight to the control room every day.'

'Prepare yourself for quite a sight,' the brother said. 'This is one heck of an operation.'

Harrison started to make his way to the white door next to the portrait, but the Lamb brother stopped him with his forearm.

'Sunnyvale is Progress. Progress is Freedom,' the twins said at once, as they looked up at the portrait.

'Oh yeah,' Harrison mumbled. 'Sunnyvale is Progress. Progress is Freedom.'

'Good,' the brother said. 'Now let's go through. After you, comrade.'

*

For the second time in recent months, Harrison's mouth literally opened in surprise and wonder as he entered a room. This time, the sight was even more stunning than the haven.

He was stood in the centre of a huge, sweeping space, extending as far as the eye could see both left and right. It was a splendorous stretch of limestone pillars and arches, up to an impossibly high ceiling dotted with gold bosses, which glimmered in the sunlight streaming through the stained-glass windows. The floor was well-worn limestone, with dark tiles zigzagging in some kind of pattern.

Harrison was now flanked by the Lamb twins, who had noticed his awe. 'A mason who worked on this building once described it as a symphony in stone,' the sister said. 'It catches people's eye when they walk past. It's the centrepiece of the city, which makes it a perfect fit for Sunnyvale. We're the centrepiece of people's lives, you see? The fulcrum of society. The drivers of positive change.'

Harrison didn't reply, as he was too busy taking in his surroundings. His first impression had been to marvel at the beauty of the stone infrastructure, but he was now equally blown away by the more modern additions within the building.

Every inch of space was seemingly accounted for. There was only a narrow strip of floor ahead which he could walk down to reach Alexa's office in the old Chapter House – either side of the little walkway were gargantuan storage units, reaching hundreds of shelves up into the air, finishing just centimetres short of the majestic ceiling.

There were dozens of these huge shelve units stretching to the building's perimeter. They were perfectly white, and looked to be made of MDF. Sturdy, but lightweight. Each unit was numbered, and consisted of hundreds of lockers built into the shelves, some small enough to contain a handful of the tiniest stock, others large enough to house a flat-screen TV.

Scores of workers buzzed on the ground around them, collecting items from the robotic arms that could speed up, down and across the units to find whatever was needed in a matter of seconds.

A grey-haired, hunched man hustled past Harrison with three packages in his arms, accidentally knocking his shoulder. He was wearing an all-in-one uniform, adorned with the Sunnyvale logo, as well as a Smart Shroud and a hard hat. He apologised immediately, and his sunken, bloodshot eyes met

Harrison's for a moment. And then he continued on his way, scurrying as quickly as his frail legs would carry him.

'He stank of alcohol,' the brother said, shaking his head. 'And did you see his yellow fingernails?'

'He stank,' the sister echoed. 'I wish they'd vet who works here more carefully – we shouldn't be letting any old fool in. I don't even know why we still have all these workers in here. Surely the robots could do everything quicker?'

'They've trialled that countless times,' the brother replied. 'The machines are obviously infinitely quicker at getting stock from the shelves, but we still need the workers to transport the items from the warehouse to the drones outside. It's one of those weird anomalies where it's quicker and cheaper to have humans doing it, largely because each warehouse has a slightly different layout.'

'So technology isn't always progress, then?' Harrison said lightly, before he was able to stop himself.

On his left, the Lamb brother looked like he was about to say something, but then just cleared his throat. On his right, the Lamb sister looked puzzlingly at her feet, wondering if she had misheard what Harrison had said.

'It was just a joke,' Harrison said boldly. 'You don't need to go all weird. You've heard a joke before, haven't you?'

'Humour is very subjective,' the brother said. His tone was neutral.

'Suit yourself,' Harrison said. 'We've still got five minutes, I'm going to explore the warehouse a bit. I'll meet you in the office. It's just straight on, through there, right?'

'I would feel more comfortable if we joined you,' the brother said. 'It would be irresponsible of us if you got lost and were late for your first Monthly Meeting. I don't want to spoil anything, but it is well known that this will be your first.'

'Suit yourself,' Harrison said again.

He turned to his left and started down a walkway which was just wide enough for the three of them side by side. It was like he was a young child being chaperoned by his parents.

'This was called the nave,' the sister said. 'It's been used for burials, processions, graduations, concerts. You could fit up to fifteen hundred people in here. Now, it's Sunnyvale's space. The last time you ordered anything from us, there's a good chance it came from one of these shelves.'

They continued walking by an endless procession of units, each with its own set of worker bees, rushing and sometimes pushing past with their hands full. The robotic arms were zooming in every direction to retrieve items from lockers, dropping them off into a basket on the floor, and then whizzing off again.

It was a mesmerising process, with everything operating in hypnotic synchronicity. Order within chaos. Or was it chaos within order? The warehouse workers – in their matching overalls, Smart Shrouds and hard hats – were scuttling constantly from one place to the next, barely pausing for breath, let alone conversation.

They reminded Harrison of Oompa-Loompas, from *Charlie and the Chocolate Factory*. Pop had read the book to him as a child, and he had rediscovered a battered paperback version in the haven. He was about to point out the similarity to the Lamb twins, but remembered that Roald Dahl, the book's author, was *verboten*. He could remember the Sunnypedia entry:

> ~~Roald Dahl (1916-1990)~~ *was a British novelist, short-story writer, poet, screenwriter, and wartime fighter pilot. The private or commercial consumption and/or distribution of his work has been prohibited. Anyone in breach of this ban will be charged under the Sunnyvale Terrorism Act of 2057.*

They reached the west front of the building, with sunlight bathing their faces in a warm glow. It was coming through a spectacular stained-glass window.

'This is newly installed,' the sister said. 'These old buildings often had windows like this, depicting silly religious scenes. We initially planned to demolish them completely, but then your mother – sorry, Mrs Snow – had the wonderful idea of keeping the stained glass, but changing the image.'

Harrison looked up and examined the window. The Great Liberator looked back at him. It was an identical image to the one on the portrait in the lobby: the piercing green eyes, the horn-rimmed spectacles, the small, feminine nose, the close-lipped smile and the black beret.

'Sunnyvale is Progress. Progress is Freedom,' the twins parroted simultaneously.

'This is a masterpiece in glass artistry,' the sister said. 'And it wasn't easy locating the few experts in the West who are capable of such a feat. We've done the same to the window on the eastern wall too – it used to be called the Great East Window. Now, it's even greater. All the other windows have been left as they are, which is a shame. But it's not practical to change every single one. There are a hundred-and-twenty-eight in total.'

'Mrs Snow's idea was so well received,' the brother said, 'that they're looking to implement it in all other Sunnyvale warehouses across the West, wherever possible. And it's partly why the Great Liberator is so keen to visit us in the summer. That will be quite the occasion.'

*

Alexa's office was equally as breathtaking. It was a large, open, octagonal space, surrounded by the old, original stained-glass windows. The elaborate ceiling swept the eyes upward, and there were ancient carvings on the limestone walls.

The only furnishing was a solid oak desk at the far end, facing the entrance, with a swivel chair and a computer. It was minimalist to the extreme. There were about seventy people standing around, talking in small pockets and creating a low hum of chatter. Harrison recognised most of them from the control room, but he hadn't had a substantial conversation with any of them.

Elliot Patrick was stood casually with a group of colleagues, languidly using his hands to help tell a story. His punch line was met with an uproar of obsequious laughter.

'You were so lucky to have Elliot Patrick as your mentor,' the Lamb brother said. 'He's valued very highly. I don't know why he's based in York, to be honest. The guy could be anywhere he wanted.'

'I think he's dreamy,' the sister said. 'He's got that geek chic look about him.'

'He's also the richest man you've ever set eyes on,' the brother laughed. 'I'm sure that has nothing to do with it.'

Harrison made his excuses and did a quick lap of the room, admiring the architecture and catching glimpses of people's conversations. He was stood in front of the oak desk, inspecting the original, immense stained-glass window behind it, when he noticed something next to the computer monitor.

It was a ceramic-framed photograph, facing away from him. He surreptitiously glanced behind each shoulder to make sure he wasn't being watched – everyone seemed engaged in their group conversations – and picked it up. He was taken aback by what he saw.

It captured a happy moment about fifteen years ago, when he was a five-year-old with puppy fat and a mop of brown hair, and his mum was beaming behind him. She was holding him up for the picture, and clearly struggling with his weight.

It was a lovely, normal mother-son photograph, which is why it had taken Harrison aback. Very little about his relationship with Alexa was lovely and normal. He had never seen this picture before, and there were very few sentimental mementoes around the townhouse. Why had she chosen to keep it in her office? He had always seen her as something of an automaton, especially when she was in her work attire, but clearly there was a maternal instinct too. It was lurking far beneath the tough exterior, but it was there.

Harrison returned the photograph and wiped a speck of dust from his eye. As he did so, the general hubbub stopped, and he heard the click-click of high heels on the tiled floor.

'Afternoon everyone,' Alexa said loudly, as she entered her office. 'Sorry to keep you waiting, but I was speaking to the Great Liberator via my Smart Sensor.'

There were titillated 'oohs' and 'aahs' around the room, and the small groups began whispering feverishly to each other. Alexa let the intrigue spread.

'He's very much looking forward to his visit in August,' she said. 'And I assured him everything would be spick and span for his arrival. I can trust all of you to give a hundred per cent for this, can't I? It's a big moment for each of us, professionally and personally.'

'Yes!' the enthusiastic response came, firstly from the Lamb twins, and then from everyone else. The cries of 'Yes' then morphed into cheers and whoops, and the grand room was quickly filled with cacophonous excitement.

Alexa raised her right hand and the noise abated. She then moved the hand over her heart, and said: 'Sunnyvale is Progress. Progress is Freedom.'

The crowd responded immediately, and repeated the mantra three times in unison. Harrison, perhaps for the first time, was swept along with the emotion. He joined in wilfully, and felt pride at how deeply Alexa was respected by her colleagues. She was a leader, and she was in her element. And she was his *mum* – in her own peculiar way – as the loving photograph illustrated.

Alexa raised her right hand again, and the din died down. 'Now it's time for normal business,' she said. She clicked her fingers, and eight formally-dressed waiters entered the room carrying silver platters. 'Please help yourselves to our vegan assortment of drinks and snacks,' she said. 'And, if you'll please excuse me, I'm now going to hand over to Elliot Patrick to continue leading our Monthly Meeting.'

She turned on her heels and departed as efficiently as she had arrived. People were soon nibbling on small snacks, and looking towards Elliot, who walked unhurriedly into the middle of the room.

'Hi guys,' he said, in his nasally voice. 'There's only one real order of business, today. And then we can enjoy mingling.'

He scanned around the room, until his eyes settled on Harrison. 'I'm happy to welcome Mr Harrison Snow to his first Monthly Meeting,' he said. 'He recently passed his probationary period, and he's already proving himself a valuable asset to the Sweeper team.'

Harrison smiled sheepishly and felt his cheeks redden. 'Congratulations,' Elliot said. 'Welcome to the Sunnyvale family.' Harrison muttered a quick 'Thank you', and the room erupted into applause.

'Now, without any further ado, let's enjoy the food, drink and company,' Elliot said. 'It's a chance to let your hair down and get to know your comrades better. This is more than a *job*, remember. It's your life.'

The Lamb twins rushed over to Harrison with gushing smiles. 'Sorry if I let it slip earlier,' the brother said. 'We knew you'd be getting a shout-out for passing your probationary period, and I didn't want you to miss it.'

'I appreciate it,' Harrison said.

'I love the Monthly Meetings,' the sister said. 'It really does make you feel part of a *family*, doesn't it?'

Harrison would have laughed with scorn half an hour ago, but he was softened by the surroundings and the smiles, and the intoxicating atmosphere of seventy people radiating goodwill.

'It really isn't so bad, is it?' he said.

'We're having some drinks at our place this evening, if you'd like to join?' the sister said. 'It'll mainly be people from work – it's nice to see each other outside of the office. Do you fancy it?'

'Yeah, why not?' Harrison replied. 'Count me in.'

9

The Monthly Meeting continued in high spirits through the afternoon, and all the way until the end of Harrison's shift. He then made his way to the Lamb twins' flat on the outskirts of the city, in a self-driven taxi with a handful of colleagues.

'I could get used to days like today,' he said. 'Getting paid to stand around and have a laugh.' He was stood with the Lamb brother in the lounge area of his flat, which had white walls and neat furnishings. It wasn't quite as minimalist as Alexa's office, but it certainly wasn't cluttered. It was dominated by the largest domestic Sunnyvale Smart TV Harrison had ever seen, mounted on the wall.

'The leadership at Sunnyvale know the importance of developing a familial work atmosphere,' the Lamb brother said. 'It means we all work that little bit harder for each other. One afternoon of lost productivity pales in comparison to that.'

Harrison turned and looked at the Smart TV. 'That's nearly the size of the one on the outside of HQ,' he said. 'It's like you have a cinema room.'

'That was the intention,' the brother said. 'My sister thinks it's a bit over-the-top, but I love it. I'll put it on later and you can see how immersive it is.'

'Sounds good,' Harrison said. He was a little light-headed from all the vegan champagne, and he was enjoying the after-party. There were perhaps twenty other people milling around the flat, and there was low drum-and-bass music playing in the background.

'What's it like living with your sister?' he said. 'I'm an only child so I wouldn't know.'

'We're very close,' the brother said. 'We were born

together in a Smart Baby Pod. It made the news actually, as we were the first twins to be born in one.'

'Cool,' Harrison said. 'I was born in one too.'

'Sadly, our mother died when we were toddlers,' the brother continued. 'So we were essentially orphans. It means our bond is closer than most siblings, even other twins. We had to look after each other.

'But it's not all doom and gloom. Luckily, our mother was a Sunnyvale employee here in York, and they've looked after us ever since she passed. They arranged foster parents for us, paid for our education and provided us with jobs at HQ after leaving school.'

'That's amazing,' Harrison said.

'Indeed,' the brother replied. His round, brown eyes were honest and intelligent. 'So when my sister and I talk about Sunnyvale as a family, it probably means more to us than most.'

'I can imagine,' Harrison said. 'What role are you doing? I see you in the control room every day but I've never thought to ask what you actually do.'

'We're part of Elliot's team, like you,' he said. 'We're well-versed in all the Sweeper duties, including editing Sunnypedia. But recently we've been branching out to data and analytics. We've always been good at maths so it's a natural fit. How can we make Sunnyvale more efficient? Are our delivery systems as smooth as possible? How can we effectively map and suppress dissent?

'These questions are nothing new, of course,' he added. 'But they're always at the forefront of our mind. Sunnyvale is a restless and relentless beast. It's all about marginal gains, and staying ahead of the game. It's a pleasure to be part of that. I, quite literally, owe my life to Sunnyvale's success.'

'Impressive,' Harrison said. 'I have no idea which particular area I'd like to work in. I just turned up and did what

Elliot told me.' He chuckled lightly.

'You're new, there's plenty of time to work out all of that,' the Lamb brother replied. He patted Harrison on his shoulder.

'I need to stock up on more drinks and snacks. Feel free to introduce yourself to anyone, don't be shy. We're a friendly bunch.'

'Yeah, I can see that,' Harrison said.

He turned around and a tall redhead, about the same age as Harrison, was helping herself to a snack. Her shiny, flowing hair was like something out of a Sunnyvale Shampoo commercial, and she glanced up at Harrison with an innocent, disarming smile.

He felt his pulse quicken. 'Hi, I'm Harrison,' he said, stretching out a hand.

'Nice to meet you,' she replied, shaking his hand gently. 'I'm Amberley.'

She was only a few centimetres shorter than Harrison, with a physique like a swimmer, and she seemed confident and shy at the same time.

'I'm quite a new employee at Sunnyvale,' he said. 'So I don't know many people here.'

She laughed politely. 'I bet I know even fewer,' she said. 'I work at Sunnyvale too, but today was literally my first day at the York office.'

'Oh wow,' Harrison replied. 'That's quite a first day.'

'I know,' she said. 'I've worked for Sunnyvale down south for two years already, and we have Monthly Meetings there too. I got a transfer up to this branch, just for a new experience.'

'What are your first impressions?' Harrison said.

'HQ is incredible,' she said. 'One of the most amazing buildings I've ever seen. And everybody seems very nice.'

'Yeah, they are. What job will you be doing here?'

'I'm training to be a Sweeper,' she said. 'In fact, I was

hovering behind you for a reason. Mr Patrick told me today that you would be overseeing my induction. He said it would be a chance for you to prove how well your own probationary period had gone.'

If it had been anyone else he would have felt aggrieved at the extra hassle, but he smiled at the thought of working with Amberley. 'Sure,' he said. 'This is the first I've heard of it, but it sounds good to me. I'm still learning myself, but I can definitely work through the basics with you.'

'Great,' she said. 'I was stuck in warehouse logistics before. This should be much more exciting.'

'Yeah, that's one way of putting it,' he said.

*

The party continued late into the evening, and Harrison had spoken to various colleagues for the first time. Most of them had joined Sunnyvale from university, he learned, after enrolling in their generous graduate scheme. It came with a plethora of benefits.

'They know how to make you loyal,' one colleague said. 'I'd run through a brick wall for them. I believe in everything we do, of course. But the money helps.'

Harrison nodded knowingly. 'How long have you worked for Sunnyvale?'

'Eight years,' the colleague replied. He was well-spoken, with a strong jawline and short, dirty blonde hair. 'I've worked there all through my twenties, and it's the best place for an ambitious person to excel. I have university friends who have gone into politics, would you believe it? They still believe in the old system, bless them.'

'What do you mean by the old system?' Harrison said.

'Oh, you know, voting and democracy and MPs and

constituencies and the House of Commons, and all that malarkey. Even though it's staring them in the face, they fail to realise that those days are over. They're *done*. The man we shared a drink with today – Elliot Patrick – is more powerful than any British Prime Minster ever has been. But some people fail to see the obvious. I would pity them, but most of them are obnoxious twits anyway.'

'What else have your friends done?' Harrison asked. 'Most of mine don't know what to do after finishing school.'

'Oh, the usual,' he replied. 'Some are lawyers – because the world needs more lawyers, of course. Some have gone into finance. But they don't understand where the *real* action lies. They're all pieces on a chessboard. Most are pawns, a few are bishops or rooks, and there's even the odd king or queen. But we're the grandmasters, overseeing it all. And, ultimately, all the pieces get swept into the same box at the end of the game.'

'Elliot Patrick said something similar,' Harrison said. 'About us being able to control the mob.'

The well-spoken colleague nodded his head. 'That's right. For the greater good, of course.'

'Why don't your old friends realise the obvious, as you put it?' Harrison said.

'Ignorance,' he replied quickly. 'It takes a certain kind of character to realise the opportunities available at Sunnyvale. You either have it or you don't. They think working for a big bank in London is exciting, without appreciating those banks have been negated by *us*. The aspiring politicians are in it for the power, without understanding – yet – that they're accountable to *us*.

'All roads lead to Sunnyvale eventually. It's not a secret, but it's amazing how many supposedly intelligent people can overlook this simple fact. You must be about twenty-one, right? You're smart to be working for us now. You'll be gaining light-years of valuable experience compared to your peers. One way or another, they'll all be working for Sunnyvale one day.'

'You think Sunnyvale's growth will continue forever?' Harrison said.

'Yes,' he said. 'The moment of critical mass has already been reached. I see nothing in our way.'

Harrison paused. 'What do you mean when you say we've negated the banks, and we control the politicians?' he said. 'How exactly does this *control* work? Elliot Patrick explained to me how we could alter the Prime Minister's Sunnypedia page. Is this what you mean?'

'That's a good example, yes,' he said. 'We control the message, which means we can control minds. And, as I'm sure you know, we're the most generous funder to both major parties. Anybody who doesn't meet our strict standards of approval won't get anywhere near the levers of power. Presumably you've heard all the stuff about post-capitalism? I like to say we now live in a post-democratic society too.

'Beyond that, forget about the individual politicians themselves. We've helped create a political *climate* where only certain discussions are allowed to be had. There's still political debate, but it's very strictly on our terms. Ever heard of the philosopher Noam Chomsky? He said: "The smart way to keep people passive and obedient is to strictly limit the spectrum of acceptable opinion, but allow very lively debate within that spectrum." Clever, right?'

'We want people to be passive and obedient?' Harrison said.

'They're Chomsky's words, not mine, or Sunnyvale's,' he said. 'But you can appreciate how effective that is, I'm sure.'

'And what about the banks?' Harrison said.

'We've long outgrown the traditional banking system. The creation of SVPs was a masterstroke in that sense. There's an old maxim in the world of economics: "Whoever controls the issuance of currency controls the nation." The banks, like everything else, are now just silly old relics. We allow them to exist, in their fancy sky-high offices in the City, but they're largely redundant.

'It's been this way for several years now, but the Sunnyvale Era will illustrate it emphatically. I'll be having a hell of a New Year's Eve party, that's for sure. You should come along, it'll be one crazy night. The future is ours.'

Harrison was intrigued, but he was growing increasingly tipsy. He found himself grinning at Amberley from across the room, and she returned the smile bashfully. Suddenly, the Lamb sister grabbed him by his arm.

'Come on everyone,' she said exuberantly, as she gathered people in the lounge area. 'It's time for karaoke.'

She flicked on the cinema-like Smart TV, which flooded the room with light and sound. A catchy instrumental was playing, and song lyrics were scrolling down the screen.

'For any newbies,' the sister said above the din, 'this is just a little ditty my brother and I put together. He has a friend who works as a DJ, and he did the background track. Please join in with us!'

Harrison looked around him uncertainly, as did Amberley. They moved closer together, and shared puzzled expressions, as the twenty other guests flocked towards the TV with enthusiastic smiles. The music was annoyingly catchy, and the group burst into song.

Harrison laughed at the absurdity of the scene before him, and saw the lyrics on the screen as they flashed by. They were chanted by the group, like an incantation:

Sunnyvale makes us happy,
Sunnyvale makes us free,
Open your eyes and you will see,
We're here to stay for eternity.

We give you one big guarantee,
We're swift with our delivery,
We're comrades, and we agree,
Working here is full of glee.

Join us now, and make the plea,
For Sunnyvale, take the knee,
For Sunnyvale, take the knee,
For Sunnyvale, take the knee.

We're one big happy, family,
We're one big happy, family,
We're one big happy, family,
One, big, happy, familyyyyyyyyyyy.

They repeated the song at least four or five times, and Harrison was dragged into the huddle. It was an orgy of drunkenness and togetherness, as they sang and sang with their arms draped around each other's shoulders.

Harrison was pushed close to Amberley and whispered in her ear: 'They should add a line ending in "Amberley", it would fit in with the rhyme.' They laughed and joined in with the singing, as Harrison found himself swept along – not for the first time today – by the fervour and emotion of the group around him.

His forehead, beneath his floppy fringe, was coated in sweat, and his cheeks were flushed. He was light-headed with alcohol and an intoxicating sense of fellowship.

Part Two

10

A few weeks ticked by. It was now a bright and balmy July. Plans for the new Sunnyvale Era, just over five months away, were gathering momentum. It would largely be a symbolic act, but there would be some practical changes too.

The calendar, of course, would alter. 2084 would be Year 1. The archaic terms Before Christ (BC) and Anno Domini (AD) were already extinct, but their replacements would be brushed aside too. Any date prior to Year 1 would have the suffix BSE (Before Sunnyvale Era).

Sunnyvale Points (SVPs) would become the sole currency throughout the West. It had initially started as a cryptocurrency, but it had swiftly evolved into society's main asset and medium of exchange. Most other currencies had died out anyway – apart from those on the black market – and the new era would officially confirm it.

Furthermore, as the circular telescreen on Coney Street regularly reminded passers-by, Sunnyvale were: Virtuous, Altruistic, Liberal, Ethical.

As such, the new era would see an even greater proliferation of policies of social engineering. Quotas were essential in a fair and just society, and the Great Liberator was overseeing plans to extend them into every sphere of education and employment. It was the only way to overcome historical prejudices and imbalances.

Increasingly, robots and AI were the beneficiaries of these measures. To deny them equality was discrimination. Some referred to it as 'species-ism'. Every living being – whether human, animal or computer – was equal in the eyes of Sunnyvale.

The Great Liberator had earmarked a visit to York in

August, for Sunnyvale's anniversary, as the perfect opportunity to make a globally televised speech about the range of measures they were looking to introduce. The awe-inspiring HQ in the city centre, formerly a religious building of some sort (or so he had been briefed by one of his advisors), would form the ideal photogenic backdrop.

*

Alexa Snow was starting to feel the pressure of her new role for the first time. She now had less than a month to ensure HQ in York was flawless for the Great Liberator's arrival, but she was also spending a lot of time on the road visiting similar sites around the country.

It was her fifty-sixth birthday, and her celebrations were modest. She didn't like to advertise her age in the cut-throat corporate world in which she operated, and her only guest for a birthday meal was her son. She was dressed casually by her standards, in jeans and a loose-fitting collared shirt, but her hair and make-up were characteristically meticulous.

It had been several weeks since they had last spoken, due to Alexa's life on the road, and she thought it was a good opportunity to find out more about Harrison's early progress at Sunnyvale. It was the first time he had been back in the townhouse since he moved out in April.

Harrison sat at one end of the large dining room table, and his mother at the other. He poked wistfully at his cauliflower bake. 'This is delicious,' he said unconvincingly, as he raised his glass of water in the air. 'Happy birthday, Mum.'

'Thank you, Harrison,' she said.

The house was as immaculate as ever. Harrison's room had always been the only messy part, which had caused regular arguments over the years.

'What have you done with my old room?' Harrison asked.

'Not much,' she said. 'It's just a relief to see it so clean. It's a bigger room than I appreciated. All your clutter made it look smaller.'

She put down her fork and looked at Harrison. He braced himself for the inevitable questioning about his career. Right on cue, she said: 'I was hoping we could have a chat about your future, Harrison.'

'Sure,' he replied. He knew resistance was futile. She never had a night off, even on her birthday.

'How have you found working at HQ? I'm glad you've passed your probationary period.'

'It's been fine,' he said. 'They're long days in the control room, but Elliot has been a good mentor. It was a relief to pass the probation and be given a full contract. It's nice to have the positive feedback.'

'Great,' she said. 'You're in a coveted position. Sweeper jobs are highly-sought after. We have dozens of enquiries every week from Sunnyvale employees wanting to switch departments.'

'I am lucky,' he said. 'And I should thank you for the opportunity. I was pretty aimless before, but now I have a purpose each day. I'm growing up.'

He cringed inside at his brownnosing, and he didn't even know himself if he was telling the truth or not. He had been instinctively sceptical of all the talk of comradeship, but the Monthly Meeting – and the after-party with the Lamb twins – had altered his perspective somewhat. Was it really such a bad thing that people enjoyed their work and liked pulling in the same direction? Had he been too cynical and misanthropic initially? What were his alternatives, anyway? He had a job most people his age could only dream of.

His answer seemed to have momentarily pacified her, and he excused himself to use the toilet. The townhouse was spread over three floors. The kitchen was on the ground floor, and the nearest bathroom was only a short walk down the hallway. Harrison, though, couldn't resist a quick detour to the lounge on the first floor, to see if anything had changed since he'd moved out.

Everything appeared to be the same: the gigantic Smart TV, the four-piece sofa with extendable footrests, the silver-framed mirror. It was still typically minimalist, but with a few flourishes, like the couple of expensive paintings above the fireplace. The only new item was a bouquet of flowers on the window sill, which were probably for Alexa's birthday.

Harrison walked over to the window to check out the river view. It was a serene evening, and rays of sunshine were reflecting off the mirror-clear water. He found himself leaning down to smell the flowers. Some were dark pink, some were light pink, and they all had green stems and shoots. There was a large red flower in the middle, which he guessed must be a rose.

Attached to the rose was a small piece of string with a message tag. The flower company's name was on one side, and on the other it said:

Dearest Alexa,

You're a bloomin' awesome lady. Happy birthday.

Roses are red
Violets are blue
We're Sunnyvale's future
And I need you.

From E,
X

Harrison stifled a laugh. He had never considered his mum to be a romantic lady, and it was jarring to see her associated with a lovey-dovey message like this. Some poor sap was besotted with her. She had been single throughout most of Harrison's life, and he certainly wouldn't begrudge her love and happiness if it came her way. But he just couldn't picture it.

He left the lounge and used the bathroom. Only when he was washing his hands did the obvious occur to him: *We're Sunnyvale's future*. She was in a relationship with someone at work. His brain scrambled to work out who it could be. The options were fairly limited: overall, there were a few hundred staff at HQ, but most of them were the Oompa-Loompas in the warehouse, and he couldn't imagine she would deal with them very often. They were largely out of sight, and well down the pecking order.

It was possible she had met this mysterious lover on one of her other site visits, but the chances were relatively slim. *Bloomin' awesome*. Aside from the awful pun, who would use the word 'awesome'? The English and American versions of the language were becoming increasingly similar, but it was still a distinctly American term. And clearly this person's name began with the letter E.

It left only one realistic candidate: Elliot Patrick.

*

Harrison made his way back to the dining room, uncertain whether to laugh or to smash the table with frustration. He wisely opted to do neither, and to pretend that he had seen nothing.

'There's more cauliflower in the kitchen if you want?' Alexa said.

'No thanks, I'm pretty full.' His brain was whirring, but he wrestled to keep his composure. *Does it really matter who she's dating? It's her choice. It's none of your business. An argument could end badly.*

'Is there any pudding?' he asked, trying to sound normal.

'No, there are sufficient nutrients and calories in this cauliflower,' she said. 'If I binge on sugar-filled deserts I'll start losing my looks, and people will begin to question my age. There's an impression at work that I'm still in my forties, and I'm happy for that to continue.'

'But didn't you help come up with the advertising campaign for Sunnyvale's new range of deserts?' Harrison said. 'Surely you must have got some free stock?'

'Just because I help sell them, doesn't mean I have to eat them.'

A long silence.

'You saw the flowers, didn't you?' Alexa said.

'What do you mean?'

'You saw the flowers on the window sill in the lounge. I heard you go in there.'

Harrison shuffled in his seat. 'Yes, I did,' he said.

'What do you think?'

'I think it's none of my business.'

'I agree,' she said. 'But it's an issue that will have to be addressed at some point. We may as well do it now.'

Harrison shuffled and squirmed some more.

'Elliot and I have been seeing each other for several months,' she said. 'It's one of the reasons he's based in York when a man of his abilities could choose to work anywhere in the West.'

Harrison stayed silent.

'I'm not as young as I used to be,' she said. 'And he's going places. He's a great catch. He's a very talented man. There's talk already that he could be the Great Liberator one day. Not any time soon, of course. But down the line.'

'Do you see yourself as the next great power couple?' Harrison said.

'Why not?' she replied. 'I have a great deal of experience to share with him. I bring the steady hand. He brings relative youth and freshness and vigour. It's a mutually beneficial arrangement. If you play your cards right, you could benefit too. It's no coincidence that you had him as your mentor. Being my son, and Elliot's mentee, could put you in a uniquely powerful position.'

'Do you love him?' Harrison said.

'Love?'

'Yeah, love. You know what the word means, don't you? Surely I don't need to explain it.'

'I've already told you,' she said. 'I'm very fond of him. We make a good team. We have a mutually beneficial arrangement.'

'Unable are the loved to die, for love is immortality,' Harrison said.

'What on earth are you talking about?'

'It's from a poem by Emily Dickinson. Don't you think it's beautiful?'

'I don't understand it,' she said.

'If it proves so, then loving goes by haps. Some Cupid kills with arrows, some with traps.'

'Harrison, stop it. What is this nonsense?'

'It's Shakespeare, Mum. *Much Ado about Nothing.*'

She looked at him with suspicion.

'I don't know what you're trying to pull,' she said. 'But enough is enough. The last person I know who used to talk like that was your grandad, and look how he ended up.'

11

The following Sunday, Harrison was sat on the sofa watching his Smart TV. He received a notification, simultaneously on the TV and his Smart Sensor, that an urgent security broadcast was incoming. The message was read by a middle-aged female news reporter, with a neutral, robotic voice and a neutral, robotic face. She said:

> *This is a special crime update. Two men in London have been found guilty of terrorism-related offences. Steven Robinson, 53, and Jim Cooper, 55, are charged with spreading subversive literature and propaganda.*

> *Their crimes were discovered by the Sunnyvale Smart Security team, and they face charges under the Sunnyvale Terrorism Act of 2057. They appeared in court this morning, where they confessed their crimes to a Sunnyvale Smart Judge.*

> *It is part of a wide-reaching crackdown on dissent ahead of the momentous restructuring of the calendar across the West in the new year. Sunnyvale's Chief of Truth, Elliot Patrick, says there will be a 'zero tolerance approach' to terrorism.*

Elliot Patrick's face and voice then took over from the reporter's:

> *The first of January will represent the start of a historic new era. The Sunnyvale Era. And we can only function as a free and safe society if we ruthlessly stamp out illegal dissent wherever we find it.*

> *These two men are dangerous, they are threats to our peace and*

security, and we have not hesitated in applying the full force of the law. Sunnyvale is Progress. Progress is Freedom.

The suspects' mug shots appeared in hologram form. The two men looked dead-eyed and defeated, as if a confession had just been browbeaten out of them. Their eyes lingered, staring straight at Harrison's, until a little *blip* signalled the end of the broadcast, and the hologram vanished.

*

Harrison was sat at his usual desk, on the edge of the semi-circle, the next morning. He hadn't exactly *enjoyed* his work at Sunnyvale so far – from day one, he had found Elliot Patrick to be smug and supercilious – but it wasn't a bad life.

The Monthly Meeting had certainly altered his perspective. If his mum was a successful leader, why couldn't he be one too? He was part of the Sunnyvale family now – this is what he did. The pay and benefits were considerably more generous than he could get anywhere else, and he was faring better than any of his friends (he still spoke to them occasionally through his Smart Sensor).

But the arrest of Steven Robinson and Jim Cooper had rattled him out of his acquiescence. Steve and Jim. They were the two men he had passed on to Elliot a few months ago. Harrison had always viewed his work as abstract and virtual, but it was now suddenly very real.

He remembered listening to their full conversation, after the AI had labelled it Unknown, and he had ascertained that they were two labourers working in the centre of London. Most construction work was now done exclusively by machines, but there were still certain jobs that required the human touch (Harrison knew nothing about the specifics, as the nearest he had ever come to manual labour was when he had to set up a Sunnyvale Smart TV).

He was shocked to learn that these two men were now classed as terrorists. In the snapshot of their lives he had listened to, all they had talked about was their useless boss, their need for a drink after work and a brief mention of their families. The limerick and the joke lasted all of twenty seconds.

Elliot Patrick sauntered into the control room in his usual manner, in his usual attire, with his usual coffee cup. Harrison gave him a couple of minutes to set up in the corner office before knocking on the glass door.

'Come in,' Elliot said.

Harrison entered and closed the door behind him.

'How can I help you?' The tone of Elliot's voice suggested he didn't want a lengthy conversation, so Harrison remained standing.

'I saw you on the news yesterday,' he said. 'In the crime update.'

'Ah, yes,' Elliot said lightly. 'No doubt you were hoping to be named as the intrepid employee who kick-started the whole investigation? To confirm, they are the two men you picked up on in your first week here. Or was it your second week? Either way, it was good work. But we can't individually name-drop employees on the news.'

Harrison was bemused. 'I don't want any credit,' he said. 'I just had a few questions about what the security team found. I don't think they were the smartest guys ever, but I didn't get the impression they were terrorists.'

Elliot looked up from his computer and fixed his thin brown eyes on Harrison's.

'And do you think your impression of a five-minute conversation is more important than a full investigation led by the security team?' he said.

'No,' Harrison replied. 'I was just curious about what evidence they found.'

'That's none of your concern,' Elliot said. But then he seemed to warm slightly. Perhaps he couldn't resist showing off his work, or perhaps he remembered he was talking to Alexa Snow's son. 'For the sake of your professional curiosity, I can share a little bit,' he said.

'We trawled through their digital profiles and found a long history of dissent. It seemed they had something of a competition going on, or a game. They would pass on, and sometimes invent, various anti-Sunnyvale 'jokes' to each other.' Elliot mimed quote marks when he said the word 'jokes'.

'They were full of hatred, bigotry and propaganda. It was something of a private endeavour between the two of them, but we also uncovered evidence of them spreading their bile to other colleagues and members of the public. We arrested them, they confessed to their crimes and then we made their arrest public. Simple.'

'But surely you found something else?' Harrison said. 'I was expecting you to say they were planning an attack or something.'

'I don't appreciate your accusative tone, Harrison,' Elliot said sharply. 'A healthy interest in Sunnyvale's processes is one thing, but I hope your questioning isn't slipping into timorous doubt? We can't afford any reluctant passengers here. You're either fully on board with us or you're not.'

Harrison paused and considered his options. His mouth was dry.

'Of course not, Mr Patrick,' he said, eventually. He normally called him Elliot.

'Please forgive me. I'm still new here and I was only asking out of curiosity. I'm proud that my work has had such an important end result.'

Elliot nodded and his thin, brown eyes switched their focus back to his computer.

Harrison closed the door behind him and silently cursed himself for being such a spineless coward.

12

Romances in the Sunnyvale workplace were frowned upon, but they were common. Working there invariably required long hours, most of it confined to one particular room with the same people, and human nature did the rest.

Alexa Snow wasn't the only one in a relationship with a colleague. Harrison was too.

He had been showing Amberley the ropes ever since her arrival, and the work rapport swiftly developed into something more. She was different to the rest of his colleagues. He could occasionally crack a joke in the control room, and she would laugh generously. The Lamb twins would pretend not to hear.

He had been single for a long time, and the array of dating and sexting apps at his disposal had lost all appeal. The most popular app for his generation, 'Sex Scores', allowed users to match with people in the vicinity. Crucially, it included a five-star rating system for their sexual performance, as adjudicated by their previous matches.

A good night would earn a user five stars and a boosted reputation; a clunky night with little chemistry could see them lose status in the quasi-Darwinian playground. Harrison was hovering around the three-and-a-half mark, but he had shied away from using the app for some time. A scathing one-star review a year ago had brought down his average, and eviscerated his confidence. But none of that mattered now.

It was August, and Harrison had the lounge windows open as he and Amberley relaxed on the sofa after work (she was a regular visitor to his bungalow).

She was mocking how sparse and drab the place was. Other than a Smart TV in the lounge, a Smart Fridge in the kitchen and a smattering of items from his old bedroom, Harrison had left the house as it was when he first found it.

'Harrison,' she said. 'One weekend I'm going to come round with a friend of mine who's an interior decorator. This bungalow is so bland! It's like you're living in a monastery, or whatever those places were called. The only cool thing about it is that you have a cat. And, even then, a dog would be better.'

'I like to live simply,' Harrison said. 'And I don't tell you how to style your place when we're round there.'

'That's because it's already perfect,' she said, with a mischievous smile. 'You can't improve on perfection, as you should already know by dating me.' She smiled again and kissed him on the cheek. They had eaten their food on the sofa together, and their empty plates were now on the table in front of them.

'If you look for perfection, you will never be satisfied,' Harrison said. 'Leo Tolstoy wrote that.'

'Well, this Leo guy never met me,' she said, as she continued to kiss him. 'And how do you know so many quotes and facts? It's like dating Sunnyvale Smart Search.' (This was the name of the West's leading online search engine.)

'I like to read whenever I can,' he said. 'I wasn't great at school but I'm trying to make up for lost time.'

'Ooh, what do you like reading? Show me your E-Reader.'

'I actually like to get physical copies if possible,' he said. 'They're hard to find but it's worth it.'

'I haven't seen a physical book since I was a toddler,' she said. 'Show me, please. Where do you keep them? What do you read?'

Harrison clammed up. It was a fine balancing act when he was spending time with Amberley – his feelings were growing stronger for her, but he couldn't yet afford the risk of showing her the haven and revealing that he was breaking the law.

Ultimately, they had only been together a short while.

'This and that,' Harrison said. 'Anything to take my mind off work on an evening. They feel like such long days in the control room.'

'They do,' Amberley said. 'It hurts my eyes when we step outside after a shift. Where are all these books, then? I can't see any in here, and I don't remember seeing any in your bedroom. I would have noticed.'

'Oh, I don't tend to keep them,' he said. 'Once I've read one I'll replace it straight away. Otherwise they can clog up the place.'

'There isn't much chance of you clogging up this bungalow,' she said. 'I've never seen a place so empty. It's like a ghost lives here.'

Harrison forced himself to laugh, but his thoughts wandered to Pop. He couldn't shake the regret of not seeing him for so many years before he died. He had the underlying feeling that there was some kind of important message he'd missed.

*

The following Sunday, Harrison had a plan in place to see how much he could trust Amberley. He was slightly ashamed at being so paranoid, but he had a lot to lose if he misjudged her, and she had come into his life so quickly. He wouldn't put it past Elliot Patrick to have planted her in the office, as a kind of femme fatale.

He had promised her a surprise, and told her to arrive at his bungalow at two o'clock sharp. The only clue he provided was that she shouldn't eat after breakfast.

She was ten minutes late, standing on the doorstep with a buoyant smile. It was a fine summer's day, and she was wearing denim shorts and a yellow top. Her red hair was in a ponytail.

'I've been thinking all weekend about what it could be,' she said excitedly. 'Obviously it's something to do with food. Are we going to a fancy restaurant?'

She stepped into the hallway and inhaled deeply through her nose. 'Home cooking. I can smell it. I didn't know you were much of a chef.'

'I'm not really,' Harrison said. 'But I'm hoping the fact I'm giving it a go is romantic.'

'It is,' she said, with a peck on his cheek.

They walked straight through the hallway and into the kitchen, where the smell grew stronger. There were pots, pans, knives and chopping boards all over the counter, and various things were bubbling and steaming.

'My grandad used to witter on all the time about his favourite meal when he was growing up,' Harrison said. 'It was called a Sunday roast.'

He walked over to a pan full of thick, brown liquid and stirred it. 'I came across an old recipe book of his, and I've done my best to recreate the meal. It consists of vegetables – we have carrots, leeks and broccoli – mashed potato, roast potatoes and Yorkshire puddings. It's like a pancake mix but the puddings rise and come out all round and fluffy. And this liquid here is the gravy.'

Amberley seemed intrigued and confused in equal measures. 'Doesn't that pancake-style mix include eggs?' she said. 'I live a vegan lifestyle, as is our duty as Sunnyvale citizens.'

'I knew you'd say that,' Harrison said. 'I found the eggs in one of the cupboards, behind all the cat food. They're still in date. And if we're going to break the rules, let's go the whole hog. A hog is slang for a pig, by the way, so the pun was deliberate. Except instead of a pig, we're going to have cow.'

Harrison opened the oven door and a rush of steam rose to the ceiling.

'This,' he said dramatically, 'is a joint of beef.' It had a dark brown exterior, with a thick layer of fat, and juices were flowing down through its sinews. The meaty smell spread through the kitchen and the whole bungalow. 'We're going to lather it in gravy. It's the centrepiece of our meal. Doesn't it smell wonderful?'

Harrison could see that Amberley was battling an internal dilemma. She hesitated for a long moment, rooted to the spot, and said: 'Let's go for it. It will be interesting to try it, if only once.'

She sat down at the wooden table, where a plate was waiting, along with a knife and fork. 'You seemed so unassuming when we first met,' she teased. 'I never knew you'd end up becoming such a bad influence.'

'I'm full of surprises,' Harrison said. 'This is just about ready. Dinner shall soon be served, madam.'

He turned off the oven and removed the beef from its tray onto a wooden board. He turned off the glowing rings on top of the oven, drained the water from the vegetable pans, and added a dash of salt and pepper to the mashed potato. The Yorkshire puddings had been done earlier, and they sat in an eight-hole muffin tray.

He took Amberley's plate and piled on generous helpings, leaving a sizeable gap at the side for the meat. He placed the plate in front of her, before carrying the wooden board of beef and presenting it on the table. His chair was opposite hers, and the meat sat between them like a prize.

There was a long carving knife on the table, and he began to slice through the beef from top to bottom at an angle. It was still oven-warm, and the juices were rolling down it. It was dark pink on the inside. He scooped three slices onto Amberley's plate.

'Help yourself to the gravy,' he said, pointing to a boat-shaped container on the table. 'Bon appétit.'

Amberley hesitated again with the beef in front of her, but then she started to tuck in. Harrison smiled and did the same after piling his food high. They barely said a word to each other until their plates were empty.

'That was delicious,' Amberley said, as she placed her knife and fork down. 'Where on earth did you get the beef? I'm amazed at how good it tasted. I always imagined it would be disgusting.'

'It was in the freezer when I moved in,' Harrison said. 'It's pretty easy to get on the black market, I think. I've wanted to cook it for weeks, but I thought I'd save it for a special occasion.'

'That's very sweet,' she said. 'I would kiss you to say thank you, but I want some seconds.' She swivelled off her chair and started refilling her plate with all the trimmings.

She's a keeper, Harrison thought. The early signs were good. If Amberley could be properly trusted, she wouldn't tell anyone about the meat. If she did grass on him, he would be distraught but the repercussions wouldn't be too severe. He would certainly be reprimanded, but he doubted it would cost him his job. It would probably involve a hefty fine, a warning and a stern telling-off from his mum.

He could just explain how he didn't buy the beef himself, how curiosity had got the better of him and then he would apologise profusely. It would all blow over, but it would confirm, either way, whether Amberley could be trusted with a secret. He was going to give it a week to see if there would be a backlash.

He felt guilty for being so devious, but it was the only way he could measure whether she could be fully brought into his life and, more specifically, into the haven.

13

A week passed, and there had been no stern hand on Harrison's shoulder. To celebrate this – as well as Amberley successfully completing her probationary period – Harrison suggested a Sunday trip to the countryside.

He wanted to go to the White Horse, a famous chalk feature etched into the Yorkshire hillside about thirty kilometres north of York. He had gone at least once every summer with Pop, and the photograph on the mantelpiece had reminded him of those trips. It was the one with Harrison as a toddler, hoisted on Pop's shoulders, with the stunning view behind them.

'What's this place called?' Amberley asked, as they made their way there in a self-driven car.

'The White Horse,' Harrison said. 'It's made out of chalk, on the North York Moors, and you can see it from a long way away. We'll be able to spot it soon. It's a nice place for a walk.'

It was late morning, and the sun was high in the spotless sky when they arrived. Birds darted and arrowed overhead, but otherwise they were completely alone. They were at the bottom of some uneven stone steps with a sharp incline, leading up to the chalk horse.

'We can walk up there now if you want,' Harrison said. 'Or we can save the view for the end.'

'The end? What are we going to do first?' Amberley said.

'You'll soon see,' Harrison teased. 'Follow me.'

He made his way downhill, back in the direction they had come. Amberley jogged in pursuit, until they were side by side.

'Do you have another surprise in store?' she said. 'Is there a whole cow waiting for us in those trees?'

Harrison laughed, and adjusted the straps on his rucksack

as he walked. 'There may be a few horses grazing, actually,' he said. 'But we're not going to eat them, don't worry.'

After about half a kilometre downhill, Harrison turned right, past an old wooden gateway. They had no specialist walking gear – just shorts, T-shirt and everyday trainers – and the weather was soothing. It was a pleasant, summertime stroll.

They continued on their tree-lined pathway, flanked by overgrown fields, past a derelict farmhouse and alongside a beck.

'I like to imagine I'm here when I'm in the control room,' Harrison said. 'With the sound of the water flowing, and greenery all around.'

'I know what you mean,' Amberley said. 'I'm starting to look forward to the weekends more and more. Don't get me wrong, I'm happy I moved up here for the new job. But it's pretty demanding, isn't it?'

'Absolutely,' Harrison said. 'It's more than a job, after all. It's a *family*, and a way of life.' He looked across at Amberley to see her reaction, but she was focusing downwards on each stride. There were plenty of uneven rocks and crevices lying in wait for the unwary walker.

'I was really cynical about all of that when I first started,' he continued. 'Then I got sucked into it for a little while. It's difficult not to, isn't it? How have you found it all?'

'It's nothing new for me, I suppose,' she said. 'I've been working for Sunnyvale for a few years now. I just go along with it. If nothing else, it's because I've never met a colleague who didn't. It's just what we have to do. We have to buy into it fully.'

'How did you find your seminar with Elliot?' he said.

'Again, it was nothing new. I had the same speech from my boss at my old branch, give or take. It's just part of the job.'

'I know,' he said. 'But what do you think of Elliot personally? He can be a bit arrogant, can't he?'

'From what I keep hearing, he's some kind of super-genius,' she said. 'So it's no surprise he's a bit full of himself. Apparently he talks to the Great Liberator all the time.'

'*Super-genius*,' Harrison muttered sardonically, under his breath.

They continued through the trees in contemplative, and peaceful, silence, until they reached a broader, gravel path. The trees on their right were growing taller and thinner, and the vast moors in the distance were coming into view.

They crossed a huge field, surrounded by the hills, and walked by another trickling beck. Soon, they had arrived at Harrison's intended destination.

'Is this where you want us to stop?' Amberley said.

'That's right,' Harrison replied.

They were stood on a grass embankment, overlooking a near-circular lake. The water looked pure. There was a backless wooden bench close to the water edge, and the sun was shining directly onto it.

'I thought we could have a picnic here,' Harrison said. 'It's a favourite spot from my childhood. My grandad would teach me how to skim rocks into the lake, and sometimes he would bring his binoculars to spot birds.'

'Aw, it's sweet that you were so close to him,' she said. 'Do you miss him?'

Harrison took off his rucksack and unzipped the main compartment. He removed a couple of small juice boxes and some foil-wrapped sandwiches, placing them on the wooden bench, and then took out a patchwork blanket. He unfurled it on the floor, a couple of metres from the ebbing water.

'Yeah, I never grew up with a dad, so I always looked up to him. He was good to me,' he said.

'I didn't have a father either,' she replied. 'Were you also in a Smart Baby Pod?'

'I was,' Harrison said tentatively. He had never discussed it properly with anyone before, aside from briefly telling the Lamb brother that he had been in one.

'I understand why it was so convenient for my mum,' he said. 'But there's also something slightly unsettling about it. I'm always quite confused about her, to be honest. I think she's finally a little bit proud of me, now I'm working at Sunnyvale, but shouldn't her love be unconditional? I don't know what to think.'

'I'm sure she's always loved you,' she said. 'But yeah, I've always had my doubts about baby pods too.'

'It's like something out of *The Matrix* or *Soylent Green*,' Harrison said.

'The what?' she replied. '*The Matrix*? And Soy-what? What are they?'

'Oh, nothing,' he said quickly. 'Let's get started with our picnic. It's not quite a Sunday roast, but it will have to do.'

*

When they finished eating, Amberley took off her trainers and socks and waded into the lake, until the water reached her knees.

'It's not as warm as I'd hoped,' she laughed. She playfully splashed Harrison. 'Come on, join me if you dare.'

He jumped up from the blanket – not bothering to remove his shoes and socks – and sprinted into the lake, past Amberley, until he was shoulder-deep.

'I've swum in this lake dozens of times,' he said. He took off his T-shirt and threw it back towards the picnic area. 'Join *me* if you dare.' He dove under water, turned and kicked, and emerged twenty metres into the distance.

Amberley smiled confidently. 'Do you remember how you once told me I have the physique of a swimmer? Well, it's because I *am* a swimmer.' She kicked effortlessly into a smooth breaststroke, and was level with Harrison in a matter of seconds.

'You forgot something,' he said. 'You don't want to get your T-shirt wet, do you?'

'It's already a bit late for that,' she laughed. 'But I see what you're getting at.' She pulled off her T-shirt, scrunched it into a ball and launched it as far as she could back to their spot.

'You didn't expect me to call your bluff, did you?' she said. Harrison grinned, grabbed her hips underwater and pulled her lithe body towards him.

'I had a feeling you would,' he said. 'You're not exactly the shy and retiring type. Now, how about your shorts? And your bra?'

'Don't push your luck.' They kissed while treading water, their bodies tight up against each other, until Harrison's legs started to ache.

'Amateur,' she said. 'I can feel you straining already. I best let you focus on staying afloat.'

She swam off, fluently. Harrison tried to swim after her but he was no match for her grace in the water. He still went jogging occasionally, but he was far from an athlete.

'OK, OK, you win,' he shouted.

'What's that?' she replied. 'I'd like that in writing please.'

'You win,' he shouted emphatically, and then he burst into laughter, swallowing water. He composed himself and continued to tread water, coughing and spluttering.

As he did so, he saw a tiny speck on the horizon, far above the trees that surrounded the lake. It was a small, dark object – contrasting the clear, blue sky – gliding in a straight line. The speck grew larger, and a low buzzing sound soon followed.

'It's a bloody Stinger,' Harrison said, pointing in its direction. 'What's it doing out here?'

Amberley spun around and looked up, and the Stinger was soon directly above them, perhaps thirty metres in the air. It remained still, and the incessant buzzing sound was loud and irritating.

'What the hell do you want?' Harrison shouted, but he knew it was futile. He tried to splash it, but the water didn't reach.

His legs were filling with lactic acid, and he began to flail rather than tread water. 'Fuck off,' he screamed at the drone. 'Just fuck off!'

'Relax, Harrison,' Amberley said. 'Let's just swim calmly back to our spot. It's not far.'

She hooked her arm under his and they gently made their way towards the edge of the lake, until they could stand up in the water. The drone had followed them overhead, but it kept its distance.

Harrison made the last few strides onto dry land. His shorts were sticking to him, so he shook himself off like a dog and bent down as if taking off his soaking trainers. Instead, he picked up a fist-sized rock from the floor. It was jagged and heavy in his hand. He pivoted and swivelled around in an instant, like a discus-thrower, and launched the rock with as much velocity as he could.

It crashed into the Stinger, high in the air, with a dramatic thumping sound – *thud* – and Amberley let out a little scream of surprise. It buzzed loudly for a second, and then it fell, crumpled, into the lake.

'Harrison!' Amberley exclaimed, startled and shaken. 'What on earth have you done? Damaging Sunnyvale Smart Drones is a criminal offence. And you're a Sunnyvale *employee!*'

'It was annoying me,' he said. 'It's just a bunch of carbon fibre and plastic. Who cares?'

'You could get in trouble,' she said. 'That was stupid, very stupid.'

'I'll just say it was an accident,' he said. 'I was skimming rocks and the bloody thing got in the way. It's not my fault it got too close.'

14

That night, Amberley was sleeping over at Harrison's bungalow. The incident with the Stinger had deflated their mood, and she was annoyed that they could both be facing disciplinary action at work the next day.

'It's no big deal,' he said, as Amberley changed into her pyjamas at the end of his bed. 'How can they prove anything? The Stinger's video stream will show me throwing a rock. I'll explain how I was trying to skim it across the water, or I was seeing how far I could launch it.'

'What about when you were telling it to "Fuck off"?' she said.

'I'll say I was screaming that at you, because you were beating me at swimming. Again, how can they prove otherwise?'

'It's pretty obvious what you did, Harrison. I'm not telling you off, but I really don't think you'll get away with it. Plus, it means our relationship is going to be open news now. You know what the office is like for gossip. Tomorrow is going to be a nightmare.'

Harrison sat on the end of the bed and put his arm around her. 'Who cares what they all think anyway?' he said. 'They can gossip as much as they want.'

'You don't understand,' she said. 'It makes me look like a climber, a golddigger. I've only been here five minutes, and I'm already seeing Alexa Snow's son. It's hardly a subtle career move, is it?'

'It's not like that at all,' he said. 'I know that, and that's all that matters.'

Amberley sighed deeply and rested her forehead in her hands. 'Maybe we should slow things down a bit,' she said. 'Until this incident blows over.'

'But why?' Harrison said. 'I don't see how it changes anything.'

'It does, whether you like it or not,' she said. 'A little break will do us both good anyway. It's been so intense. I'm in a new city, starting a new job. That's enough on anyone's plate, at least for a short while.'

Harrison moved a hand through his wavy hair, adjusting the floppy fringe, and nodded his head in reluctant agreement. 'If that's what you want, so be it. Please stay the night, though. It's already late, and your work clothes for tomorrow are here. There's no need to go traipsing back to your place.'

She turned and kissed him on the lips. She smelt of shower gel and moisturiser, and Harrison ran his hand through her soft, red hair. 'I'll stay tonight,' she said.

*

An hour later, they were dropping off to sleep, side by side in the double bed. The bungalow was dark and silent, and the bedroom window was ajar in a desperate attempt to get some cool air circulating. It was a humid night after what had been a sultry day.

Harrison's legs ached from his escapades in the lake, and he was asleep quicker than usual. Amberley had also dropped off, and was breathing rhythmically.

The peace was suddenly punctured when a figure jumped onto their bed – Amberley screamed and Harrison shouted 'Woah!', as he scrambled for the lamp on the bedside table.

He turned it on and they both exhaled with relief when they realised it was Aslan. He had jumped in through the open window. Amberley let out a smaller scream when she saw the cat had brought a little present.

A half-dead mouse was trying to scuttle away on top of

the duvet, but Aslan kept it in check with his paw. He looked up at Harrison with his intelligent, green eyes, as if to say: 'This is for you. Aren't I a clever and grateful cat?' His pupils were fully dilated: he was in hunt-mode.

Amberley was now hunched and recoiling in bed.

'Harrison, get that thing away from me.' He laughed and shooed Aslan off the covers, before picking up the mouse by its tail and walking through to the kitchen. He unlocked the back door and let the mouse free outside, then stroked the cat's head.

'Thank you for your gift, Aslan,' he said. 'But feel free to just get me a pair of socks next time.' He filled the ceramic feeding bowl and gave him another stroke, and then laughed again as he re-entered the bedroom. He wanted to keep the mood light.

'It's just his little way of saying thank you,' he said. Amberley was already replacing the duvet cover with another one from the wardrobe. 'That mouse could have been anywhere,' she said. 'And I've closed the window, so it won't happen again. Do you have a fan, to keep us cool?'

'Yeah, I think so.' He returned to the hallway and had a root around the closet (it was slightly fuller than it had been when he first moved in) where a neglected, old fan was sitting on the top rung of a stepladder.

'This'll do,' he said, as he brought it into the bedroom. 'It looks pretty knackered, but it should do a job.'

'This is why I prefer dogs,' Amberley said. 'What kind of a name is Aslan anyway? I've never heard it before. Why couldn't he just be called Fluffy or Snowflake or something?'

'It's not *his* fault we didn't appreciate the mouse,' Harrison chuckled. 'It's just his nature. And I don't know why he's called Aslan – I never even knew my grandad had a cat. Come on, let's get back to sleep.'

*

It was around three o'clock when Harrison's instincts woke him up, again. He sat bolt upright, and was instantly alert. Amberley lay next to him, undisturbed and sleeping serenely.

Aslan. He *had* heard the name before. He was sure of it. He gently moved the duvet aside and slipped out of bed, careful not to knock Amberley. She made a little snoring nose as a floorboard creaked, and he tiptoed out of the room, leaving the door ajar.

He crept quickly but carefully through the hallway and kitchen, then unlocked the back door and stepped into the garden. It was still a sticky and humid night, and he was more than comfortable in just his pyjama shorts. It would have been too much of a kerfuffle to grab a T-shirt or his dressing gown.

He typed 1811 into the keypad and made the familiar walk across the shed and down the hatchway. The automatic light filled the room and he climbed down the ladder until his feet met the thick, cream carpet.

Aslan, Aslan, Aslan, he repeated to himself, as he strode over to the bookshelves. They contained hundreds of books, and since discovering the haven he had only had time to work through a few dozen. But he would know what he was looking for when he saw it.

He scanned each shelf metronomically, rapidly absorbing each author and title, dismissing them and moving on to the next. Dickens – *no*. Austen – *no*. Milton – *no*. Woolf – *no*. The back of his mind was screaming at him. *It's there somewhere!*

He was onto the third tier of the last shelf, and doubt was clouding his mind for the first time. Was he barking completely up the wrong tree? Had Pop's eccentricity started to rub off on him? Was living here making him paranoid – a rock-throwing lunatic, no less?

Shelley – *no.* Greene – *no.* Solzhenitsyn – *no.* Lewis – *no.*
Wait, Lewis.

Harrison plucked the book off the shelf and held it in both hands, like he was clasping the Holy Grail. The front cover was a hand-sketched drawing of four smiling schoolchildren, all gathered around a proud, thick-maned lion, who was looking directly at the reader.

'*The Lion, The Witch and the Wardrobe,*' Harrison said. 'By C.S. Lewis.'

Aslan, the heroic lion, was one of the main characters in the story. He could now remember Pop reading out his dialogue in a low, guttural voice. It was another long-forgotten memory the haven had unlocked.

It was a dog-eared, crinkled paperback version, much in keeping with most of the books surrounding it. Harrison sat in the armchair, planning to sample a chapter or two before calling it a night. He would sleep more soundly now he knew the origin of his cat's name. It had always tinkled the tiniest of bells, and it was satisfying to hear it properly rung.

As he tenderly opened to the first page, a white envelope, folded in half, fluttered onto his lap. He picked it up, and saw 'Harrison Snow' neatly written in fountain pen on the front.

It was hard to tell whether his mind or his heart was racing quicker, as he unsealed the envelope and pulled out a sheaf of A4 papers. At the top of the first page, was written:

> *This letter is intended for Harrison Snow's eyes only. If it falls into the wrong hands, please do the decent thing and leave it unread.*

From the depths of his childhood memories, he recognised Pop's handwriting.

*

Dear Harrison,

I can only hope this letter finds you healthy and well. It is towards the end of 2082 as I write this. I can feel my health slipping every day, and I suspect within a year my brain and body will be overwhelmed by illness, and I will be dead. I must assure you, however, that everything in this letter is true. Please do not doubt my integrity or my sanity. I am old but I am clear of mind, at least for the moment.

There's a good chance your mother will have left you with the hassle of sorting out my bungalow and possessions. It is on this assumption that I have put the shed's entrance code on Aslan's collar. In turn, I am hoping you made the connection with the name Aslan and have gone straight to The Lion, The Witch and the Wardrobe on the bookshelf, in which this letter is enclosed. I spent many happy hours reading the Narnia stories to you when you were a young boy.

As I hope you remember fondly, I love any puzzle, game or treasure hunt. But I didn't set this all up for fun. It was the only way I could think of to contact you safely. I have been under constant, close surveillance for longer than I can remember, and any attempt to reach out to you would have severely jeopardised your future.

I am 'persona non grata' in this sunlit society of ours, and I didn't want to smear you by association. The very fact you're my grandson will already ensure you're on a list of possible threats, and any contact with me in recent years would have made things significantly worse for you. Of course, Alexa decreed that I could no longer see you or her anyway, so any relationship would have been difficult regardless.

I am writing, therefore, to say that I love you, and I am desperately sorry that it's been over ten years since we saw each other. The absence has slowly sapped my soul. It's been even crueller knowing you live such a short distance away. There was one time, perhaps five years ago, when I was sure I saw you in the distance. You had grown so much. But, for the reasons mentioned above, I was wary of even saying hello, even if it was desperately tempting. The risk was too great.

I am also writing to share a little bit of our family story, in the hope that it will help you on your journey to adulthood. I tried my best in your early years to fill the role of your non-existent father, and this letter is a small attempt to fill the subsequent, decade-long void.

I'll begin with a direct warning: be very aware that freedom in our society has essentially extinguished. Sunnyvale's claim that their idea of 'progress' is equitable to 'freedom' is a lie of the greatest magnitude. It is one, unfortunately, that Alexa has swallowed whole. This is my biggest regret as a father. I have failed her.

She has a strange form of Stockholm Syndrome. I don't know how much she has ever told you about her upbringing, but her mother and I were once digital utopians of the most evangelical kind. We worked for different companies in the Big Seven – before they merged to become Sunnyvale – and we believed we were making the world a better place. We were handsomely rewarded for doing so, and we even named our only child after what we viewed as a great technological triumph.

I can't pinpoint exactly when the doubts started to creep in, but gradually the wool was pulled from my eyes (have you ever heard this phrase before?). To use another expression from my childhood, I began to realise that the Emperor was wearing no clothes. Sunnyvale doesn't always necessarily mean progress, and this form of progress doesn't necessarily lead to freedom. In fact, the opposite is very often true.

Think, for a moment, about the Smart Sensor currently implanted in your wrist. It permanently records and files everything you say, everywhere you go, and everything you do. It is a 24/7 surveillance tool. (I installed signal-blockers into the shed's insulation, so you should be safe down here. But still be vigilant.)

Think – really think – whether this is justifiable, or in any way helpful to the cause of personal or collective freedom. It is the direct opposite of freedom! The West was built on the concept of liberty. In the USA, this concept was enshrined in the Constitution, and the Declaration of Independence. In the UK, one could argue it stretches back (at least symbolically) all the way to 1215, when the Magna Carta first curtailed the absolute power of the monarch.

Liberty is the lifeblood, the foundation, of humanity. It is precious, and takes centuries to build. Clearly, it takes only a few short years to dismantle. Sunnyvale has made us all serfs. They control what we buy, what we read, what we say, what we think, what we feel and what we do. Their influence is utterly unprecedented in human history. It is an evil beyond the comprehension of our forefathers.

Alexa had grown up with all the trappings of the comfortable lifestyle afforded by our line of work, and she rebelled when her mother and I began to extricate ourselves from it. She couldn't understand why we would sacrifice a large house, respectable status and good jobs in an exciting field for ostracised misery. All for the sake of our so-called principles.

Of course, we weren't able to move on without a fuss. We were forced to take lie detector tests upon our resignations, and this revealed our growing hostility to the technopoly-totalitarianism we saw growing around us. They attempted to threaten and bully us into staying, but we remained resolute.

Their power wasn't quite as omnipotent as it is now, and we were able to try to build new lives. We downsized to this bungalow, but shortly thereafter your grandmother died. I have no doubt that the stress caused by our decision led to her illness and death, and every day I have to live with that burden. Did we do the right thing? Was it worth it? God rest her soul.

Alexa moved out to forge her own path. I have always admired her grit and focus. She's intelligent and ferociously strong-minded. It's just a crying shame those virtues are channelled in the support of Sunnyvale, and everything they represent. I tried on hundreds of occasions to get her to reassess her allegiance, but she's utterly convinced of their goodness. And she's astute. She knows that to advance in life she has to play the game. She has to play by their rules.

I tell you this not to drive a wedge between you and Alexa, but because I have a duty to tell you the truth. I hope you love her, and she loves you, and she can somehow be a good mother to you. But I urge you not to follow in her footsteps.

If my transformation from digital utopian to sceptic and pariah seems sudden, please trust that it was an agonising, gradual process. It took years for me to wake up. I can scarcely do justice to what it felt like. It started with a few trickles of doubt, and eventually the floodgates opened.

I saw things develop that I'd read about with horror as a student. If anything, the dystopian warnings of Orwell, Huxley, Bradbury, Koestler, Kafka and more had grossly underestimated the potential of a technopoly-totalitarianism.

The rise of the Internet, and of the forces that would grow to control the digital world, were beyond even the most fertile of imaginations in the twentieth century. But they were right in the sense that naked power and rampant utopianism are a deadly mix. All of these authors are represented on the bookshelves around you – some of their works were very difficult to find – and I implore you to read them.

I created a pseudonym, inspired by characters from two of those books: Guy Smith. I envisaged myself as an underground agitator; a fearless rebel giving a voice to the voiceless; a martyr willing to sacrifice everything to spread truth. I had nothing to lose, after all. My wife was dead, my daughter had disowned me, and I wasn't allowed to see my only grandchild.

There were others out there who felt the same as me. I wasn't totally alone. We had some small success in spreading subversive literature, and arranging clandestine gatherings. I was even invited to move to a small island community, who live without any modern forms of technology. But York is my home city, and I'm an old man. I'm happy to die here. I refuse to flee.

Despite the thrill of some modest success, it was like firing a pea-shooter against a full battalion. Actually, it was like firing a pea-shooter against a whole army. The largest army the world has ever seen.

Sunnyvale's strength grows every day, and there's nothing we can do about it. I'm not a defeatist, but I'm also not deluded. The vast majority of the public in the West are unaware of what freedom means. Freedom of thought, freedom of speech and the right to privacy are dead. In both concept and reality. We became flabby and careless, and now there's no going back.

The response is even worse than ignorance and apathy: it's an open embrace. People are happy to be servile. They are happy to have their opinions shaped and monitored by their overlords. They are happy to be dazzled by an endless stream of technological goods. They are happy to see the silencing of those who dissent. The ghastly Sunnyvale Smart Shrouds are their muzzles.

A lot of this has stemmed from good intentions. Those with 'offensive' opinions should be punished, they thought. They should be held accountable for their views, and exposed accordingly. Many of those who rushed to this cause meant well. They just wanted a nicer, kinder society in accordance with their worldview. Virtuous. Altruistic. Liberal. Ethical.

But there was a malevolent underbelly. 'Offensive' became a term which encompassed anything and anyone they disagreed with. This mindset was weaponised with frightening alacrity. And it grew hand-in-hand with the rise of Big Tech, culminating in Sunnyvale's formation in 2056. It was a symbiotic process. The result is technopoly-totalitarianism.

Decades ago, there was still a chance of change. But the authorities were utterly ruthless in their denunciation of dissenters. They were systematically blackmailed, censored, deleted and cancelled. Now, the war is won and they barely need to bother anymore. They're just sweeping up the last remnants of defiance.

I'm a powerless old man who will die soon. I pose no threat to them, and they know it. Otherwise, I wouldn't even be here to pen this letter.

I don't know what type of young man you have grown up to be, but the child I remember was curious, clever and independent-minded. I can only hope those traits have stayed with you. And I wish you luck, and all my love, as you make your way in this increasingly dark and desperate world.

Please enjoy this room. I call it my shelter, and I hope its existence can be our secret.

Yours Forever, and in Freedom,
Pop

P.S. There are Smart Sensor removal services on the black market, and I've known of people who have removed it themselves (be careful if you do so). If you get challenged, say you had an allergic reaction to the implant and you're happy to wear the microchipped glasses. The glasses are just as intrusive, but they can be conveniently 'lost' or left behind from time to time.

P.P.S. If you want more answers, remember Truth is a Fool's Gold.

15

Harrison dropped the sheaf of papers on his lap, and closed his eyes. How could he have missed the clue with Aslan's name? He should have read the letter months ago, as Pop intended, when he first discovered the haven.

There was so much new information for him to assimilate: *Pop had been an 'underground agitator'? Having previously worked for Big Tech? Freedom of thought, freedom of speech and the right to privacy are dead?*

Harrison thought back to his swim in the lake with Amberley, crassly interrupted by a Stinger. Why was that any of Sunnyvale's business? He looked down at his right wrist, where the Sunnyvale Smart Sensor was implanted. His whole life was stored in that little microchip: his thoughts, his dreams, his hopes, his flaws, his mistakes and his memories. And it could all be analysed, as if it was some code on a computer screen, by the likes of Elliot Patrick.

He thought of Steven Robinson and Jim Cooper, whose lives had been ruined by a couple of tame jokes. *No*, he accosted himself, they hadn't *been* ruined in a passive sense. *He* had ruined them. By reporting their conversation to his superiors.

He thought of the Sunnypedia articles he had drafted and doctored, all to maintain some unspoken balance of power. *We can make the mob applaud, we can make the mob hiss.* He thought of the chest-thumping comradeship, the dopamine-fuelled Monthly Meetings and the stained-glass portrait of the Great Liberator, smugly overlooking the worker bees.

He was disoriented, his mind swirling with recollections and recriminations and regrets. He was supposed to be at work in less than six hours. What the hell was he going to do?

He was shocked out of his stupor when the ceiling above him started creaking, and when two feet appeared on the top rung of the ladder. In all the excitement, he had forgotten to lock the doors behind him.

*

Amberley said nothing for several minutes. She paced around the room, occasionally picking a book off the shelf, or analysing one of the record sleeves, or looking at one of the wooden-framed photographs on the mantelpiece. Harrison sat, deadly still, on the blue armchair, still reeling from Pop's letter, and not even knowing where to begin with an explanation. He poured himself a glass of whisky from the decanter, and rested his eyes.

'Harrison, we need to talk,' she said, eventually. He kept his eyes closed, and reached out to hand her Pop's letter. She took it off him, confusion etched on her face, and read it carefully.

When Harrison sensed she had finished, he opened his eyes. Her hair was frizzy and unkempt, and her eyes were alert with concern. Her hand was shaking as she returned the letter to him.

'Just for knowing what I know, I would lose my job,' she said. 'Or worse.'

'That's the price you pay for following me down here,' Harrison said.

'I was worried!' she said. 'I woke up and you weren't there! I had no idea I'd end up in some time warp, some underground shelter with a load of forbidden books and music. Why didn't you tell me, Harrison?'

'What was I supposed to say?' he said.

Harrison downed the rest of his whisky and stood up. His floppy hair was comically askew.

'Let's just take a deep breath,' he said. 'It's been a jarring night for both of us. We can get a few hours' sleep and think about all this in the morning. It won't do us any good to stand here debating till dawn.'

*

Harrison woke shortly before quarter to eight. His shift in the control room was set to start at nine. He was pleasantly surprised at how easily he had managed to fall back asleep after all the commotion – it was like his brain was so overwhelmed it just needed to shut down for a while.

He yawned and stretched, and looked to his right. The other half of the bed was empty.

'Amberley,' he shouted. 'Are you in the kitchen? Please can you put the kettle on if you are?'

There was no response, so he jumped out of bed and walked through to the kitchen. There was nobody there. He backtracked into the hallway, and leaned to look into the bathroom, which was also empty. He checked the spare bedroom and the lounge, to no avail.

The house was as still and silent as when he had first visited, shortly after Pop's death.

'Amberley,' he shouted again, but he knew it was futile. She must have slipped out when he was asleep. He sighed and re-entered his bedroom, to check if any of her clothes were still there. They had all gone, as had her handbag, and any other sign of her presence in the bungalow.

The electric fan in the corner was still whirring, so he leant over to switch it off. As he did so, he noticed a scrap of paper on his bedside table. It looked like it had been torn from a notebook, and scribbled on hurriedly. For the second time in a few hours, he was reading a note left for him.

Harrison,

You're a great guy and the last few weeks have been fun. But there's a lot for me to take in, and I think we need a break from each other. I have some annual leave to take, and I'm going to visit my family down south.

Sorry. Take care.

Amberley x
(Please remember I'm sorry xx)

Harrison scrunched the scrap of paper into a ball and threw it on the floor. He didn't have time to stew over Amberley: he was due at work soon, and he had a decision to make. Could he turn up and pretend everything was normal? Could he possibly get through the day – dealing with the Lamb twins, Elliot Patrick, and maybe even his mum – after what he had learnt overnight? And would he be disciplined for damaging the Smart Drone? Would Amberley be questioned for her involvement?

He felt like he had a hundred questions, and precisely zero answers. *Relax*, he told himself. *First things first, people call in sick all the time. No big deal.*

He called HR through his Smart Sensor (this would just be a voice call; he had decided not to make it a video call). A lady answered, speaking in clipped tones. 'This is the Sunnyvale HR department. How may we help you, Mr Snow?'

'Hi, I'm calling to let you know I won't be able to make it into work today, I'm afraid.' He was speaking in an affected under-the-weather tone, with the occasional sniffle for added authenticity. 'I've picked up a bug and I'm struggling to get out of bed. The last thing I'd want to do is spread it to other people, this week of all weeks.'

It was Monday, and the Great Liberator's momentous visit was set for Friday.

'Thank you for letting us know, Mr Snow. We will update your digital profile and inform your colleagues. Get well soon. Please call us with an update later this week.' A little *blip* signalled the end of the call.

He had bought himself at least a few days. *Now what?*

16

His first instinct was to get his Smart Sensor removed. Pop's warning had been like a slap to his face: he had no privacy, no autonomy, no semblance of individuality, if he had this *thing* implanted in his wrist. (Plus, they would be able to monitor his health data and ascertain that he wasn't actually ill.)

He had been indulging in a bizarre doublethink, whereby he had listened to other people's personal conversations through their Smart Sensors (and had them punished for what they had said), but had never fully realised that the same could happen to him. He was working for the good guys, right? He was one of the watchers, not one of the watched. But he now understood that this was an illusion.

Even if the signal-blockers had ensured his time in the haven was safe, everything else he had said or done would be fair game. A fellow Sweeper could, right now, be listening to his conversation with Amberley the previous night. It would become clear that he *had* deliberately attacked the Stinger (as if it wasn't already obvious) and he would have to face the repercussions.

It wouldn't take much to unravel the whole story: the discovery of the haven, his mounting confusion and disillusionment with Sunnyvale, Pop's letter – all of which would build into an ever-growing suspicion that Harrison was becoming an enemy of everything they stood for.

His only hope was that it would be so trivial as to be unworthy of investigation. Even with Sunnyvale's unfathomably vast resources, they couldn't constantly target everybody. They only arrowed in their focus – with the precision of a laser beam – on those who justified the attention. He just had to stay under the radar, and he might be fine. After all, Stingers must occasionally break or fail of their own volition on a daily basis across the West.

In that case, would he be better off keeping the Sensor? Would he draw too much attention to himself by claiming he had suddenly suffered an allergic reaction to it? Where would he even begin to get it taken out?

Pop had mentioned there were removal services on the black market. Were there particular places in town where these markets operated? Who could he trust? He had lived a sheltered life, as the son of one of the city's wealthiest people, and he had no streetwise network to tap into. His old friends, who had all attended the same exclusive private school as him, would be equally as useless.

He now felt like he had a *thousand* questions, and precisely zero answers.

He walked into the lounge and slumped onto the sofa, as the fresh morning sun shone through his bay windows. He held his right arm out, with his hand facing downwards, and looked at the top of the wrist where the microchip was implanted. There was a small, square shape just underneath the surface of his pale skin, exactly where his wrist met his hand.

He wondered how painful it would be to remove it himself. If it was in the bottom of the wrist, with all the veins and the arteries, he wouldn't dare go near it. But the top of the wrist would be less risky – there were still nerves and tendons that would be better left undamaged, but it was certainly viable. According to Pop, other people had managed to do it themselves.

The indecision was starting to make him feel nauseous, and he decided – suddenly – that it was the time for action. He was sick of being a coward. He strode purposefully out the back door, entered 1811 into the keypad, and headed straight for the toolbox in the corner of the shed. He had walked past it many times, on his way down to the haven, but had never had cause to open it before.

It was a squat, steel box, the size of a briefcase, and he picked it up by its handle. He also reached for a green, plastic box nearby with the words 'First Aid' stencilled on it. He carried both boxes back to the kitchen and placed them on the wooden table, before closing his eyes and breathing deeply.

'Come on,' he said to himself. 'Cowards die many times before their deaths. The valiant never taste of death but once.'

He opened the toolbox's steel lid, revealing a neat arrangement of hammers, nails, screws and bolts. He felt like some kind of nightmarish surgeon from a horror movie, as he carefully removed a pair of diagonal pliers from the box. They had a thick, red tubular grip, and sharp metal pincers, designed to cut through copper, brass, iron and steel wire. Human skin wouldn't put up much of a fight.

He scanned the rest of the toolbox to see if anything else would be more suited to the job, and the screwdriver caught his eye. Rather than cutting open his skin with the pliers and removing the microchip, the screwdriver could burrow in, making a little indent, and shovel it out instead.

The screwdriver looked new and unused, but he grabbed a sterile wipe from the First Aid box nonetheless, and thoroughly cleaned its metal tip. He did the same with the pliers' pincers, which felt smooth and lethally sharp.

He steadied himself again. Pliers or screwdriver? Screwdriver or pliers? It would all be over in a matter of seconds, if he could just pluck up the courage. The chip was only just under the surface of his skin.

He felt another wave of nausea in his navel, as if he was taking a sweeping turn on a rollercoaster, and his legs nearly gave way from underneath him. He held on to the edge of the table for support. His face had a sickly pallor, and sweat was gathering on his forehead.

He forced himself to stand up straight, and shouted 'Come onnnnnnnnnn!' as loudly as he could, like a tribal war cry. In one swift motion, he grabbed the screwdriver from the table, stabbed into the top of his wrist, twisted and burrowed for a few seconds (for what felt like an eternity), dug out the microchip and sent it flying across the floor.

Blood poured from the wound, and he immediately wiped it down with another sterile wipe, before rolling a self-adhesive bandage round and round and round, until it was tight and thick. Without pause, he stepped over to the chip on the floor and crushed it with his foot. He stamped on it six, seven, eight times, until it was splayed into tiny pieces.

He looked across at the table, at the screwdriver and pliers, and then down at his bandaged wrist. And then he vomited everywhere.

*

At Sunnyvale HQ, Alexa Snow strode through the warehouse, past the row upon row of white, shelved units, towards the western entrance. She had three aides walking in her wake, struggling to keep up with her pace. The click-click of her heels echoed up to the high ceilings, and the warehouse workers warily kept their distance.

'It's essential that the Great Liberator arrives through the ornate western doors,' she said. 'First impressions are very important. It means the very first thing we can show him is the stained-glass portrait.'

'Noted, ma'am,' one of the aides said. 'We've had the arrival plan arranged for months.'

'Talk me through it again,' Alexa said.

The aide was a young man, around the same age as

Harrison. He was wearing a suit that was too big for him, and he cleared his throat nervously.

'The Great Liberator will enjoy a leisurely breakfast at his hotel on Friday morning,' he said, checking his Smart Sensor for the schedule. 'One of our cars will pick him up at eight-thirty, and he should arrive at HQ less than ten minutes later. We've built in some time, just in case there are any delays. There'll be big crowds in the city centre, especially outside HQ, which may slow the car down.'

'How many people are we expecting?' she said.

'Thousands,' he replied. 'We've ensured that the response will be appropriately enthusiastic. It's the Great Liberator's first visit on our soil, after all.'

'What next?' she said, as they continued their march inside the building's perimeter. They had now passed the western entrance and had turned back towards her office, in the old Chapter House.

'The Great Liberator will enjoy a first-hand tour of the site, led by you and Elliot Patrick. There will then be a special Monthly Meeting in your office, which he will attend. There'll be vegan champagne, and a three-course lunch. It's a chance for all the staff here to meet him, or at least to be in the same room as him.

'And then he will make his globally-televised speech on the steps outside the western entrance, at midday sharp. All major media will be there, of course. And the crowds will still be rocking. We've organised something of an all-day festival to maintain their enthusiasm. Music, magic, entertainment and the like.

'Once the speech is done, our car will transport the Great Liberator back to his hotel, and in the evening he'll be on his jet, flying to his next site visit. It won't have the fanfare of ours though – this is the headliner, the big one. It's all been meticulously planned, with enough in-built leeway for any surprises, and we expect the day to run as smoothly as clockwork.'

'Very good,' Alexa said. 'How is everything looking security-wise?'

'Clean as a whistle,' he said. 'But we're being extra vigilant. Even the slightest hint of a threat is being treated very seriously. There is no scope for failure on Friday, ma'am. It's the biggest day of all our lives. We won't let you down.'

*

Harrison cleaned up the mess on the kitchen floor, returned the toolbox and First Aid kit to the shed (keeping a fresh roll of bandages in his pocket), and stood up straight. He was proud of his bravery in removing the Smart Sensor, but he still had a thousand unanswered questions.

Pop's voice was playing on a loop in his head. *Sunnyvale has made us all serfs. We became flabby and careless, and now there's no going back. Technopoly-totalitarianism.*

And what on earth did he mean by saying 'Truth is a Fool's Gold'? Pop and his bloody puzzles. Even in his letter from beyond the grave, he couldn't resist a riddle.

'If you're ever in a pickle about something, go for a walk,' was something else Pop regularly said. 'It clears the head.'

Harrison grabbed his trainers and set out for a stroll along the riverfront, planning to trace the same route he took on his occasional jogs. There was the chance he could bump into a colleague, who would enquire why he was off work, but he could always say a doctor had advised a walk in the sunshine to see off his bug.

He was in a pickle, alright. And he very much needed to clear his head.

*

Harrison ambled past the spot where Pop had tried to teach him how to fish, and he smiled broadly. The sun was on his face, the River Ouse was calm and clear, and he was enjoying an exhilarating sense of freedom at being without the microchip in his wrist. He felt lighter.

He even began to whistle, and tried to push all the heavy, existential questions from his mind. It had been a life-changing twenty-four hours, but he felt strangely at peace. He wasn't just walking, he was *sauntering*. He sauntered past flocks of geese, which nipped away at the lush riverside grass, and sauntered by stone bridges that had stood for centuries.

Whatever happened hereafter, he was proud to be the grandson of Joseph Snow, of Guy Smith, the fearless underground agitator and protector of civil liberties. It had a better ring to it than just being another generic Sunnyvale Sweeper, hunched over a computer screen and taking nasally orders from Elliot Patrick.

He had sauntered nearly all the way to the city centre, which was dangerously close to Sunnyvale HQ. It was late morning, and his stomach was growling with hunger – in all the drama, he had forgotten to eat breakfast. It was time to head back to the bungalow, and take stock.

Suddenly, a familiarly ominous buzzing sound filled the sky overhead. A Stinger. In all likelihood, it was just delivering a package, but Harrison was fearful of taking risks so soon after removing his Smart Sensor. He didn't dare look up, but he could hear that it was coming closer.

A Tudor-style house was on Harrison's right, with a ground floor fronted with stone and a first floor with white render. Its steep, tiled roof was obscuring the Stinger. In just a few seconds, the drone would be unobstructed, and it would be close enough to identify and scan his face. He had no option but to leap towards the house.

He flattened himself against the wall, covered by the roof's shadow, but it wouldn't be enough to evade the drone's sophisticated technology. He edged around the corner and clasped a brass doorknob. He twisted and pushed, and practically fell through an old-fashioned doorway, stumbling through the entrance. After gathering himself, he realised it wasn't just an old, nondescript house. It was a pub.

Every conversation halted as Harrison tripped gracelessly into the room, which was low-roofed and dark-timbered. There were about ten men dotted around, all in their seventies or eighties, some perched on stools at the bar, others sitting stoop-shouldered at tables. One was smoking a tobacco cigarette, which is something Harrison had never seen before. Nobody was wearing a Smart Shroud or a pair of Smart Spectacles.

It was light and warm outside, but it was cool and dim in here, and the bald-headed landlord looked at Harrison with a rugged, unimpressed face. He was a few decades younger than the clientele, and he had a Neanderthal-like skull.

Eyes followed Harrison as he made his way to the bar, the wooden floor creaking beneath his trainers. His face was scarlet: he was conscious of the bandage on his wrist, and of the conspicuous way he had flopped into the room. He reached the bar and leaned on it, trying to look casual.

'Can I have a beer, please?' he said.

The landlord looked at him for several moments. Harrison was only twenty, but he was fairly tall and well-built, and his voice was deep.

'A pint?' the landlord said, in a thick Yorkshire accent.

'Yeah,' Harrison replied, without knowing what he meant.

The landlord reached for a glass, pulled a brass pump and filled it to the brim with dark, amber ale. His hands were as huge as the joint of beef Harrison had cooked for Amberley, and his fingers were calloused and coarsened.

'And I'll have one of whatever they are,' Harrison said, pointing to a row of snacks, in silver packets, stacked behind the bar. He hoped they would take the edge off his hunger.

The landlord plonked a packet next to the pint, and Harrison inspected it.

'Is this a vegan snack?' Harrison said.

The whole pub suddenly erupted with laughter. Ten men guffawed and snorted, and the smoker's laugh turned into a fit of coughing. The frail one nearest to Harrison – who was on a barstool, arms propped on the counter – turned and looked with quiet amusement on his weathered face.

His bloodshot, sunken eyes met Harrison's, and his expression suddenly changed into one of surprise and fear.

'It bloody well isn't a vegan snack,' the landlord said emphatically. 'They're pork scratchings.'

'Good,' Harrison replied. 'That's good. I'm sick of us being told what we can and can't eat or drink.'

The mirth quietened down, and Harrison took a sip of his pint (he still wasn't sure if this was the name or measurement of the beer). It was somehow smooth and bitter at the same time.

The old man next to him was now looking down at his drink, as if he wanted to blend meekly into the surroundings, but Harrison had caught his strange alteration in expression.

'Excuse me,' Harrison said quietly. 'Do you know me from somewhere?' The landlord had gone to the back and nobody could overhear their conversation.

'Please leave me alone, young man,' he said. 'I'm not doing anybody any harm. Leave me be.'

Harrison frowned and took another sip of his pint. 'I don't mean to intrude at all,' he said. 'I'm just confused as to why you looked so shocked when you saw me.'

'Bollocks,' the man said severely, or at least as severely as he could with his frail voice. He sounded wheezy and short of breath.

'I know you work for Sunnyvale,' he said. 'I saw you in the warehouse recently, parading around in your suit. If you're here to arrest me or to close down this place, get on with it. I couldn't care less anymore. The only thing I don't understand is why you're doing it now. I thought it was easier to leave us old folk alone? We don't bother anybody. We sit here and drink a few pints. So what?'

Harrison's mind flashed back to his warehouse tour with the Lamb twins, when one of the overall-wearing workers had knocked into him. He remembered the bloodshot, sunken eyes that had met his.

'Slow down,' Harrison said. 'I'm not here to arrest anybody. I'm on a day off, and this is my downtime. I'll spend it how I want.'

The old man didn't respond, but he seemed slightly calmed. He had grey, thinning hair, and he was wearing a battered pair of jeans with a shabby, colourless, collared shirt. The sleeves were rolled up, and his pale forearms were pocked with liver spots. His fingernails were yellowing and his hand was shaking slightly as he reached for his drink.

'How old are you? If you don't mind me asking,' Harrison said.

'I'm old enough to remember when people respected their elders,' he replied.

Harrison rolled his eyes, and moved from the bar to a wooden table in the corner, which had just been vacated. The beer was slipping down nicely, and he wondered how many times he had walked past this building without ever thinking what was behind the old-fashioned doorway. The pork scratchings were salty and crunchy, and added to his thirst.

He finished the drink, savouring the last sip, and caught the barman's eye. 'I'll have another, please,' he said. The landlord gave a short nod, and grabbed a fresh glass. There was no music playing, and conversation was at a minimum, but the place had a relaxed air about it. Aside from the drama of Harrison's arrival, it was clear nothing much had happened in the way of action today. It was likely nothing of action ever happened much.

Harrison walked over to the bar (he thought it might be pushing it to expect the grizzled landlord to hover over his table like a waiter) and fetched his fresh pint.

'How are you planning on paying for these drinks?' the landlord said.

Harrison cursed himself. Nearly every monetary transaction he had ever made had been through either his Smart Spectacles or his Sensor, and he had never thought of the logistical problems arising from the latter's removal.

He held up his right wrist. 'I'm really sorry,' he said. 'I've had a problem with my Smart Sensor, which normally works automatically. I don't know how else I can pay.'

The landlord looked apathetic. 'Hand me that beer back, then,' he said. 'I'm a generous man, and I'll let you off for the first. But you can't have any more.'

The frail man at the bar reached into his jeans pocket and removed a tattered leather wallet.

'I'll cover his drinks, Jamie,' he said. 'They're on me.' He took out a crisp, rectangular note from the wallet and placed it on the bar. Harrison caught a white background and a flash of purple, but nothing more.

'Are you sure?' the landlord said. 'That's a bloody rarity. I thought I saw moths fly out that wallet a second ago.'

'I'm sure,' the old man said lightly. The landlord took out an ancient-looking till from under the bar. He handed him a similar note and a handful of silver and copper coins in return.

Harrison was speechless with surprise. Eventually, he said: 'Are they coins? And notes? I've never seen old money before. And thank you for the drinks. To what do I owe such generosity?'

'You don't seem like a bad lad,' the old man said. 'And it's about time I got a round in. There's no point taking money with you to the grave. Not that I have a great deal of it.'

'Well, I'm very grateful, thank you. I'm Harrison, by the way. What's your name?'

'Stan,' he said. 'Were you named after Harrison Ford?'

'Who?'

'Ah, it doesn't matter,' he said. 'He's probably banned now anyway. Or cancelled, or whatever they call it. It's hard to keep track nowadays.'

Stan reached again for his pint, and his hand was still trembling. It looked like he had some kind of nerve problem, or maybe a disease like Parkinson's.

'I'm sorry to ask again, but how old are you?' Harrison said. 'I'm wondering if you knew my grandad.'

'I'm seventy-nine,' he said. 'Born and bred in York, so there's a good chance I will know him if he's from round these parts.'

'His name was Joseph Snow, or Guy Smith,' Harrison said. 'He was a bit older than you, though. He died earlier this year, aged ninety-ish.'

'Never heard of him,' Stan said. He was content to sit in peace and quiet, never forcing conversation, and Harrison allowed himself to fall into this staccato tempo. They continued talking, but sometimes minutes would elapse between each spurt of conversation.

'How long have you worked at Sunnyvale?' Harrison said. 'It looks like hard work for a man your age. No offence.'

'I've worked there coming on four years now,' he replied.

'It's bloody knackering, but I have no choice. I have to pay the bills somehow.'

'Can't you retire soon?' Harrison said.

Stan let out a little snort of derision. 'Retire? No chance. There are no pensions anymore, lad. It's work until you drop. The second you're no longer useful, off you go. I'll be shuffling off this mortal coil before long.'

'Mortal coil? What do you mean?'

'It's Shakespeare, I think. It's just a saying.'

'You know Shakespeare?' Harrison said excitedly. 'What's your favourite play?'

'Nah, nah, I don't know anything like that. I was never any good in school. It's just a famous saying, my old man used to say it. I'll be dead before long. I'll pop my clogs. I'll buy the farm. You know what I mean.'

'What's it like working in the warehouse?' Harrison said.

'We're nothing more than ants scuttling around in the dirt and the mud. Or maybe we're more like cattle, being herded this way and that. Either way, we're certainly not human beings.'

Harrison didn't know what to say in response. 'Couldn't you do something else?' he offered, weakly.

'Like what?' Stan said. 'I'm seventy-nine, I have two knackered knees, more medical problems than you can shake a stick at and no qualifications. The only thing stopping me from living on the streets is that damned job. And at least I can come in here on my days off.'

'There must be other work you can do though?'

'Look around you, lad. There's barely any real work left. My dad was a butcher, like his dad before him, and like his dad before him. That's long gone. My mum worked at the city library, near Museum Gardens. That's long gone. I'm as useless as an old donkey with a broken leg. It won't be long till I'm put out my misery.'

'Bloody hell, you're miserable,' Harrison said. 'But it's actually quite refreshing compared to all the "Sunnyvale is Progress. Progress is Freedom" stuff. I hope you remember to say that every time you walk past the stained-glass window?'

'Do I bollocks,' Stan said, and he let out a quiet laugh. 'I just keep my head down and count down the hours till my next pint in here.'

'What was life like before Sunnyvale?' Harrison said.

'What do you mean?'

'Things must have been different. My grandad says he saw the world change in ways he could never have imagined.'

'It's hard to say,' Stan said. 'I've never really thought about it. It just happened. You can't fight it, can you? It's big business, big money. It's pointless getting all angry or annoyed.'

'But so many freedoms from your childhood have vanished,' Harrison said. 'You're lucky that they even let you have this space, which is breaking about ten laws. It's only because you're old and unthreatening.'

'As long as I can have a quiet pint in here, I'm fine,' Stan said defiantly. He scratched his forearm with his yellowed fingernails, and shuffled off to use the toilet.

The conversation had petered out, leaving Harrison frustrated, but he fancied another pint before heading back to the bungalow.

'One more, please,' he said to the landlord, who was at the other end of the bar, trying to fix a faulty pump.

'Last orders for me,' Harrison said, shouting after Stan. 'I'll call in sometime soon to pay you back for these drinks. I really appreciate it.'

'Aye, you're not a bad lad,' he replied.

*

Fifteen minutes later, Harrison drained the last few drops of his drink – he was back at his corner table, to give Stan some peace – and looked out the window to see if he could spot a Stinger. The coast appeared to be clear, and he was ready to make a move.

'See you,' he said to the landlord. 'Thanks again, Stan,' he added, which was met with a nod.

He reached the old-fashioned doorway, and turned around to face the low-roofed, dark-timbered room.

'Excuse me, everyone,' he said loudly. 'Does anyone know anything about the phrase "Truth is a Fool's Gold". Is it some old saying, or something? My grandad said it to me before he died and I'm trying to work out what it means.'

He was met with silence. Ten men looked at him over their pints and said nothing, until a croaky voice from the shadows said: 'I used to be a chemistry teacher. Fool's gold is a mineral called pyrite. It can have a superficial resemblance to gold, hence the name.'

'Thanks,' Harrison said. 'Can you think of any relevance to my grandad's quote?'

'Not without more context,' the croaky voice replied.

'Where can you find pyrite?' Harrison said.

'All over the West. It's the most common of sulphide minerals and you can find it in many different types of rock. Igneous, metamorphic and sedimentary. It's also known as iron pyrite: one part iron and two parts sulphur.'

'Cheers,' Harrison said, but it didn't feel like much of a breakthrough.

'You're thinking too literally,' the landlord said in his booming voice. 'Fool's gold is just a metaphor for thinking something is more precious and valuable than it is. Like, when my old man bought this pub years ago, he thought he was onto a goldmine. But he was a fool. Instead, I make a pittance of pennies every month and spend all my time with this miserable lot.'

The room erupted with laughter, as it had done when Harrison asked about the pork scratchings. He thanked everyone again and emerged, blinking, into the early afternoon sunlight, straining his ears and his eyes for any sign of a Stinger.

17

He made it back to the bungalow, unspotted and unscathed, though a little tipsy. It was like, just for an hour or two, he had been transported to a different world. A world where real men – crabby and cantankerous, but *real* – still existed. It was a thrill to see what old money looked like, and to experience somewhere where a black market existed. It may have even been where Pop purchased his joint of beef.

Truth is a Fool's Gold. The riddle was niggling him, and he wouldn't be able to relax until he had done some more digging. Could it really have something to do with a mineral found in rocks? Or was the landlord right in saying it was a metaphor? Surely Pop wouldn't insinuate that the truth was unimportant, or that it was some kind or mirage? The more he thought about it, the more he tangled himself in knots.

Aslan came and sat on his lap, purring loudly. Harrison inspected the belt-like collar around his neck, and the metal disc, to see if he had missed another clue. '1811' it said on one side, and 'Aslan' on the other, but otherwise there wasn't a blemish. He stroked Aslan's head gently – who closed his eyes and continued to purr – and racked his brain. Nothing was forthcoming. Not even the slightest hint of a solution.

Without his Smart Sensor, he had lost the ability to search online through Sunnyvale Smart Search, or on Sunnypedia (which he had lost trust in anyway, having seen how it worked from the inside).

He used to own different handheld devices too, but the Smart Sensor had made them all redundant: everything was stored on that little microchip. It had been one of its great selling points – no fuss or clutter; everything held safely in one place;

permanent connectivity – but now it seemed foolish to keep all his technological eggs in one basket. One glitch and he was back in the Stone Age.

He was on the sofa in the living room, but he had an urge to head down to the haven. If he had missed the original clue about *The Lion, The Witch and the Wardrobe*, there was a chance he'd overlooked another one. At the very least, he fancied some whisky to add to his earlier beers. The alcohol in his system was both numbing his frustration and accelerating his imagination, which he didn't think was a bad mix in the circumstances. He needed to keep working on the clue without tearing his hair out.

Aslan let out a little burble of displeasure as Harrison stood up, brushed the hairs off his lap, and marched out the back door. Moments later, he was pouring himself a whisky, and falling into the blue armchair. *Pyrite. Sulphide minerals.* That had to be a red herring? What possible link could it have to 'Truth'? But it was all he had to go on so far.

From his vantage point on the armchair, he scanned the bookshelves for anything that could help. Perhaps there was a novel called *Fool's Gold*, or some kind of science book that could point him in the right direction with pyrite. *One part iron and two parts sulphur.* Did that mean it had some kind of chemical formula? He strained his brain, and sipped his whisky. What was that big chart called, with all the elements listed on it? Where each element has a letter?

He stood up and worked up and down the bookshelves again, ensuring nothing slipped past him. There were novels, biographies, poetry collections, history books and all sorts of miscellaneous titbits, but he couldn't see anything about chemistry, or science in general.

The thickest book on the top shelf was a fat, well-worn dictionary. Harrison had thumbed through it many times, marvelling at the time and effort it must have taken to compile nearly every English word ever uttered by a human being. It was an old version, published many decades before even Pop was born, with a tatty and battered cover.

Next to it, there was a reference book of some kind. It was nearly as chunky as the dictionary but not quite as old, dating from around Pop's childhood. It listed everything from capitals to US presidents to old currencies (Harrison knew that the old money he had seen in the pub was called 'pound sterling'), to famous quotations and historical figures and sporting records. It was like a primitive, paper version of Sunnypedia.

Most of the things alluded to in the book were so alien to Harrison that he hadn't seen much appeal in flicking through it much, even though he respected the toil it must have taken, but he realised it could now be his only decent source of scientific information.

He stretched and pulled it down from the top shelf, opening to the contents page. He moved his thumb down several rows until he reached the letter S – underneath the heading 'Science' it read:

Chemical Elements – 1185
Periodic Table of Elements – 1186
Chemistry: General Information – 1187
Geochemical Abundances of the Elements – 1188
Mathematics: General Information – 1188
Physics: SI Units – 1190
Derived Units – 1191
Physics: General Information – 1191

Harrison flicked feverishly to page 1185 and raced through the list. The headings for each chemical element were 'Name', 'Symbol', 'No.', 'Name Source,' and 'Discovered or isolated by'. He located the two he needed:

iron – Fe – 26 – Anglo-Saxon word - prehistoric
sulphur – S – 16 – sulphur – known to the ancients; first
recognised as an element by Antoine Lavoisier 1777

One part iron and two parts sulphur = FeS_2. Could FES stand for something? It rang no immediate bells, and he couldn't think of a viable way to search it.

Iron (26) + two parts sulphur (16 + 16) = 58. Did the number 58 mean anything? He turned to the page listing the periodic table of elements. 58 was cerium, a metallic solid. It meant absolutely nothing to Harrison. It looked like a dead end.

He grabbed an old A4 notebook and tore out a sheet of lined paper. He wrote 'TRUTH IS A FOOL'S GOLD' at the top, and started experimenting to see if it was an anagram he was supposed to solve.

For twenty minutes he scribbled, and grunted and groaned. He had the word 'altruist', which linked to Sunnyvale's mission statement, but the remaining letters didn't surmount to anything. He then had 'astrologist', which felt like a breakthrough, but turned out to be another blind alley.

The alcohol was no longer numbing his frustration, it was fuelling it. He downed the whisky in his glass tumbler, poured himself another, and downed it again. It stung his throat and his chest, but he didn't care anymore. He tore the paper into tiny pieces, and then took the thick reference book and threw it violently across the room. It crashed into the waist-high pile of boxes in the corner, the top one of which had the word 'Monopoly' written on it. The games burst open and their contents sprawled all over the carpet. Counters, dice, cards, fake money. Harrison kicked at them with fury.

Every time he felt he was getting closer to understanding Pop, he was pulled away. It was one step forward, and a giant leap back.

He was thrilled and inspired by his letter, but he was also daunted by it. It cast a shadow over his life and his choices, and it could never be unread. He knew too much, and there was no turning away from the truth.

*

Harrison woke at dawn, with a dry mouth and a drilling headache. He was in the blue armchair, and the whisky decanter on the small table next to him was empty. If yesterday had been a day of action and anger, today promised to be a day of stasis. He was hungover, deflated and bereft.

He missed Amberley, who had departed his life as quickly and dramatically as she had entered it. He had scared her off with his weirdness. He thought of the Lamb twins, powering through every day at work with a permanent smile. They never seemed to have existential crises.

Why was nothing ever normal in his life? He had grown up in a privileged bubble, with a distant mum, and a whole cupboard-full of family skeletons just waiting to be discovered. He was annoyed at Pop too. Surely there was some way he could have made contact when he was still alive? All the riddles, the smoke and the mirrors, seemed like an egotistical game as much as anything – as if Pop was a showman, and Harrison was his eager, top-hatted assistant, hanging on his every flourish of magic and dash of hand.

He was sick of it all. He barged upstairs, out into the garden, and failed to notice it was a beautiful August morning. The sun was peeking its head above the horizon, like an angel slowly rising from her nightly slumber, ready to cast the sky, and the day, in its bright orange hue. This time of the morning belonged to the birds, who sang their tuneful chorus like a heavenly choir greeting the day.

Harrison burped, scratched his backside and grabbed some breakfast from the fridge. The last thing on his mind was the riddle and what it could mean. The magnitude of Pop's letter had overwhelmed him. His brain's response was fight or flight. Last night, he had fought with all his acumen; right now, he had mentally fled the situation.

He thought of Stan's bloodshot, sunken eyes. *You can't fight it, can you? It's big business, big money. It's pointless getting all angry or annoyed.*

Harrison grabbed his food, set himself up on the sofa in the lounge, and turned on the Smart TV. The e-sports football World Cup was still taking place. He escaped into it for the next forty-eight hours, as dawn turned to day and then to dusk, until it was dawn, day and dusk again.

18

Thursday morning at Sunnyvale HQ was a rush of activity. The number of overnight cleaners had been doubled, and they were still finishing up when the first office staff were arriving. The stained-glass window on the west entrance was gleaming in the morning sunlight, and the old building was humming with anticipation.

Even the warehouse workers, who were generally too exhaustedly occupied to feel involved in broader happenings, had noticed a shift in mood. The number of people walking around in suits, and with stern faces, had increased markedly, and the worker bees instinctively quickened their pace as they shuffled to and from the storage units.

Alexa Snow was completing another lap with her aides, as if the walking would burn away her nervous energy. She was on the cusp of the biggest day of her life, and she was leaving nothing to chance.

'We need to make sure these cleaners are out of here earlier tomorrow,' she said. 'Tell them to get started an hour ahead of schedule if they need to.'

'Yes, ma'am,' her male aide replied.

'And make sure the toilets are spotless. I want them clean enough to eat off,' she said. 'He may need to go when he first arrives, and I want him immediately struck by our professionalism.'

'Noted, ma'am.'

They hiked back into her office, where a long, light-wooded dining table was already waiting for tomorrow's three-course lunch. 'Check the table has no wobbles,' she said. 'It can be precarious on the tiled floor. I often have to adjust my desk.'

'Will do, ma'am.'

She sat in her swivel chair, at the far end of the office, and jiggled her leg restlessly. She was confident in her team, and in her own meticulous planning, but she would only relax once the visit had gone smoothly.

Her aides waited dutifully for a few moments, before discreetly leaving her to her thoughts. She was alone in her cavernous office, with its remarkable ceiling, and its arched windows, and its thousand-year history of solemn reflection and quiet. For the first time in her life, just for a moment, she was tempted to pray. But she stopped herself and laughed inwardly at her silliness. She would be meeting the Great Liberator tomorrow, and there was no higher power than that.

Footsteps echoed from across the room. Elliot Patrick was walking towards her desk, fiddling with his glasses.

'You're here earlier than usual,' Alexa said.

'Even I'm feeling the nerves a bit,' he replied. 'I've talked to the Great Liberator many times, but hosting him for a visit is different altogether. Are you confident about our tour with him?'

'Of course,' she said coolly. 'We should be proud of what we have here – it's one of the most magnificent sites in the West. And we're running a tight ship. He's going to love it.' Speaking so assuredly made her feel better, and her anxiety began to abate.

'We're going to be stood right behind him when he makes his speech,' Elliot said. 'Billions of people will be watching. They'll associate our faces with leadership and progress. It bodes very well for the future.'

'Indeed it does,' she said. 'That reminds me, please can you bring Harrison in from the control room when he gets here? I need to talk to him about what we expect tomorrow. I haven't seen him in a while.'

Elliot shook his head. 'He hasn't been in all week. He called in with a bug on Monday and there's been no sign of him since. His little girlfriend Amberley has been off too – she's taken her leftover annual leave from her previous role. It's pretty clear they're bunking off work together.'

'This week of all weeks,' Alexa sighed. She picked up the ceramic-framed photograph, portraying her with Harrison when he was a chubby toddler. 'I give that boy so many opportunities, so many chances. I was planning to have him stood next to us, behind the Great Liberator, during his speech. Can you imagine any other new employee getting such a leg-up?'

'You're too soft with him,' Elliot said. 'He's spoilt. He hasn't had to work from the bottom at Sunnyvale like us two. And don't forget he has some of your father's blood in him. I've never fully trusted him. I've advocated significant surveillance from day one.'

'Let's not overreact,' Alexa said. 'I'll call in at lunchtime and make sure he's coming in tomorrow, no excuses. He'll listen to me. He's turning twenty-one soon, and it's time he stood up to his responsibilities.'

*

The knock on the door jolted Harrison out of his malaise. He had been in an almost vegetative state for two days, cocooned from the outside world, and the table in front of the sofa was strewn with soda cans, wrappers and crumbs.

Rat-a-tat. Rat-a-tat. The sharp knocking continued, and Harrison peeled himself off the sofa. He was wearing a baggy pair of shorts and a stained vest. His hair was messy and greasy, and there were dark bags under his eyes.

'Harrison, it's me,' Alexa called through the door. 'I know you're in there, you can't avoid me.'

Harrison's mind flashed with panic, scrambling for options, but he had few alternatives to letting her in. If he went

AWOL, any suspicions about him would be confirmed. He was very much alert and awake again.

He turned the handle and Alexa stepped into the hallway, in her usual attire. She stood still and looked around, uncharacteristically quiet, as if memories were swirling in her head.

'Hi Mum,' Harrison said. 'Make sure you stay back. I don't want to infect you.'

'You do have a bug then?' Alexa said.

'Of course,' Harrison replied. 'I felt ill over the weekend and when I woke up on Monday I could barely get out of bed.'

'So your girlfriend Amberley isn't here?' she said, as she started to pace through the bungalow, checking each room.

'No. We broke up actually. I haven't seen her in a while.'

'Oh,' Alexa said, momentarily uncertain of herself.

'How did you know about us two anyway?' Harrison said. 'We hadn't told anyone.'

'Don't be naive, Harrison. Subtlety isn't one of your strong points.'

I know more than you realise, he thought.

'What happened to your Smart Sensor?' she said, frowning. The bandage was still wrapped around his right wrist.

'This is what caused the bug I think,' he said. 'I had an allergic reaction to it. My arm was numb and tingly, and then I had a headache and fever. Soon, I was vomiting. I went to hospital and had to get it removed. I was going to explain all this when I was back at work.'

'Right,' she said, unconvinced. 'That's strange. Why didn't this happen when you first had it implanted? Did the doctor explain why there was a delayed reaction?'

'It's quite common apparently,' Harrison shrugged. 'Ultimately, it's a foreign body under the skin. I can wear Smart Spectacles for now, and then I'll talk to the doctors about having a Smart Sensor put in the left wrist. Some left-handed people prefer this anyway, apparently.'

Alexa stayed silent for several moments. 'Well, you look awful,' she said eventually. 'And this place stinks. I'll open a few windows. Go and have a shower and we'll have a chat on the sofa in twenty minutes. Chop chop, I don't have all day.'

'A chat about what?'

'About tomorrow,' she said. 'It seems to have escaped you that we're on the verge of the biggest day of our lives. Come on, hurry up.'

*

He was cleaned, scrubbed and clear-headed after his shower. (Or at least as clear-headed as he could be considering recent events.) Alexa was perched with her legs crossed on one end of the sofa, and Harrison sat at the other end. There was a wide gulf between them.

They each clutched a glass of iced tea. 'I remember this used to be Pop's favourite drink,' Harrison said, but Alexa offered no reply.

'We're in his house,' Harrison said. 'The least we could do is talk about him a little. We can't just pretend he didn't exist.'

The bay windows were open, and a light breeze fluttered through the lounge.

'Actually, it can be better to pretend some things never existed,' Alexa said.

'Really?' Harrison replied. 'Does cleansing the past make you feel better?'

'It's not about feeling better,' she said. 'It's about moving forward. A society that looks backward will *become* backward. The same is true for individuals. Otherwise, we'd still be hanging from trees and beating each other to death with rocks.'

'Progress, then, is the defining human condition?' he said.

'You could put it like that,' she said. 'It's a quest for perfection.'

'Do you believe perfection is attainable?' he said.

'Yes,' she replied. 'At the very least, we must work towards it.'

'And anything that gets in the way is expendable?' he said. 'Including your own parents? Not only should they be expunged from our lives, they should be expunged from our *memory* too?'

'You don't know what you're talking about,' she said. 'If anything, I was much too lenient with your sainted Pop.'

'One man's utopia could be another's dystopia,' Harrison said. 'How are you measuring progress? What do you mean by perfection? Can't you acknowledge, at least, that your father used to enjoy a glass of iced tea? Or are you incapable of acknowledging this simple memory?'

'OK,' she said, with gritted teeth. 'Your grandfather enjoyed iced tea.'

'What else did he enjoy?' Harrison said. He was in a playfully rebellious mood. He didn't want to give anything away, but he was sick of always being the one on the back foot.

'What else did he enjoy?' he repeated.

'All sorts of nefarious things,' she said. 'He was a strange man. I never really understood him.'

'Just because you don't *understand* something, it doesn't necessarily make it bad,' Harrison said.

Alexa frowned again. 'Here you go,' she said. 'You sound a lot like him sometimes. I don't like it.'

'Just because you don't *like* something, it doesn't necessarily make it bad.'

'Harrison, stop it. Just stop it. I don't have time to play any silly games. I'm here to talk to you about our plan for tomorrow. It's important.'

'Go ahead,' Harrison said.

'After he's had a tour of HQ, the Great Liberator will be joining us for a special Monthly Meeting. It's a three-course meal, and he'll be sat next to Elliot and I. I'd like you to be nearby too. I'm sure if you just had an allergic reaction and a fever you won't be contagious in any way. It'll be fine.

'Then he's making his televised speech outside the western entrance. Again, I'd like you to be in the vicinity. There should be me, Elliot and you all in the shot. We can't underestimate the good this could do our careers in the long-run. It's symbolic. We're waiting in the wings, supporting the Great Liberator. And we're ready to take over when the time comes. We're a dynasty in waiting.'

'Sounds like a good plan, Lady Macbeth,' Harrison said.

'What? Lady who?'

'It doesn't matter,' he said. 'So, tell me, in how many years will Elliot be the Great Liberator? Ten? Five? Two?'

'We can't put a timescale on it,' she said. 'It doesn't work like that. And there are no guarantees. He's one of several good candidates, but I know he can do it.'

'And what happens when he is at the top? What's the plan then?' he said.

'In what sense?'

'If you're pursuing power, surely there's a purpose underlying it? In what direction will our great dynasty take Sunnyvale?'

'We'll keep doing what we're doing,' she said. 'The Sunnyvale Era will herald a Great Leap Forward in our society. We'll maintain that progress.'

'Splendid,' Harrison said sarcastically.

'What's got into you recently?' Alexa said. 'Here I am presenting a great life on a platter – full of achievement and worth and purpose – and you're still behaving like a sulky teenager. You're twenty-one soon, you need to grow up.'

'I agree,' Harrison said. 'It's time for me to become a man.'

'Good,' Alexa said, but then she frowned once again, wondering if they were on the same page. She was never quite sure with Harrison nowadays.

'I've put a lot on the line for you,' she said. 'Your attitude and aptitude are a very direct reflection on me. You need to buckle up. I've worked for decades to get where I am today. And yet you behave like you're the one doing *me* the favour.'

'I never asked you to do anything for me,' he said. 'I never asked for any of this.'

'That's right,' she said. 'It's just been fed to you on a silver spoon. And, like an ungrateful toddler, you try to swat it away. I fed you, I clothed you, I sent you to the best school in the city, and I got you this lucrative job. Now, I'm securing our future, *your* future, by working with Elliot. Do you have any idea how fortunate you are?'

'Yes, yes. My life is a bed of roses. I should be skipping around the room, in a frock, thanking you for being such a wonderful mother.'

'You're impossible,' she said, shaking her head. 'Just make sure you're there tomorrow. Showered, suited and on your best behaviour. This is a once-in-a-lifetime occasion. And when this is over, we need to have another serious chat about how we go forward. Your behaviour is childish and unacceptable, bordering on the dangerous. For now, just do your duty tomorrow. And don't show me up.'

'OK, Mum,' he said. 'Just one more thing. Do you remember how on your birthday I quoted from Emily Dickinson? I came across something else she wrote.'

Harrison put his iced tea down and dramatically cleared his throat. He said:

There is no Frigate like a Book
To take us Lands away
Nor any Coursers like a Page
Of prancing Poetry –
This Traverse may the poorest take
Without oppress of Toll –
How frugal is the Chariot
That bears the Human Soul –

Alexa looked at him, expressionless. Her slate-blue eyes met her son's.

'I don't understand you, Harrison.'

'I know you don't, Mum. I know you don't.'

19

Harrison felt better after his shower, and his showdown, with Alexa. He was still in a state of flux about what to do next, but at least he had thrown her off balance a little.

He was in the haven, tidying up the mess he had caused in his drunken anger a couple of nights ago. The thick reference book was open and face-down on the floor, with many of its pages crinkled and damaged.

The contents of the board games in the corner were strewn all over the carpet, and a handful of counters and pieces had rolled under the blue armchair. He was on his knees stretching to reach them, inwardly scolding himself for losing his temper the other night. All it had done was cause him further hassle.

He was packing up the Monopoly box, which was still slightly crumpled, and placing the fake money back into the various slots. There were crisp, rectangular notes for £5, £10, £20 and £50, and they looked strikingly realistic.

Hang on, Harrison thought. He cast his mind far back to when he had played the game as a young child – he could remember Pass and Go, the jail, an old boot, and the different denominations of fake money. Each note was a distinctly different colour, he recalled, and they were small and easily torn.

The notes in front of him all had a white background, and they weren't made out of cheap paper. They felt like they would be hard to tear, and they all had an image of some kind of queen wearing a crown. Was it Elizabeth, or whatever she was called? He knew that the royal family used to be a lot more important than they are now, and it would make sense to have the monarch's face on a banknote. Overall, they just looked *official*.

He was sure he hadn't seen them before when playing Monopoly; instead, he had seen them in the pub, just a few days ago. Stan had taken a note out of his wallet, exactly like one of these, to pay for his drinks. This wasn't Monopoly money. It was real money. Old money. Black market money.

Harrison scooped the pile of notes out and started counting them. Minutes later, piled neatly in order of value, he had thirty-one £5 notes, forty-two £10 notes, thirty-three £20 notes and fourteen £50 notes. He scribbled on a nearby notebook to add them up. He had £1935 in total.

This didn't mean a great deal, as he had no idea of the relative value of pound sterling compared to SVPs. But it looked like a decent haul, and he had Pop to thank again for another fun discovery. Just when he thought he was done with the games and the secrets, he had stumbled upon another little treasure trove.

He piled the money into one thick stack, secured it with a rubber band, and stuffed it into his front jeans pocket. It just about fit, but there was a noticeable bulge.

'First things first,' he said to himself. 'I have a favour to repay.'

*

The pub was quieter than it had been on Harrison's first visit, but everything else was the same: the low ceiling, the dark-timbered beams, the tranquil atmosphere and the Neanderthal-like skull of the landlord.

'Hello again, young man,' the landlord said. He was leaning an elbow on the bar, and wearing a tatty lumberjack shirt.

'Afternoon,' Harrison replied. 'Has Stan been in today?'

'No.'

'Do you know if he will be?'

'I don't keep track of my customer's schedules. But I get

the impression Stan lives a simple life. He's either at work or in here, so there's a good chance he'll be in after his shift.'

Harrison had no idea when the warehouse workers normally finished, but decided to stay for a while nonetheless.

'You fancy some more free drinks from him, do you?' the landlord said.

'Quite the opposite, actually,' Harrison said. 'I was going to pay him back.' He pulled out the stack of money from his pocket and slammed it onto the bar.

The landlord quickly pushed the wedge of cash back to Harrison with his calloused, shovel-like hand.

'If you know what's good for you, you won't advertise your newfound riches,' he said. 'Have some common sense, lad.'

Harrison scanned the room, and there was only one old man for company. He had a hearing aid in, and his head was resting against the dark wooden backboard behind his chair. He seemed to be snoozing.

'Sorry,' Harrison said. 'I have no concept of what this money is worth. It's nearly two thousand pounds. Is that a lot?'

The landlord chuckled, deep from his barrelled chest. 'It's certainly enough to cover Stan's drinks for a while,' he said. 'I wouldn't keep it all in one stack, if I were you. We get some dodgy characters in here sometimes. It comes with the territory.'

'OK, thanks,' Harrison said.

'Where'd you come by such cash, anyway?' the landlord said. 'It's becoming increasingly rare as time goes on.'

'It was left to me by my grandad.'

'Ah. The grandad who likes his deathbed riddles? Truth is a Fool's Gold.'

'Well remembered!' Harrison exclaimed in surprise. 'Impressive.'

'I have a decent memory,' he said. 'They're long, slow days in this pub. I do a lot of crosswords. It passes the time.'

'I see,' Harrison said. 'Well, I've got no further with it. The pyrite thing was a blind alley. I'm trying not to dwell on it, really.'

'It was niggling me yesterday,' the landlord said. 'You know when something burrows into your brain and won't leave you alone? It happens with songs all the time. I think they call it an earworm.'

'Tell me about it,' Harrison said. 'I know the feeling very well.' *Sunnyvale is Progress. Progress is Freedom. Sunnyvale is Progress. Progress is Freedom.* Sometimes it seemed to play on an incessant loop in his head.

'Anyway,' the landlord continued. 'I was completely wrong when I said you were thinking about the riddle too literally. If anything, you weren't thinking literally enough.'

'What do you mean?' Harrison said.

'I mean that I've solved it,' the landlord said, matter-of-factly.

20

A private jet landed expertly in a remote, abandoned airfield, and the owner unbuckled the seatbelt on his leather chair. It squeaked as he stepped out of it, and he quietly thanked the pretty stewardess who had overseen his comfort during the smooth transatlantic flight. He had wanted for nothing.

Within moments, the side door opened and hand-railed steps were released down to the tarmac. He stretched his shoulders and his neck and exited the plane. A beefy security team covered his every movement, and a litany of aides and hangers-on followed him down the steps.

It was a lovely summer's day, making a mockery of the warnings he had heard about this little island's famous rainy weather. It was eternally grey and bleak, he had been told, but his first impressions were of a calm, blue sky, dotted with puffy clouds.

A trio of self-driven limousines waited on the tarmac, long and sleek and black. They each had a pair of flags on either side of the bonnet, with the Sunnyvale logo on them.

The Great Liberator, wearing sunglasses and his trademark beret, stepped into the middle car. He was flanked by his dark-suited security team, and joined by his Chief Personal Assistant.

He settled into the luxurious leather seat, and swapped his sunglasses for his regular, horn-rimmed spectacles. The Chief Personal Assistant sat directly next to him, and one of the security team spoke into his Smart Sensor. 'All clear,' he said sharply, and seconds later the convoy began its short journey. The five-star hotel was less than twelve kilometres away.

The Chief Personal Assistant was a lady aged around thirty. She had a blonde bob, and she was wearing a navy pant suit. She lightly cleared her throat and looked at the Great Liberator. 'I'm glad you slept on the flight, sir. Tomorrow is a big day. If I may, I was hoping this would be a good time to go over your itinerary for the trip. I know you like to be thorough.'

He gave a slight nod in return.

'This first visit to York is the headliner of your whole tour,' she said, in an American East Coast accent. She had the assured air of an Ivy Leaguer. 'Your anniversary speech tomorrow will be shown all over the West as a compulsory announcement on the Smart Sensors.

'There'll be the usual site tour and three-course lunch. Please note that this particular branch has a huge stained-glass window of your portrait, which you'll be expected to comment on. We're considering adding something to your speech about it, but at the very least make sure you thank Alexa Snow and Elliot Patrick in person.

'They're long-serving comrades and they'll be leading your tour. I know you've spoken to them both before. They'll be looking forward to the honour of your visit.'

The limousine carried smoothly and silently on its way. The tiny hum of air conditioning was the only background noise.

'Your speech has been written by the Sunnyvale Smart Speech software, of course,' she continued. 'And you'll be able to go over it in the hotel tonight with the team. It must be word-perfect. Once it's ready, we'll share a copy with all media outlets so it can lead the news tomorrow. "Great Liberator charts Great Leap Forward in historic speech", and so on.'

The assistant checked the schedule on her Smart Sensor. 'After York, you'll be visiting four other sites in consecutive days across Europe. We can go over the specifics for each one in due course. For now, all our attention is focused on tomorrow. This is the biggie. If you don't mind me saying, sir, this is the most important visit and speech of your tenure so far.'

The leading member of the security team – a burly brute who looked like he'd come straight from being a defensive tackle in the NFL – then lightly cleared his throat, just as the assistant had done earlier. It was a small, polite way to ask permission to talk.

'All our security is looking good, sir. We'll be the only guests in the hotel, and we've done a full sweep of the building. The Sunnyvale site itself is already secure, as it's one of our own, but we'll be liaising with the team there and conducting another full sweep before your arrival in the morning.

'There'll be big crowds there tomorrow, but we'll have plenty of Stingers in place and lots of boots on the ground. Every face will be accounted for. The online surveillance team are on top of everything too, sir. We have extra eyes on the East, and the West is covered as always. You're the safest man on the planet right now, sir.'

'Don't say that,' the assistant said. 'It sounds like you're tempting fate.'

'I have full faith in our team and the work we do, ma'am,' the security man said. 'It was merely a statement of fact. Failure is not an option.'

The assistant checked her Smart Sensor again. 'We'll be there any minute, sir. Make sure you eat well and get a good rest tonight. I've arranged for your favourite meal in the hotel restaurant: lobster and corn on the cob.'

The Great Liberator was a pescetarian, rather than a vegan, which meant he could eat fish. It was just one of the many privileges afforded to the most powerful man in the West. He sat looking straight ahead, with his hands resting on his knees, and gave a tiny nod of his head, discernible only to those who had worked with him for a long time.

The assistant looked out of the tinted, bulletproof window and spotted the spectacular Sunnyvale HQ overlooking the city.

'Isn't it beautiful?' she said, pointing in its direction. 'It towers above all the other buildings in the vicinity, but not in a way that's crass or overbearing. It stands with beauty, dignity and grace.'

She smiled, full of awe. 'It's the perfect symbol for Sunnyvale.'

*

Harrison laughed uncertainly. 'This is another one of your jokes, isn't it?' he said. 'What's the punch line?'

The landlord scratched his thick, round skull and smiled. 'Not this time, lad. I save my best jokes for an audience anyway. They would be a bit wasted today.' The old man at the back was still snoozing soundly.

'It'll be easier to show you,' the landlord said. 'Follow me.'

Harrison frowned, unconvinced. But he ducked under the flip-up countertop and stood up behind the bar, where the landlord was beckoning him through to the back.

'My dad took over this pub well before I was born,' he said, in his gruff accent. 'And he saw York go through a lot of changes, most of them for the worse. He was a bit of a collector, or a hoarder, and he kept many things from his childhood and adolescence. They comforted him, I think.'

'My grandad did the same,' Harrison said. They walked through a dank-smelling store room, full of cardboard boxes and wooden crates and empty barrels, and into a smaller utility room. It was empty apart from a stainless steel sink, which looked old and out of action.

The ceiling was so low that the landlord's head was nearly touching it.

'I don't know if anything he kept was illegal,' he said. 'You know what it's like nowadays. But, just to be safe, I keep it in the loft up here. It's a while since I've been up, so there'll be lots of dust.'

There was a little cord hanging down from the ceiling, which the landlord pulled. A rickety wooden ladder emerged, reaching down to the floor. 'This is eerily similar to what my grandad did,' Harrison said.

'It was pretty common, I reckon,' the landlord replied. 'You can tell people that things are no longer allowed for public consumption, but it's another thing to make them destroy them completely. We're sentimental creatures, really.

'After you,' he added. 'I'm slightly worried the ladder won't take my weight anymore.'

'You promise this isn't a practical joke?' Harrison said. 'You're not going to lock me up there and have a good laugh with your pals?'

'I promise,' he replied impatiently. 'Get on with it, I can't leave the bar unattended for too long.'

Harrison stepped onto the first rung, and the ladder felt sturdy enough. He made the short climb upwards, and poked his head up into the windowless loft.

'Oh, don't forget this,' the landlord said, as he threw a torch up into Harrison's midriff, which he just about clung on to.

Harrison clambered into the open space, careful to balance on the wooden beams, and flicked the torch on. The loft was layered in dust, and overwhelmed with cobwebs, damp and rot. It was nothing on the luxury of Pop's neatly arranged haven, with its thick carpet and its warm ambience.

'What exactly am I looking for?' Harrison called down. He was surrounded by perhaps a dozen cardboard boxes, all soggy and disintegrating.

'Give us a sec,' the landlord replied, and his head popped up a moment later. He heaved himself up with a groan, and shook his head. 'I've let this become a right tip.'

He was also carrying a torch, and he shone the light straight ahead to the far end of the loft. The wooden beam creaked under his considerable bulk.

'Most of this stuff is personal to the family,' he said. 'Photo albums, school reports, childhood drawings, all that type of stuff.' He picked up an old photograph from one of the boxes and shone the torch on it.

'This is my old man,' he said proudly. 'People always say how much we look alike.' Harrison murmured his agreement. His father had the same huge skull and rugby player shoulders.

'But I won't bore you with the family stuff,' the landlord said, returning the picture to the cardboard box. 'There was one occasion when my dad really went out of his way to save something that had nothing to do with us directly.'

Several careful strides later, they were at the far end of the loft. A grey, woollen blanket covered a large item (or perhaps many small items).

'Think back to the riddle,' the landlord said. 'Truth is a Fool's Gold.'

'OK,' Harrison replied, but he couldn't yet see any link.

'It's a tough one for someone your age, to be honest,' the landlord said. 'You'd have to be some kind of music historian. An obsessive. Or you'd have to have access to a load of old albums and LPs.'

Harrison's mind raced to the assortment of black discs, and the music-playing device. There were so many more clues in the haven, it seemed, than he had first realised.

'It took me a while to recognise it myself,' the landlord said. 'But the riddle got in my head. It became an earworm, as I said earlier. And it became an earworm because it reminded me of a particular song.'

The landlord whipped off the blanket, creating a cloud of dust, and pulled out a record sleeve, much like the ones in the haven. It had a white background and a strange painted image of a dolphin in the middle.

In black capital letters at the bottom, it said: FOOLS GOLD 9.53.

In black capital letters at the top, it said: THE STONE ROSES.

The Stone Roses. Damn it. Harrison was sure this was in Pop's collection in the haven, but he had never got round to listening to it. Frustration bubbled to the surface again. Did Pop expect him to read *every* book, watch *every* DVD and listen to *every* song? It would take years to do the haven justice, and he still had a life to lead in the meantime.

'It's a start,' Harrison said. 'But I'm sure it can't be the only song with that name. It could be a coincidence. Are that band linked to the Rolling Stones in any way? Their names are kind of similar.'

'No,' the landlord said. 'The Stone Roses are from the nineteen-eighties. They're from Manchester. Both great bands but very different.'

'There's no apostrophe in the song title, but there is in the riddle,' Harrison said.

'Forget that,' the landlord said. 'Now you're thinking too literally again,' he chuckled. 'The apostrophe is irrelevant.'

'What am I supposed to be seeing?' Harrison said irritably. 'Is it the image? What does a dolphin have to do with anything? Is it the 9.53? Is it some kind of code? Is there a clue in the lyrics? I don't know the song, so how am I supposed to work anything out?'

'Again, it's hard for someone your age,' the landlord said. 'Your grandad didn't like to make things easy, did he?'

'No,' Harrison said sulkily. 'Please, just tell me.'

'The things my dad saved – including this – were from a music bar, just around the corner. It was taken over by Sunnyvale and turned into a coffee shop, much to his annoyance.'

'Oh yeah, my grandad hated that too,' Harrison said. 'He used to go there loads, apparently.' He thought of the picture on the marble mantelpiece, of a teenaged Pop in a leather jacket, with a group of lads and one tomboyish girl.

'That bar was called The Stone Roses,' the landlord said. 'In tribute to the band, presumably.'

The landlord shone his beam over the pile of items that had been covered by the blanket. It was like a memorabilia jumble sale: framed photographs, signs, posters, albums with crazy artwork. All sitting together in one large heap.

'It hasn't been kept very well, which is my fault,' the landlord said. 'But my dad felt he had to do something to rescue all this before it went to the tip.

'I don't know why he had such a soft spot for the place. He liked his music, sure. But he also went to plenty of other pubs and bars in the area. I think it was just the final straw when Sunnyvale were taking over everything in sight. Plus, it was practically on his doorstep. It was his little act of resistance. His small way of preserving something that Sunnyvale wanted to consign to the scrapheap.'

'This is all well and good,' Harrison said. 'But I still don't understand how it solves Pop's riddle. Even if he was alluding to the long-lost music bar, how does it link to 'Truth'? I'm not convinced.'

'The beauty of a clever crossword clue,' the landlord said. 'Is that the two parts of the clue can be solved in different ways. 'Fool's Gold' leads you to the Stone Roses bar. A place. 'Truth' leads you to something else...'

'To what?' Harrison said.

'A person,' the landlord replied.

'Jamie, hello? Jamieee? Anybody there?' a faint male voice called from the distance. It sounded like a customer at the bar.

'Bloody hell,' the landlord said. 'I leave the front unattended for five bloody minutes.' He stormed past Harrison and climbed down from the loft, brushing dust from the front of his lumberjack shirt.

Harrison hurried after him and sneezed loudly.

'I have to get back,' the landlord said, striding through the musty storage room. 'Anything could be happening in there.'

'But wait,' Harrison said, rushing in his wake. 'How am I supposed to find this person? What should I do?'

'Head over to the coffee shop where the Stone Roses bar used to be,' he said. 'You should find who you're looking for.'

'OK,' Harrison said breathlessly. He followed the landlord back behind the bar, where a couple of old men were stood waiting. They light-heartedly berated the landlord for his shoddy service.

Harrison waited for them to be served their ale, and then shook the landlord's hand. It was about as large and as coarse as a baseball mitt.

'Thanks for your help,' he said.

'For what?' the landlord replied, with a wink. 'You never heard anything from me.'

Harrison pulled the wedge of cash out of his pocket and placed it on the bar.

'I have no idea how much this is really worth, but please put it on a tab for Stan's next visit,' he said. 'And anything left over can go towards your new loft renovation.' He laughed and walked out of the pub, into the enduring August sunlight.

*

The coffee shop was, quite literally, just around the corner. A short walk along the riverfront and a left turn up a sharp incline brought him to its front door.

It was indistinguishable from the scores of Sunnyvale coffee shops in York, or the millions across the West. There was the glass-panelled door, the ubiquitous logo, and the clean, white, sterile decor. The building had three floors, but the coffee shop only took up the ground floor.

Harrison stepped through the glass door and took a table by the left-hand wall, giving him a view of the whole room. There were only two customers inside, and no staff, as everything was machine-made. He wouldn't be able to buy a drink, without his Smart Sensor or a pair of Smart Spectacles, so he kicked his chair back and tried to sit casually, as if he was waiting for someone (which, in a sense, he was).

He muttered to himself, as he so often did when he was dealing with a dilemma. *Truth, Truth, Truth.* He sat for a minute, but nothing happened. The two people in the room were sitting separately, and both wearing Smart Shrouds. One was a lady aged around fifty, with a heavyset physique and tired eyes. She kept lifting up her Shroud to take sips of her coffee.

The other customer was a teenage girl, with short, dark hair. She was talking to someone through her Smart Shroud, and Harrison could make out snippets of the conversation. It was some stuff about a project at school.

He didn't think it was likely that the answer lay with either of these two, but he forced himself to be patient. The landlord had seemed pretty certain that he had solved the riddle, and the solution was in this very building. Ten minutes passed, then twenty, then thirty. The other two customers had gone, and Harrison found himself alone, in more ways than one.

Was this all an elaborate joke by the landlord? Would he head back to the pub, only to be met with uproarious laughter from the regulars? (It would be filling up now, he reckoned.) How could he have been so naive? It would be annoying and embarrassing, but at least it would put him out of his misery.

He sighed, swore under his breath, and left the table. He would take his licks from the landlord, enjoy a couple of ales and take stock again back at the bungalow. The afternoon sun was still burning brightly as he exited the coffee shop and started the brief downhill ascent.

He made only a metre or two before something caught his peripheral vision. There was a door to his left, painted green but flaking and cracking after many years of neglect, and an entrance panel mounted on the brick doorway that framed it. It seemed like there were flats above the coffee shop.

There were four slots on the panel, with four names written inside them.

Flat 1 – A. Williams
Flat 2 – G. Henderson
Flat 3 – A. Short

Harrison scanned down to the bottom panel. It read:

Flat 4 – T. Ruth

Harrison smiled and looked up at the sky. 'You and your bloody riddles, Pop,' he said. 'Couldn't you have told me this without all the drama?'

He pressed all four buttons on the panel, and a crackly, buzzing sound came back. 'Hello,' a male voice said through the static. 'Please can you let me in?' Harrison replied. 'I'm delivering a pizza.'

There was another buzzing noise, and Harrison heard the door's mechanism unlock. He pushed it open, and started climbing the wooden stairs, which took him upwards and left above the coffee shop. The walls were uncared for, bordering on grotty, but there was the warming smell of coffee and cocoa emanating from below.

He got the impression it was a cheap place to rent, and he could imagine Stan heading back to somewhere like this after his shift in the warehouse (or his shift in the pub). Unpretentious and unspectacular, but not uncomfortable.

He reached flat number four and rang the doorbell.

21

The doorbell's jingle resonated through the flat. Harrison immediately heard movement on the other side of the door, but it sounded tentative. Light footsteps. Almost definitely a woman's. He could sense her stood just behind the thin layer of wood, weighing up whether to open or not.

Eventually, the door creaked ajar. It was still on its chain, and a lady's head appeared in the gap.

'Who is it?' she said. She was older than Harrison expected, at least in her eighties, but she had a firm voice. Her short hair was white, underneath a bowed bandana, and her face was heavily wrinkled. Despite her ageing features, he could tell that she had once been attractive. She also looked vaguely familiar.

Her eyes settled on Harrison's face, and she visibly gasped. A short, instinctive intake of breath that looked like it could have knocked her sideways if she wasn't holding on to the door.

'Do you know me?' Harrison said. 'Why do you look like you've just seen a ghost?'

She recovered herself in a second and looked at Harrison's right wrist, which was still covered in the thick white bandage. 'Are you wearing a Smart Sensor?' she said.

'No,' Harrison replied. 'I was until recently. Hence the bandage.'

'Please come in, Harrison. We have a lot to discuss.'

Harrison stood still, calculating every possibility. Instinctively, he didn't feel threatened by an old woman, and she had a trustworthy air about her. But how did she know his name?

Please come in, Harrison. It was familiar and friendly, and Pop had pointed him in this direction. Ultimately, his curiosity outweighed any caution or suspicion.

She closed the door to remove the chain, and then opened it wide, beckoning him in with her outstretched arm. 'Quickly, quickly,' she said.

Harrison obliged. He took a deep breath and stepped into her flat.

*

It was a well-kept one-bed studio apartment. It smelt of incense and perfume, and it was decorated in pinks and yellows and oranges, but in a way that was tasteful rather than gaudy. There were candles and ancient clocks, a tie-die duvet cover on the double bed in the corner and a couple of turquoise armchairs facing a faux fireplace.

Above that, there was a bizarre painting of swirling colours in a spiral pattern, which momentarily enraptured Harrison's attention. For a small place, it nearly overwhelmed the senses with its psychedelic styling. Conspicuously, there was no Smart TV.

'Please take a seat, Harrison,' she said softly. She had regained her composure very quickly from the initial shock, and she was remarkably mobile for a lady of her age. She was swift, supple and assured.

'Who are you? How do you know my name?' Harrison said, still standing.

'Would you like a drink, dear? I have squash. Or I could do us both a coffee? I make it much better than those damn machines downstairs.'

'I'm not doing anything until you tell me who you are,' Harrison said.

She smiled warmly. 'I see you're just as direct and restless as your grandfather,' she said. She took a seat in one of the turquoise armchairs and gestured to the other. 'Straight to business.'

The chairs were both facing the faux fireplace, but at a slight angle towards each other. Harrison perched rigidly on the end of the seat.

'It's probably best you don't learn my real name,' she said. 'Just call me Tessa. Like your grandfather, I adopted a pseudonym when I became – how shall I put it? – *noteworthy* to the authorities. I thought Tessa Ruth was as good a name as any. T-Ruth, as in Truth. We had pretentions of grandeur, back then.'

'You knew my grandad?' Harrison said.

'Oh yes,' she said. 'Very well indeed. We go back a long, long way. I know you as well, Harrison. You were such a livewire of a young boy. Very bold and inquisitive. Your hair is still the same, and your eyes. And I bet your smile is too. Butter wouldn't melt. You've grown into a very handsome young man.'

'You knew me when I was younger?'

'That's right,' she said calmly.

'How?' Harrison said. 'I don't remember you. No offence.'

'None taken,' she chuckled. 'I'll start from the beginning. I must warn you that you may not like everything you hear. Feel free to leave now if you're of a sensitive disposition.'

Harrison looked back at her. Her short hair – as white as her alabaster skin – looked subconsciously familiar, as did her smile. And there was something tomboyish about her mannerisms.

'You're the girl from the group photograph at the gig,' he said. 'When you were teenagers, holding beer bottles.'

'I am indeed,' she said. 'And I bet you know the photograph from the White Horse too, with you being hoisted on your grandad's shoulders? I took that one. That was such a lovely day out.'

Harrison's mind raced for an explanation.

'Let me elaborate,' she added. 'I can tell that your spirit is searching for answers, and it's not my place to keep delaying them.'

She sat back into the armchair and closed her eyes, as if it would help her in accessing her memories.

'Joseph and I knew each other since we were teenagers,' she said. 'We were in the same group of friends at school. Music-obsessed. Edgy. Or so we thought at the time. Outcasts and misfits, kind of. We weren't uncool or unpopular, but we weren't mainstream either. We didn't follow the crowd.

'We would use fake IDs and go to bars around York from the age of fifteen or sixteen. There was a place called Fibbers that had loads of live music, and there was The Stone Roses. That was the name of the bar beneath this flat, which is now a coffee shop, of course.'

'I know,' Harrison said. 'That was the clue Pop used to lead me to you. He wrote: "Truth is a Fool's Gold." After a few false starts, and with considerable help, I finally ended up here.'

'You still call him Pop,' she said, beaming, opening her eyes to look at him. 'That's very sweet. And yes, I can understand why he had to be cautious. He wouldn't have wanted to name me directly, in case it fell into the wrong hands. That riddle is so typical of him.'

She closed her eyes again and settled deep into the chair.

'We were all very close throughout school. I was a bit of a tomboy rebel back then, as you could probably tell from the picture, but I swooned like a damsel in a fairytale when it came to your grandfather. I hope you don't mind me mentioning there was more than friendship between Joseph and I. He was my first proper boyfriend, and I was his first proper girlfriend. They were very happy days. Young love, music, alcohol. They say youth is wasted on the young, but it wasn't wasted on us.

'We broke up when we went to different universities, as so

often happens. We lost touch for many years. It wasn't until we were in our late forties that we saw each other again. We were both back in the York area, and we walked past each other in the street. I can remember it so vividly. It was on Parliament Street, near where the fountain used to be.

'It was like a cheesy scene from a B-list rom-com. I was recently divorced, and he was married. He was working for one of the Big Tech firms. Even though he was a bit of a rock 'n roll rebel at school, he was always very intelligent, and I knew he'd go far.

'I warned you that you may not like everything you hear, and I'm not particularly proud of the next bit. But it happened, and that's life. We soon started an affair. The spark was still there, and a couple of friendly coffees quickly escalated. He was my first love, and I couldn't help myself.

'The strange thing was he was very happily married to your grandmother too. He was in love with both of us. People don't think this is possible, but it is. He wasn't some shameless womanising philanderer. He doted on your grandmother – he was a good husband to her, and he was a good father to Alexa. But we had such a connection and a history that he was drawn to me too. It wasn't easy for him. Nor for me.

'This continued for many years. It wasn't ideal for me being the outcast mistress – it's not exactly how I envisaged my life. But it happened, and it was better than not seeing him at all.' She bowed her head and exhaled loudly. The trip down memory lane seemed to be fatiguing her.

'Please keep going,' Harrison said.

'Meanwhile, the world around us was changing,' she said. 'Everything seemed so divided and divisive, and Big Tech was creeping more and more into people's lives. Joseph and his wife were going through all sorts of drama at work. They wanted out, but it was very difficult. How much of this part do you know?'

'Pop wrote that they had started off as digital utopians,' Harrison said. 'But gradually they grew uneasy and disillusioned. He said they managed to leave their jobs but had to downsize, and the stress of it all led to my grandma's death. This was before Sunnyvale even existed.'

'That's pretty much it, in a nutshell,' she said. 'It was a tough period for everyone. Joseph was distraught. He felt like he'd broken up the family. His wife was dead, and Alexa was adamant that they had made a mistake. She later went her own way, of course.

'I hesitate to say I helped him through it all. I don't want it to sound like I swooped in to fill your grandmother's shoes the second she passed away. It wasn't like that. But our relationship continued, and we built something of a new life together. He had nobody else. And I loved him, always.'

'How come I've never heard of you?' Harrison said. 'Why hasn't my mum said anything?'

'Occasionally, when you were very young and staying with Joseph, I would visit too. We would spoil you rotten. We managed a couple of trips to the seaside and, of course, the White Horse. Your mother got wind of this and banned me from seeing you.

'Alexa and Joseph stayed in touch for some years afterwards – I don't think she ever quite knew the extent of his underground activities – but their relationship became more and more strained. Eventually, some trivial argument over the automatic surcharge on coffee was the final straw. She cut him off completely. It's just the way she is, I'm not surprised I've never come up in conversation.'

'What happened with you and Pop then?' Harrison said. 'Why didn't you live together? I live in his bungalow now, and there was no sign of a female presence there.'

'We did for a while,' she said. 'But I never felt comfortable sleeping in his marital bed. It just didn't feel right. Perhaps we'd been so used to our previous relationship, when he would come specially to see me at my place. I saw this studio advertised and decided to move out. I thought it was very fitting, as we have many memories in this building. He enjoyed coming round as regularly as he could.'

'So you were in contact with him until the day he died?'

'I tried to be, but he really wasn't well for the last year or so. I hadn't spoken to him for several months. Getting old can be very cruel. His mind was slowly disintegrating, and he wasn't always very pleasant to be around. I looked after him as best as I could, and I offered to move back into the bungalow to nurse him, but he preferred his independence. Plus, I'm no spring chicken myself. I recently turned ninety-one.'

'Why did you both use pseudonyms? What were you doing exactly?'

'During any war, there's always an underground resistance against an occupying force,' she said. 'It happened when France was under Nazi rule. It happened, extensively and effectively, in Vietnam, and Afghanistan and Iraq. It can have a great impact, if done properly.

'We considered ourselves at war with Big Tech, which later morphed, like one great blob or being, into Sunnyvale. A technopoly-totalitarian state, whatever you want to call it. We resented and rejected the erosion of privacy, the wanton destruction of small businesses, the creepy rise of AI, the evisceration of free speech and the growing influence Big Tech were having in politics. Perhaps you have to be of my generation to understand that there was a world before the Big Seven and, eventually, Sunnyvale. Their rise was so smooth and swift and ominous, but we hoped it wouldn't be irreversible.'

'And you both happened to be very passionate about this?' he said. 'So much so that you were willing to risk your lives?'

'Politics was never really my bag. But I've always been a rebel, a bit outside-the-box. My mum was a nineteen-sixties hippy – flowers in her hair, girl power, stick-it-to-the-man, and all that. I was definitely my mother's daughter. Joseph and I talked a lot, and read a lot, and I slowly joined him as a fully-fledged resistor to the regime. He was very charismatic.'

'What did being a resistor consist of?' Harrison said. 'Pop wrote something about subversive literature and clandestine gatherings?'

'That's just his fancy way of saying we liked to share books that were banned,' she said. 'I'm sure you've seen many of them in the room beneath his shed. It's an impressive collection, isn't it?'

'It is,' Harrison said. 'I've spent many hours down there.'

'The gatherings were just meetings with others who were opposed to Big Tech,' she said. 'We'd talk grandiosely of a world without their malign influence, and how we'd rebuild society after their collapse. It was all very cloak-and-dagger. Secret locations, passwords, codes. Joseph was in his element.

'But there was never much we could do practically. We'd try enlisting journalists and broadcasters, but their funding came from Big Tech. It was the same with politicians. We'd try marches and protests, but they were quickly shut down.

'We'd plan dramatic stunts, like chaining ourselves to the doors of the beautiful Minster, now known only as Sunnyvale HQ. But the plan would never come off. We'd produce videos, podcasts and articles, and they would be censored and removed before we could blink.

'Ultimately, it was about the thrill of the chase as much as anything. And don't forget we were already getting old – I was in my fifties when we started on this path, and I was in my early sixties when Sunnyvale was formed. There was only so much we could do.'

'Do these meetings still happen?' Harrison said.

'Not that I'm aware of, but I'm out the loop now. There used to be plenty of resistors out there. But most of my generation have died, or they're just too old, and the fighting spirit has gone with them. Most people don't know anything different now. They don't question anything. And Sunnyvale's power grows relentlessly. They can sniff dissent from a continent away.'

'I know,' Harrison said. 'I work for them, believe it or not.'

'Oh my. You're not here to arrest me, are you?'

'No, no. Please don't worry,' Harrison said. 'It's my mum who got me the job. I'm very much on your side. I think. I have a lot to work out.'

22

Harrison and Tessa sat in silence for several moments. She still had her eyes closed.

'Who helped you solve the riddle?' she said.

'The landlord at the pub on the riverfront, around the corner,' Harrison replied. 'I think he's called Jamie.'

'OK, that's good. We can trust him. I've been going in there for years. We even held a few underground meetings there, many moons ago. You didn't tell anyone else?'

'Others in the room heard the clue,' he said. 'But they didn't have any context.'

'The pub is safe,' she said resoundingly. She took another long pause. Harrison couldn't tell if she was thinking or resting, or even if she was asleep. He began to feel slightly nauseous from the overwhelming smell of incense and perfume.

Then, in an instant, she opened her eyes and swept out of her chair as effortlessly as a woman half her age. She walked over to a small, pine office bureau, positioned just beneath the window which looked out onto the street, and opened its fold-out front.

'I'm still in awe of how perceptive your grandfather could be,' she said. 'During one of our last cogent conversations here, many months before he died, he told me that one day you would ring that doorbell. He also said that you would be working for Sunnyvale at the time, but that I would have nothing to fear.'

She rummaged in the bureau, pushing past stationery and piles of paper and post-it notes. She pulled out a brown, standard-sized envelope, with no markings on the front.

'He made me promise that I would give you this letter on the day that happened. I haven't read it myself.' She handed the envelope to Harrison, who was still sat in the turquoise armchair.

'Thanks,' he mumbled, with a dry mouth. 'Please can I take you up on your offer of a drink now? A coffee would be wonderful.'

'Of course,' she said, quietly moving over to the modest kitchen area. Harrison unsealed the envelope and braced himself for another message from beyond the grave.

*

Dear Harrison,

If you are reading this, it means you have solved the riddle. Congratulations, and I apologise if it was unfairly tricky. I hope you understand that I had to take precautions to protect Tessa. The authorities already know about her, of course, but there is no sense in drawing unnecessary attention.

I'm also hoping that it is proof that you are keen to learn and understand more about my life and the choices I made. But you know my story now, and that's enough about that. This letter is about the future. It's about you.

I highly suspect that you will now be working for Sunnyvale. This takes no great foresight on my part. Alexa will like you being in the fold, and no doubt she'll be grooming you for some kind of senior leadership role.

If you decide to take this route, I do not judge you. I do not criticise you. All I ask is that you destroy the letters I have left for you, and you do not implicate Tessa in any way. She is a good woman, and she deserves to live her twilight years in peace.

But I suspect, again, that you may feel a yearning to take a different route. Perhaps this is because of what you have recently learned. Or perhaps you instinctively felt something from day one. Either way, I encourage you to listen to that gut feeling. That feeling is a blessing. It means you're still a human being, intuitively craving liberty as much as you crave food, water and air.

I wrote in my first letter that the war has been won, and they're just sweeping up the last remnants of defiance. This is true. But no good cause is ever futile, even if it is lost. And maybe – just maybe – even the bleakest of situations is never quite as bleak as it seems. As long as the desire for freedom beats in one human heart, there is hope.

I will not beat around the bush. You are in a unique position within Sunnyvale. You are the son of one their most highly-regarded employees, and you have access to their inner workings. You could be the most powerful weapon the resistance movement has ever had.

The movement has waned, but it could be resurrected by you, with a little help from Tessa. She will still have a few contacts, a few morsels of information that could help you rebuild what I devoted the second half of my life to. There must still be whispers of dissent out there, and you can be the man to find them, and amplify them. And then, working from within, you can slowly bring about real change. Figuratively speaking, you can dismantle the great machine from deep within its engine room.

I call it Operation Neo. It's my desperate, last-ditch, final-breath attempt to fight the good fight.

It would not be easy. It would take superhuman levels of guile and bravery, and you would need huge, great dollops of luck. It may even be impossible, but I can't – in good conscience – let the idea slip by, even if it is asking more of you than any man ever should. I cannot go gently into that good night.

You have two paths before you, Harrison. It can only be your choice, and *may God bless you whatever you decide.*

I leave you with the words of Robert Frost, from his poem 'The Road Not Taken':

I shall be telling this with a sigh
Somewhere ages and ages hence:
Two roads diverged in a wood, and I—
I took the one less traveled by,
And that has made all the difference.

Love,
Pop

*

Harrison returned the letter to the envelope and burst into laughter. His stomach convulsed and his shoulders shook.

'What is it?' Tessa said, as she handed him a steaming mug of black coffee.

'Here, take a look yourself,' he said, as he stood up and placed the envelope on her armchair. She picked it up and settled down to read it, plucking a pair of reading glasses from the pocket of her blouse.

She reached the bottom of the letter and folded it neatly in half, returning it to the envelope. 'He's asking a lot of both of us,' she said.

Harrison laughed again. 'A lot? He's asking us to commit suicide. Tell you what, I'm at a banquet with the Great Liberator tomorrow. Why don't I just assassinate him? I'll attack him with my knife and fork.'

He continued laughing and shaking his head. 'So I have to choose between being a puppet of my mum's, or a puppet of my grandad's. That's a really healthy choice for a young man to make.'

A niggly feeling, deep in his stomach, wouldn't go away. 'It's light on specifics, isn't it?' Harrison said. 'There's very little in the way of practical advice. I'm supposed to conjure a new resistance movement out of thin air? And dismantle the Sunnyvale machine from within? *Operation Neo*. Bloody hell, Pop.'

'He was at the end of his life when he wrote this,' she said. 'He was desperate, and wasn't always the most sound of mind.'

It was Harrison's turn to instigate silence, which he wallowed in for several minutes. The stillness was broken only by his occasional sips from the coffee mug. Tessa closed her eyes again, enjoying the peace.

'You know what the most annoying thing is?' Harrison said, leaning forward. Tessa opened one eye.

'Pop is right,' he said. 'He's bloody right. He's stupidly, ridiculously, ludicrously right. There's no way I can go on with life as normal. There's no way I can devote myself to Sunnyvale, and climb the ranks like a good boy, pretending I don't know what I know. But it's a hell of a leap to do what he's asking.'

Harrison stewed and sipped some more, until the mug was empty, and he returned it to the narrow kitchen top. Tessa was still resting.

He gently took the envelope from her lap and read the letter again, this time more slowly. As he got to the end, he read the Robert Frost lines aloud:

> *I shall be telling this with a sigh*
> *Somewhere ages and ages hence:*
> *Two roads diverged in a wood, and I—*
> *I took the one less traveled by,*
> *And that has made all the difference.*

He laughed and shook his head again. 'The road he wants me to take isn't just less travelled by,' he said. 'It's literally *never* been travelled by. It's not even a road, it's a mud track covered in bushes and thorns and nettles and puddles, with a sheer drop waiting at the end.'

Tessa opened her eyes and also laughed warmly. 'This is typical Joseph,' she said. 'He didn't like to do things by half. And he loved the drama of it, sometimes.'

'I could talk in circles for hours,' Harrison said, stepping closer to Tessa's chair. 'But sometimes the truth is simple. Pop is right. I'm in a unique position, and I have to make it count. At the very least, I have to try.'

He held out his hand. 'Would you help me get started, Tessa? I think we'd make a damn good team.'

She sprang up from her chair again and met his hand with a surprisingly firm grip. 'There's plenty of life in me yet,' she said emphatically. 'Let's bring the bastards down.'

*

It was now late on Thursday evening, and the sun was finally setting on what seemed an endless day. Harrison was on his fourth black coffee, pumped with caffeine and adrenaline.

He had been discussing strategies with Tessa for hours, and she had promised to reach out to her few remaining contacts to see who, or what, was still out there in the form of resistance.

'It's important you don't arouse any suspicion early on,' she said. 'First things first, you must be Mr Compliant. Mr Goody Two Shoes. Wear your Smart Spectacles every day, but try to avoid a new Smart Sensor. Do your job well. Play the game.

'If you can, look into the Cambridge Five. They were a group of double agents at the heart of the British establishment in the nineteen-thirties and forties – years later, the CIA would study videos of them being interviewed to see how incredibly effective they were at lying. Deception is a skill, and it can be worked on like anything else.

'This won't happen overnight. You need to work yourself into a position of trust on the inside, as we build a framework of resistance on the outside. You're our secret weapon, our golden goose. If you fail, we all fail.'

'No pressure, then,' Harrison joked. He fiddled with his floppy fringe.

'I think that's enough for tonight,' Tessa said, her face betraying her age. She looked pale and washed out. 'Get a good sleep and do all the right things tomorrow. It's a big day.'

'You don't have to do this,' Harrison said. 'It's a lot to ask for a lady of ninety-one. You've left this life behind.'

'I've never felt younger,' she smiled. 'What type of rebel would I be if I gave up because of my age? If anything, it means I have nothing to lose. You're the one with the most at stake.'

He pulled her into a gentle hug. 'I can see why Pop liked you,' he said, and then he went on his way.

23

The morning of August the eighteenth started like all the other mornings that warm summer. The sun was blazing from dawn, blitzing clear the clouds from the sky, making early risers of even the heaviest sleepers.

It was sweltering by seven o'clock, as Harrison buttoned up his sharpest suit and slipped on his smartest shoes. Today was the first day of the rest of his life.

He had slept well, considering the caffeine in his system and the thoughts churning in his mind, and he looked the part: he was a fresh, enthusiastic comrade brimming with excitement at the arrival of the Great Liberator. He straightened his tie in the mirror, and neatened his hair.

With the time to spare, he decided to walk to work along the riverfront. The River Ouse shimmered in the morning sun, and he was, once again, *sauntering*. He was nervous, and uncertain, and full of doubt, but he also felt an overwhelming sense of peace in taking the first steps on his new journey.

As he neared the city centre, he noticed more Stingers overhead, swooping and circling and surveilling. He had to remind himself that he had nothing to hide. He had been off work for a few days, after an allergic reaction, but he was back – fighting fit and keen to impress. This is the narrative he had to convince himself was true.

He walked down Coney Street, past one of the many Sunnyvale coffee shops, and the old church that served as one of HQ's overflow warehouses. The ticker on its perimeter was carrying a scrolling message: 'Happy Birthday Sunnyvale!'

The streets were already filling with the general public, and a carnival atmosphere was brewing. Young children – most of them in Smart Shrouds – skipped along next to their parents, many of whom were carrying mini Sunnyvale flags on sticks. They had rucksacks and picnic boxes full of goodies, ready to capitalise on the sun and the day off work. August the eighteenth was, of course, a sacred holiday throughout the West.

Harrison turned right into St Helen's Square, where jugglers and magicians and fire-eaters were setting up their spaces, and then left up Blake Street. He turned right again, onto Duncombe Place.

He always liked to take this route into work, with the spectacular final straight. HQ stood proud and tall ahead of him. It was one of the best views of the building, and this street was evidently one of the favoured vantage points for the Great Liberator's visit. The paths were already full with the most eager families, who had claimed their territory with their deck chairs and blankets. Jingly music started in the background. The celebration – the festival – was underway.

The road itself was clear, sealed off with barriers, ready for the arrival of the sleek limousine sometime after eight-thirty. As Harrison passed the masses, waiting patiently to wave their mini flags when the time came, he wondered what each individual really thought of Sunnyvale and the Great Liberator.

What, exactly, were they here to celebrate? Were they compelled to do so, because their neighbours did? Or because they truly believed Sunnyvale were making the world a better place? How many people, in these thronged streets, would be harbouring doubts? How many of them would feel something wasn't quite right, even if they couldn't explain why?

He thought of a line from Pop's first letter. *The response is even worse than ignorance and apathy: it's an open embrace. People are happy to be servile.*

He now had a *million* questions. The more he learned, the less he seemed to know.

*

Harrison was cleared by security and made his way across to the control room. In all his keenness, he had arrived at work much earlier than usual.

Unsurprisingly, he wasn't the first one there. The Lamb twins, in perfect unison, greeted him with delighted waves and smiles from the meeting room. The glass door was open, and they were perched on the laminate table. The brother was in a white tuxedo, complete with bow tie, and the sister was wearing a billowing white dress and matching heels.

'Did I miss the memo about a dress code?' Harrison joked. They tittered politely.

'We thought we'd go all-out,' the sister said. 'It's not every day you share a three-course meal with the Great Liberator.'

'Fair enough,' Harrison said. 'Let's just hope it's not soup for starter. Imagine that spilling down your front.'

'Oh no,' she replied. 'I never thought of that.'

'It'll be fine,' Harrison laughed. 'Forget I said anything.' He checked his tie and his hair in the glass-panelled wall.

'It's good to have you back,' the brother said. 'We heard you had a bug of some sort.'

'That's right,' Harrison replied. 'It was pretty nasty for a few days, but I'm fine now. I didn't want to risk spreading it to anyone this week.'

'If I missed this because I was laid up in bed, I honestly think I'd never recover,' the brother said. 'That would be the lowest of the low.'

'The lowest of the low,' the sister echoed.

Harrison pulled out a chair from under the table and settled into it. 'I guess all we can do is wait?' he said. 'Presumably we have to stay here until after the tour?'

'That's right,' the brother replied. 'But we can head out to see his arrival. That will be epic.'

*

The clock ticked to eight-thirty and the control room was now full of excited employees, dressed in various degrees of formality.

'He'll be on his way from the hotel now,' one lady said loudly. 'He won't be long.'

They all made their way out into the scorching morning. The group pushed themselves through the thronging crowds to get close to the western entrance, where the Great Liberator would be arriving.

Harrison was sweating profusely within a minute, and he dabbed himself down with a handkerchief. The scene before him was remarkable. The streets had been busy earlier, when he walked down them, but they were now completely full, as far as his eyes could see.

There was barely a scrap of space left, as people stood and jostled for the best view, waving their Sunnyvale flags from side to side. The jingly music had been cranked louder, and people clapped and danced on the spot, jigging from one foot to the other.

Harrison marvelled at the sheer mass of celebrators – he could see thousands, and there must have been many more thousands in the nearby streets out of his view. In the distance, he spotted a huge hand-held banner: 'SUNNYVALE IS PROGRESS. PROGRESS IS FREEDOM.'

The barriered road was still empty, and all eyes were on it. The Great Liberator's arrival was imminent.

Harrison heard him coming before he saw him. A distant cheer made the group of employees stand up on their toes, searching and straining. The Lamb sister squealed with excitement.

The cheers spread closer and closer, like a Mexican wave, growing exponentially louder. Harrison dabbed his forehead with his handkerchief, and saw a black dot far ahead. It grew into a larger dot, and then it became a shiny limousine, rolling to the foot of the steps of the western entrance. The crowd waved and cheered, and cheered and waved some more, full-hearted and flush-faced.

It was chaos, joyous chaos, and Harrison found himself looking from the outside-in. He watched dispassionately as an aide opened the side door of the limousine. The Great Liberator stepped out, to a raucous reception. He was wearing sunglasses and a suit, and his trademark beret, and he waved modestly to the crowd.

He was greeted by Elliot Patrick, who looked like a teenager wearing his dad's overgrown suit, and Alexa Snow, who was in a long, blue dress with heels. They exchanged pleasantries at the bottom of the steps, and then walked as a trio to the top. The Great Liberator turned and waved again, to a huge roar, and then they disappeared through the western entrance.

*

The group of employees were back in the cooler confines of the control room.

'How cute did Elliot look in his suit?' the Lamb sister said.

'I know,' a female colleague replied. 'I've never seen him in anything formal like that.'

Harrison was enjoying the air conditioning, and had taken off his suit jacket to maximise the benefit. The room was abuzz with chit-chat. People were speculating about what the meal would be, and where the Great Liberator would be sitting, and whether they would get to speak to him one-on-one.

After a few minutes, a black-suited, muscle-bound aide

entered the control room – every conversation faltered as the congregated employees followed his progress – and headed straight for Harrison. He was one of the biggest men Harrison had ever seen, with a neck as thick as a car tyre.

'Harrison Snow, you're needed in Mrs Snow's office,' the aide said, in a deep voice.

'What for?' Harrison replied. Everyone in the room was listening to their exchange.

'Mrs Snow would like to see you. Just follow me, please.'

The Lamb brother slapped Harrison on his back. 'Looks like you might get to meet him personally,' he said excitedly. 'Amazing.'

'I doubt it,' Harrison said. 'It'll probably just be some formality I have to go over.'

He followed the behemoth into the lobby of the main building, through the warehouse (where the worker bees were toiling away like it was any other day) and to his mum's office in the old Chapter House. The long, light-wooded table now had a Sunnyvale-logoed tablecloth on it, and it was set up with china plates and silver cutlery.

The aide pointed Harrison to a wooden chair about halfway down the table, opposite a lone figure. There was no sign of Alexa Snow, nor of Elliot Patrick.

'Good morning, Harrison,' the Great Liberator said.

24

Harrison sat and looked at the most powerful man in the West. His first thought was how accurate the oil painting in the lobby was. It captured his features perfectly: the feminine nose, the piercing green eyes, the smile with the upturned lip, the horn-rimmed spectacles and the black beret.

'I've requested a meeting with you alone, without your mother's presence,' the Great Liberator said. His accent had a soft American edge.

Harrison offered nothing in return.

'Oh, I'm so sorry,' the Great Liberator said. 'Where are my manners? I'm Edward Allen, but you can call me Eddie.' He laughed in a faux self-deprecatory way, just as Elliot Patrick had done when he had introduced himself to Harrison.

The room was dormant, and the muscle-bound aide kept watch at the office door. The Great Liberator sat with his hands on his lap, his fingers interlinked. Patient and avuncular. He seemed assured and easygoing, as if Harrison could say nothing that would ruffle him.

Silence hung for several moments, until Harrison decided to break it. He wasn't going to sit there like a lackey.

'Why have you requested to see me?' he said.

'I think you know the answer to that.'

'Humour me.'

'If you insist,' the Great Liberator said, as he prodded the bridge of his spectacles with his index finger. 'You've become a threat to society, Harrison. It was foolish of you to think you could undermine us from within.

'We know all about your grandfather's shed at the bungalow. We know you had your Smart Sensor removed. We know you attacked a Stinger. We know you've been reading subversive literature, and listening to forbidden music, and slowly but surely working yourself up into a frenzy of hatred for Sunnyvale and everything we represent.

'We know about your embryonic plan to lead a resistance movement, as devised rather hastily last night with one Tessa Ruth. Even accounting for the limited preparation time, it was endearingly amateurish. You have guts, Harrison, but you're hardly Hannibal when it comes to operational planning. You sought to take on the might of Sunnyvale with a ninety-one-year-old woman as your only accomplice. It is true that bravery and stupidity are often one and the same.

'Operation Neo,' he said, with a deadpan expression. 'At least it had a creative flourish.'

Harrison stayed silent.

'I'm sure you're wondering how we know all of this,' the Great Liberator continued, matter-of-factly. 'Perhaps your lovely girlfriend wasn't quite as innocent as she made out. It is an almighty coincidence that the young woman you were assigned to mentor was mildly sympathetic to your cause, when most citizens would have reported you immediately.'

'Is Amberley safe? Have you done anything to her?' Harrison said.

'I'm merely speculating,' he said. 'Relax. Perhaps it was the lovely Amberley who did the right thing. Or perhaps it was the woman known only to you as Tessa Ruth, who you were so quick to ally with. How much do you really know about her, anyway, apart from a few stories and a photograph?

'Or perhaps it was your mother who worked it all out. There is such a thing as mother's instinct, you know? Your rebelliousness hasn't exactly been subtle. Or perhaps it was Elliot Patrick? Or your watchful comrades in the control room?

'Or perhaps nobody close to you was an informant.

Perhaps our security surveillance systems are so advanced, we didn't need one. Perhaps we've been able to back-trace your actions and conversations every step of the way.

'Or perhaps it was a mixture of all the possibilities I've just mentioned. You'll never know. An impressive feature of the extensive informant system in the old East Germany was that the guilty party could never quite be sure who had told on them. It's a very effective method.'

'Are you enjoying this?' Harrison said.

'Not particularly. I'm just doing my job. Until this morning, I didn't know anything about you. With all due respect, I have much bigger things on my plate. I don't need to know about every small threat to Sunnyvale, even those that are internal. We have an excellent security team in place, and I generally leave them to it.'

'Then why all the drama of this one-to-one meeting?' Harrison said.

'I must admit I am a little intrigued. I understand you had everything going for you. Intelligence, likeability, a very powerful family connection. And yet you decided to throw it away. Why?'

Harrison looked back at him defiantly. 'Because I chose to. Because I had to. *Someone* had to.'

'Ah, the allure of martyrdom,' the Great Liberator replied. 'I hoped you would have a more interesting explanation.'

He again prodded his spectacles, and then moved his hands back onto his lap, as if he was relaxing on a breezy porch.

'You're in quite a pickle, Harrison. We have enough evidence to ensure you can never find employment again. If we wanted, we could ensure you never see daylight again. But I never like to be unnecessarily cruel, especially to a relative of one of our finest comrades. I think I have a solution which will suit all parties.'

'Hold on,' Harrison said. 'May I, at least, ask a few

questions? Before you deign to determine my future for me.'

The Great Liberator smiled with his upturned lip. 'By all means, Harrison. Please do.'

'How do you get up on a morning knowing that you're nothing but a tinpot dictator? Does it make you proud? Does it give you a fuzzy warm feeling inside? And do you think the pretentious beret disguises the fact that you're bald? It's still very obvious, I'm afraid. Haven't Sunnyvale developed a cure for baldness yet? I should think that would be at the top of your priorities.'

The Great Liberator continued to smile, with an amused look in his eyes.

'Things are never black and white, Harrison,' he said. 'From your perspective, I'm a despot. I'm the head of an overbearing regime that crushes individual liberty for the sake of technological progress.

'Others portray me as the Great Liberator, helping lead human civilisation into a bright, new, post-capitalist era. The truth is somewhere in between, which means I have some sympathy for your point of view. You're not *entirely* wrong. But you're too young and hot-headed to understand that power is a balancing act. We do what we do out of necessity.'

'*Necessity?*' Harrison scoffed.

'Yes,' he replied. 'The creation of the internet was a landmark moment in human history. It's up there with the discovery of fire, the invention of the wheel and the development of the combustion engine.

'It began as a tool and a medium *for* the people. At the turn of the twentieth century, the iconic musician David Bowie said: "The internet carries the flag of being subversive and possibly rebellious." It was opening up the world at a dizzying rate. The Information Age was upon us. What a wonderful new dawn! Think of the possibilities!

'But the ideal quickly turned sour. The internet became a breeding ground for terrorism, and every other evil conceivable to humankind. It became an extension of human consciousness, with all the good and the bad. And there was a hell of a lot of bad.

'It made national borders redundant, and we needed a supranational infrastructure in place for the purpose of protection. We couldn't get rid of the internet, but we could control it. Simply put, Sunnyvale ensures the West's unity and security.'

'Hang on a second,' Harrison said. 'The only way for us to be safe is to live in a glorified prison, with our every move monitored by guards in the shadows?'

'That is an unfair characterisation of our society,' the Great Liberator said. 'If you're doing nothing wrong, you have nothing to hide. The overwhelming majority of western citizens are happy. You saw the jubilation on the streets today. They know the deal. Privacy is a luxury we cannot afford.'

'Privacy is a right,' Harrison said.

'But, by the same token, no man is an island,' the Great Liberator replied. 'We are all interconnected. Nothing can happen in an advanced society without interconnectivity. Take the example of a simple lead pencil. There was a famous essay written about this in the nineteen-fifties. The manufacturing of a humble pencil is a miracle of human ingenuity and co-operation, on a global scale. And most of it is unseen and unappreciated.

'You can't just opt out and say you want to be left alone. It doesn't work like that. We are all bees in the same hive. Sunnyvale is the most effective means of harnessing this inherent interconnectivity. And anyone who threatens the harmony of the hive is a terrorist.'

'This is absurd,' Harrison said. 'How can that be your definition of terrorism? How can the ruthless quashing of a citizen's non-violent political opinions be justified?'

'Very easily. If you wait for said citizen to commit violence, it's already too late. Our sophisticated algorithms, and our committed workforce, are dedicated to stamping out dissent at source. It's the only foolproof way, and the only effective deterrent.'

'What about Magna Carta?' Harrison said. 'And the Bill of Rights, and the presumption of innocence, and trial by jury, and habeas corpus, and the freedom of the press, and the American Constitution?'

'They're all noble sentiments,' the Great Liberator said. 'But they were designed for a different world. We cannot compare 2084 to 1787 or 1215. They're different universes.'

'They're not as different as you think,' Harrison said. 'As the great John Henry said: "A man ain't nothing but a man." I don't see how the passage of time has changed that.'

'I see you've been indulging in your grandfather's library. Parroting phrases you don't even fully understand doesn't make much of an argument.'

'Yes, I have. I only wish more people my age had the opportunity to do so. We've been brainwashed and conditioned from the day we were born. Only in the last few months have I felt some rays of light begin to break through. And it's given me the strength to fight back. Cowards die many times before their deaths. The valiant never taste of death but once.'

'While we're throwing literary quotes around,' the Great Liberator said. 'Have you ever heard Alexander Pope's phrase: "A little learning is a dangerous thing"? How much have you read about your country's history? Have you any idea how much danger England would be in without the broader protection and alliance of Sunnyvale?'

'What do you mean?' Harrison said.

'The balance of power was slipping further and further

eastward, and this little, rainy, windswept island was rightly regarded by those in the East as inconsequential. Worse, they were eager for revenge after centuries of British meddling.

'Do you know about the First Opium War of 1839? Although the Chinese invented gunpowder, they hadn't developed their firearms as aggressively as the Brits. They were overwhelmed by their own technology. They don't forget things like this. Without Sunnyvale, there would be no collective 'West' as we know it, and this country would be up for grabs. You should be thanking me.'

'You keep talking about security,' Harrison said. 'But it's about so much more than that. How did these companies, founded by geeks in college campus bedrooms, evolve to become the arbiter of *everything*? On what basis is such power justified? What gives you that right?'

'The people gave us that right,' the Great Liberator said. 'When they voluntarily signed up in their billions. It's simple supply and demand. We offered a service, and the people wanted it. And they used it again and again and again. We grew and they used us more, we grew again and they used us even more. Sunnyvale is the logical extension of that transaction.'

'People didn't always use your services out of choice,' Harrison said. 'They were forced to, when the alternatives were systematically taken over or destroyed. And you lured them in with your addictive features. Every click of the button was a dopamine hit, and you knew it. You consulted with gambling companies and casinos. I've read all about it.'

'We started off as businesses like any other,' the Great Liberator said. 'We were playing by the rules of capitalism. Who can criticise us for that? Anyway, we've evolved beyond all that now.'

Harrison shook his head with frustration. 'We no longer control the technology we use,' he said. 'It controls us. How can the fate of a human soul, standing trial in a courtroom, be decided by AI?'

'You overestimate human beings, Harrison,' the Great Liberator replied. 'Our justice system is infinitely fairer than it ever was before. Have you any idea how flawed our perceptions are? Historically, a jury in the American south would always look more favourably at a white defendant than a black one. Justice was never blind.

'Here's another example. A study in Israel suggested judges delivered harsher verdicts when they were hungry. They denied about thirty-five per cent of parole cases just after breakfast, but a whopping eight-five per cent just before lunch. A Sunnyvale Smart Judge is not affected by the vagaries and whims of the human mind. It is an improvement. It is progress.'

'What is the endpoint of all this supposed progress?' Harrison said.

'Harmony,' the Great Liberator replied. 'Some people say it's the pursuit of perfection.'

'Do *you* say that?' Harrison said. 'You strike me as a more practical man than many of your dogmatic followers.'

'There is a place for realism, and there is a place for dogma.'

'You're a coward,' Harrison said. 'You're dancing around the answer. I asked my mum the same question and she was unequivocal. I actually find that more forgivable.'

'I don't need to be forgiven by you, or anybody,' he replied, as calmly as ever. 'Everything I do is for the greater good. I sleep very soundly at night.'

'Do you have children, *Eddie*?' Harrison asked suddenly. He said 'Eddie' in a deliberately patronising, matey tone.

'Yes, I have a son and a daughter. They're both teenagers.'

'Do they have Sunnyvale Smart Sensors implanted in their wrists?'

The Great Liberator was momentarily unbalanced for the first time, but he quickly recovered himself. 'No, they do not.'

'That's interesting,' Harrison said. 'Do they plug into Sunnyvale e-sports or do you encourage them to play real sport outside? We're talking man to man here, there's no need to lie.'

'They occasionally do so, like everyone else. But yes, I do encourage them to play softball, baseball and the like. I play catch with them whenever I'm home.'

'Do they have social media profiles?'

'No, they do not.'

'Why?'

'Because I think they're too young,' the Great Liberator said. 'And because of their association with me. They'd be a ripe target for blackmail or abuse.'

'Do you have books in your house? Ones that are officially banned?'

The Great Liberator stayed silent.

'Are you starting to see something of a hypocritical pattern here, Eddie? Is it one rule for the masses and a different one for those at the top? Your own family should be the keenest advocates for Sunnyvale's values, right? Are you a disbeliever of your own cause? Are some people more equal than others?'

The Great Liberator laughed generously. 'I see you have your grandfather's way with words. I admire your attempts to box me in with my own logic. I dare say, again, there is some truth to what you say. But it doesn't matter. I don't have to keep justifying Sunnyvale, and myself, to the great Harrison Snow. You won't even qualify as a footnote in the history books. Your cause is over. It's finished. Your grandfather said so himself.'

'You're probably right,' Harrison said. 'But I can still look you in the eye and tell you that you're evil. Your smug self-awareness only makes it worse. I'd respect you more if you were a raving ideologue, totally convinced of the purity of your cause.

But you know yourself it's an abomination. You know you're in charge of a monster which is totally out of control. You're a modern Dr Frankenstein. Deep down, you're agreeing with every word I say.'

The Great Liberator shrugged indifferently. 'If that gives you some comfort, you're welcome to it. Let's get back to business, shall we? I called you in here for a reason, not for a philosophical discussion. I'm a busy man, and you've taken up enough of my time. Your antics are delaying this lovely lunch, which your comrades are looking forward to so much.'

He leaned forward in his chair. 'As we've established, your position at Sunnyvale is no longer tenable. We could – and perhaps should – meet your threat with full force. But, out of respect for your mother, I've come up with a generous compromise. Did your grandfather ever mention anything about the island of Jura?'

Harrison could see where the conversation was going. 'He mentioned something about an island community,' he said.

'Jura is off the west coast of Scotland,' the Great Liberator continued. 'It's become home to a community of Luddites, who have no access to modern technology. They're a strange mix of the old-fashioned Amish, of hippies, of misfits, of rabble-rousers, of troublemakers and of the occasional political prisoner.

'They're a harmless bunch. They enjoy their primitive existence, and they're no threat to us. We leave them to it. I think you'd fit in there nicely.'

The Great Liberator looked at Harrison through his horn-rimmed spectacles.

'I highly recommend you take me up on this offer. It's exceedingly benevolent of me, and I'm only going to ask you once. You have no alternative. There's no life for you here.'

'Just one more thing,' Harrison said. The Great Liberator

nodded slightly.

Harrison cleared his throat, smiled, and said:

There once was a Great Liberator,
More like a Great Dictator,
He was bald as a coot,
Slimy as a newt,
And as ugly as the Terminator.

Part Three

25

One year later

It was a humid, muggy day on the isle of Jura. Sweat was trickling steadily down Harrison's flushed face, and he swatted angrily at the air around him. 'Bloody midges,' he said.

He had nearly finished his shift delivering letters and parcels to the island's inhabitants, most of whom lived in houses stretched along the seafront in a small town called Craighouse. This is where he had first arrived, by boat, a year ago and it was where he was now based. He hadn't yet been able to call it 'home', but the place was steadily growing on him.

He glanced to his right and caught eyes with a deer. It was stood – about fifty metres away behind a chain-link fence – gently grazing on short grass, unperturbed by Harrison's presence. Harrison had been learning bits about the island's history, and he knew that the name 'Jura' may have come from the old word 'Deray', or 'Diuray' in Gaelic. It was, quite literally, 'Deer Island'.

Like everything with Jura, however, nobody could be quite sure. Other theories were that it derived from the Gaelic for yew tree, or from the Jura mountains in France, or from the names of two Danes who fought and killed each other on the island (and whose ashes were buried in urns). Mystery and mythology were now part of his everyday life, a development which he welcomed.

He slapped himself on the side of his neck and shouted in frustration at the midges which were plaguing his every step. He reached into his over-the-shoulder satchel and rooted around beneath the last remaining letter, before plucking out a bottle of insect repellent. He hastily sprayed it all over himself, coughing and spluttering loudly as he inhaled some of it.

'Morning,' a familiar Scottish voice said, as Harrison continued to clear his throat. It belonged to a diminutive, wiry elderly man who lived close to the pier, right at the end of Harrison's route (he liked to start furthest away, on bike, before working his way back and finishing the home stretch on foot.)

'It's just about the afternoon now,' Harrison replied after composing himself, glancing at his watch. 'Which means it's time for a post-work beer. Hallelujah.'

'You're not a fan of the postie shift, then?'

'I don't mind it actually,' he said. 'On a summer's day like this it's no problem getting up early with it being so light. I was out the door by half-four. And it keeps me fit. I'm more tanned than I ever was. The only problem is the midges.'

'Aye, they're little blighters.'

Harrison removed the final letter from his satchel and handed it over to the old man, who enjoyed this part of the daily routine. He never waited inside for them to be posted through his letterbox.

'If you don't mind me asking,' Harrison said. 'Who do you keep exchanging letters with? I do this shift four times a week and you get one every time, like clockwork.'

'They're from my daughter,' he replied. 'She's up in Inverlussa.' This was a hamlet about an hour-and-a-half cycle away up the eastern coast of the island. It marked the furthest point on Harrison's route.

'Why don't you go and see her?' Harrison said.

The old man suddenly looked very frail and weak. 'Oh, it's a long way for a man of my age,' he said. 'Too much hassle. We like our daily letters, it's what we've done for years.'

Harrison smiled warmly but found himself shaking his

head as he walked away. He still hadn't quite adjusted to the pace of life, and lack of technology, here. *Imagine not seeing your own daughter just up the road because it was too much hassle!*

The voice on his other shoulder then chimed in. *Who are you to judge? He's lived here for decades. He doesn't know any different.* This type of internal exchange was a regular part of Harrison's new life. He was torn between two worlds.

*

Later that afternoon, Harrison was sinking his fifth beer in succession. He wasn't normally a big drinker, but in recent months he had found solace in its numbing qualities. It tempered the never-ending arguments in his head. *Why are you here, coward? What kind of a life is this? ... Then again, what options did you have? Don't beat yourself up.*

The bar was downstairs from his living accommodation. He had his own room in a large, white building by the pier, just beyond the imposing whisky distillery. It had been a hotel in the heady days when Jura was open to visitors – the old hotel was essentially three or four conjoined houses with spacious rooms, and all the inhabitants shared a communal kitchen area and lounge. Harrison felt like he was living permanently in a hostel.

The rooms around him were largely taken by the most recent newcomers to the island. As the Great Liberator had put it, these were Luddites, hippies, misfits, rabble-rousers, troublemakers and political prisoners. Harrison often wondered which category he qualified for.

Aside from a smattering of people in Inverlussa (like the elderly man's daughter), Harrison lived alongside and amongst around a thousand people in Craighouse. It was a sizeable population – much greater than there had been earlier in the century before the rise of Sunnyvale – but humans were still vastly outnumbered by deer. (They co-existed harmoniously, though venison was – naturally – a staple of the Jura diet.)

Everything felt a bit crowded, with the old-fashioned houses packed to the brim, and every room in the former hotel occupied, and a few hundred hardy souls living in makeshift tents and shelters along the seafront.

There were procedures and structures in place in an attempt to build something of a society – everyone was expected, for example, to chip in with regular work, for which they were paid in old money – and there was a council. But it was difficult to establish any real cohesion. Ultimately, a thousand people had just gradually been dumped on a remote island and left to their own devices. Only a handful of locals remained, and their truculence was easy to spot – their beautiful, serene island had been turned into a de facto prison.

'One more beer please,' Harrison said to the landlord. 'And a double whisky, neat. Pour one for yourself too. It's the best part of living here. All that old whisky stored away in crate after crate. It's rude not to make the most of it.'

'Aye,' the landlord said. He was a man of few words.

Harrison was fond of landlords ever since his experience with the Neanderthal-like owner of the pub in York. The one who had solved Pop's riddle and led him to Tessa Ruth.

But what would have happened, he sometimes wondered, if he had never stepped foot in that pub in the first place? He only fell through the door because he was ducking away from a Stinger. If he had never met the landlord, he may have never solved the riddle, which meant he would never have met Tessa and seen Pop's second letter. Does that mean he wouldn't have been caught? Would he still be working for Sunnyvale? He had no idea at what point his actions had become suspicious.

All these thoughts whizzed through his head in seconds, until he opened his mouth and threw the double whisky down his throat. It stung, but he soon felt refreshingly fuzzy-headed. The best way to avoid uncomfortable thoughts was to stop thinking at all.

*

Another five pints later, and Harrison was comfortably numb. He stumbled to the toilet and then out into the sun, which was still beating down on Craighouse. The view was spectacular, like something from an old-fashioned postcard. The grass was implausibly lush, the sea was implausibly blue and the sky was implausibly clear. Even the midges failed to spoil his few moments of peace.

He walked towards the waterfront and found a thick tree just beyond a bike shed. It cast a long shadow, and Harrison sat down in its shade with his back against the trunk. He just about had the wherewithal to cover himself from head to toe in repellent, before promptly falling asleep. He wasn't typically a snorer, but he grunted loudly with every inhale.

26

Harrison woke to an angel. Or so he thought. He opened his bloodshot eyes and saw the blurry outline of an angelic face close to his.

'I'm sorry to bother you,' she said gently. She had a Scottish lilt to her voice. 'But we're about to play some music near here. You may be best sleeping inside. And it looks like the midges have taken a liking to you.'

It took Harrison a few moments to reorientate himself. The sun was lower in the sky, but it was still the evening. He sprang up and pretended that he had just been having a power nap.

'Thanks,' he said croakily. 'I was just resting my eyes.' He swatted at the midges and smiled sheepishly. 'I'm Harrison.'

'I'm Bonnie,' she said. Her skin was porcelain white and her dark hair was in pigtails. She was wearing a knee-length dress, a fedora hat and she had a guitar strapped to her back. Harrison also noticed a modest link-chain necklace, with what looked like a yellow guitar pick as the pendant.

'I'd like to watch you play,' Harrison said. 'When do you start?'

'Any minute now.'

'A quick whisky will be good for your vocal chords,' he said. 'Give me a second.'

He bounded back to the bar and returned with a couple of amber-filled glasses. Bonnie stayed quiet but Harrison was sure he saw the flicker of an amused smile. He held up his glass and passed the other to her.

'Bonnie,' he said. 'I've known you for five seconds. But nothing would give me more pleasure than sharing this drink with you. Cheers!'

He drained his glass immediately. Bonnie hesitated for a moment, but then downed hers just as quickly. She let out a little cough but otherwise stayed silent. She handed her glass back to Harrison and walked away with the hint of an amused smile still on her face.

*

Bonnie fronted a band of three, who had set up on the lawn of the old hotel. They had microphones and a little wooden stage. At least a couple of hundred people (including most of those who lived in tents and shelters along the seafront nearby) were gathered to watch.

'Evening everyone,' she said into the microphone. 'My name is Bonnie. I'm nineteen, and I'm born and bred on Jura. These are my two younger brothers, Phil and Callum.' They both gave a short nod at the announcement of their names.

'We've been practising together since we were children, but this is our first time playing publicly. We hope you have fun.'

The crowd applauded politely and Bonnie cleared her throat. Harrison wondered if she was inwardly thanking or cursing him for the whisky.

They started playing a slow-burning melody, which was unfamiliar to Harrison, but he was enthralled. The trio just worked. Bonnie looked and sounded magnificent, her soft features belying the authority and breadth of her voice. The crowd were soon clapping and singing along, and they continued late into the evening.

I was right, Harrison thought. *I was woken by an angel.*

*

After the show had finished, Harrison hovered around the stage until most of the crowd had gone.

'Do you need a hand dismantling it?' he said to one of the brothers.

'Nah, we've got permission to leave it here now. We're hoping to do a show every week if people are interested.'

'They're definitely interested,' Harrison said emphatically. 'Everybody loved it.'

'Aye, it was good fun.'

Bonnie glanced over from the other end of the stage, still wearing a hidden smile.

'Your sister has such a good voice,' Harrison said.

'Aye, she's talented. Our mum was very musical apparently, not that I can remember. She died when all of us were young. Bonnie remembers a little, but me and Callum don't.'

'So it's just you three and your dad?'

'Aye.'

'Where do you live?'

'Just up the road, like everyone else.' He was starting to grow impatient with Harrison's questions.

'Which house specifically? I'm the postie at the moment so I always like to know who lives where.'

'The last on the row of terraced houses, not far from the church.'

'Cheers,' Harrison said, and then he wandered over to Bonnie.

'Why am I not surprised that you're still here?' she said, with a knowing smirk.

'How much would you charge for guitar lessons?' he said.

'Who says I'm giving lessons?'

'Nobody, but it's something I've always wanted to do.'

She paused and looked at Harrison. His eyes were still

bloodshot, but he had something of a jack-the-lad charm about him when he'd been drinking.

'Seven o'clock tomorrow night,' she said. 'At our house. We'll have a trial lesson and see how it goes.'

'Perfect,' Harrison said. 'Where do you live?'

'You already know that,' she replied. 'I heard you talking to my brother.'

27

The guitar lesson was productive; Bonnie was a natural teacher, and Harrison was eager to learn. They only covered the basics, but Harrison promised to go away and practise in his spare time. There was a second-hand, worn-out guitar in the lobby of his accommodation which he reckoned he could use.

Of course, it wasn't really about the music. For the first time since his sweet, but brief, time with Amberley, Harrison was besotted. And he had fallen for Bonnie just as rapidly as he had for Amberley, which seemed a lifetime ago.

They had the lesson in the back garden, and Harrison had nipped inside to use the toilet. Bonnie followed him into the kitchen and poured them both a cool glass of lemonade.

'So you've lived here your whole life?' Harrison said, as he emerged from the bathroom. The house was old-fashioned and compact, and there were ample books, records, pictures and bric-a-brac to signify a comfortable and long-established family home.

'Yeah,' she replied softly, almost wistfully. She was leaning against the kitchen counter. 'I've literally never left the island, unless you include kayaking or fishing trips off the shore.'

'That's crazy,' Harrison said, shaking his head. 'How do you deal with that? I still can't comprehend that I'm stuck here.'

'I don't know any different, I suppose,' she said. There was still a wistful tone to her voice. 'As a young girl I read all sorts of adventure stories. Tolkien was my favourite. Jura is like the Shire, in a way. It's safe, and it's home. But there's a whole world beyond it, isn't there?'

'There is. But it's Sunnyvale's world now.'

Just as Harrison said this, a barrel-chested middle-aged man walked into the kitchen. It was Bonnie's dad, evident by their matching grey-blue eyes, and he fixed them on Harrison.

'Evening,' he said, outstretching his hand. He was roughly the same height as Harrison, but a good deal broader, and his Scottish accent was thicker than his daughter's.

'I remember when you first arrived. It took you a few weeks to get your head straight but I knew you'd come in handy. We need all the young, strong people we can get. How are you finding the postal route?'

Harrison was momentarily taken aback.

'I didn't know we'd met before,' he said.

'Aye, it was in your first day or two. Every new arrival is questioned by a few of our councillors. We try to work out their strengths and see how they can best be employed.'

'I don't remember much about the first few days,' Harrison said. 'My mind was a blur.'

'Aye, understandable. You've been doing the work rotation, right? Trying a few different jobs out before committing. Remind me what you've done so far – fisherman, labourer and now postie? Is that right?'

'Spot on,' Harrison said. 'They all have their pros and cons. At least as a postie I'm done by midday.'

'I can understand that,' he said, chuckling. 'I'm Gavin, by the way. Come through to the lounge and let's find ourselves a stronger drink than that lemonade.'

*

Gavin wasn't an overly gregarious man, but he was open and welcoming in a modest way. He trusted himself as a good judge of character, and he was keen to learn more about the young man who had clearly taken an interest in his daughter. He poured Harrison and himself a whisky from a glass tumbler, and Bonnie popped her head in to say she was going for a walk.

'Same time next week,' she said, with her hidden smile.

The lounge was then silent aside from the sonorous ticking of an old clock on the mantelpiece. The layout reminded Harrison of the haven, except it didn't have to be hidden underground. There was a sofa, and a couple of tartan armchairs, and a large oak bookcase at each wall. There was even a record player, and some board games, in the corner.

'Correct me if I'm wrong,' Gavin said, eventually. 'But I recall you come from a high-profile family on the mainland. What happened there?'

'Is this the Spanish Inquisition?' Harrison said lightly. He tried to relax into his tartan armchair. 'I only came round for a guitar lesson.'

'Sure you did, laddie. Don't forget, I was your age once. I'm not grilling you. But I'm a councillor here and it pays off to know who's who and what's what.'

'Fair enough,' Harrison said. 'My mum is very high up in Sunnyvale. She got me a job there, but I soon rebelled. I could never fully get on board. I was expelled here personally by the Great Liberator, of all people.'

Gavin whistled through his teeth. 'Christ, I didn't realise it was *that* high-profile. You really spoke to the Great Liberator? That's what they call the CEO now, isn't it?'

'Yeah, he isn't all he's cracked up to be. I had him rattled. Still, he took pity on me and sent me here, which is a blessing I suppose. It could be worse, right?'

'Aye.'

They sat in contemplative silence for a minute. Gavin was still reeling from the revelation that Harrison was privy to the higher echelons of Sunnyvale.

'It's no big deal,' Harrison said, sensing his intrigue. 'I was born into it, I didn't achieve anything. The really interesting man is my grandad. He's the one who recognised what was happening and tried to fight it. But he's dead now.'

'What was his name?' Gavin said.

'Joseph Snow. But his pseudonym was Guy Smith.'

Gavin lurched forward in his chair, like a little jolt of electricity had surged through him.

'Guy Smith? You're the grandson of Guy Smith?'

'Yep.'

'Christ, that's a blast from the past. In the early days when Jura was being turned into what it is now, his name was often on the lips of the councillors. I can't remember all the details. But I know he was invited to live here a few times. I think they used to send him the odd crate of whisky now and again, as moral support. That's when it was possible to send stuff to the mainland, of course.'

'He mentioned some of that in his letters,' Harrison said. 'But he said he wanted to stay in his home city. He didn't want to flee.'

'Aye, well I can appreciate that. It's the reason I'm still here now. There came a point when I had to choose between risking a move to the mainland – where things were clearly getting worse – or staying put. Neither were great options for my children. They're free from the very worst of Sunnyvale here, but they're still effectively prisoners. By choosing not to leave, we cast ourselves as rebels and outsiders, even if we'd never done anything to oppose Sunnyvale.'

'Did you ever see much of the mainland?' Harrison asked.

'Oh yeah. It was only about eighteen years ago when the authorities identified Jura as the perfect spot to keep their miscreants. It's not a new idea, by the way. The Americans did it with Guantanamo Bay in Cuba.

'Jura was already attracting people on the run, objectors to the regime, and all that. Nonconformists. A lot of them have never actively opposed Sunnyvale, they just wanted to live their lives away from interference. We have a few Amish here, for instance. They have their own settlement north of Inverlussa. And I'm sure you've heard people here refer to themselves as Luddites. Do you know what this means?'

'Kind of,' Harrison said.

'The Luddites were a movement of textile workers at the start of the industrial revolution. They opposed the rise of the machinery which they feared would drive them out of work. The term then came to represent anyone who was sceptical about new forms of technology. It eventually became a kind of insult, but it was embraced by those who were supposed to be offended by it.

'The movement began in the year 1811, so a few people here want to celebrate the two-hundred-and-seventy-fifth anniversary the year after next.'

Harrison laughed inwardly as he remembered the number to access Pop's shed, which was etched on Aslan's collar. 1811.

'Sunnyvale decided to turn it into one big open prison,' Gavin continued. 'Before then I was hopping over all the time. You'd either get a car ferry to Islay, and then another across to Kennacraig. Or you could get a little passenger ferry to Tayvallich.'

'And that freedom just stopped overnight?' Harrison said.

'Not quite. There was a period of a few months where every local had to weigh up whether to stay or go. Most of them went, which is fully understandable. My wife and I decided to stay. We knew there'd be no life there. At least here we could barricade ourselves from the worst of it. But there have been times when I wonder if we did the right thing, especially after she died.'

'How come they could send whisky to my grandad then?'

'For a year or two it wasn't quite as strict as it is now. Very occasional visits were allowed, for special events like funerals.

And letters and parcels could be sent to the mainland, after they'd been checked and monitored. But, inevitably, they soon put a stop to that. It always travels in one direction. Always.'

Harrison was stimulated by the conversation. It was waking dormant areas of his brain. For the last year he had tried to just live in the moment, to numb his thoughts with alcohol and to somehow moderate the battle between the voices on each shoulder.

'Have you ever wondered why they bother with this at all?' Harrison said. 'Why not just kill us, or put us in a proper prison?'

Gavin laughed heartily. 'Every day, laddie. We call it the Jura Complex – a very strange form of survivor's guilt. There are a few theories.

'Theory number one,' he said, raising a single forefinger. 'I mentioned Guantanamo Bay earlier. Had you heard of it before?'

'It rings a bell,' Harrison said. 'It came up in some book I read in my grandad's secret stash.'

'Well, the same question applies to the US. Why didn't they just kill all the prisoners? It would be easier than storing them indefinitely, right? But it's never as simple as that. A lot of the things they did there were illegal, but they still – at least ostensibly – had human rights lawyers and Geneva Conventions and all sorts of things to consider.

'Sunnyvale don't have as many of those problems, and they're much more ruthless. But it still isn't as straight-forward as it sounds. I bet they still have certain procedures to go through and boxes to tick. Here, we're out of sight and out of mind. And we lack the technology to pose any kind of threat. It's a hassle-free compromise.

'Theory number two,' he continued, raising a second finger. 'Lots of people don't buy theory number one. Sunnyvale are not known for their mercy and restraint. They're accountable to nobody. Why would they spare us? A thousand is not a great number in the scale of the West. If they really took mercy on troublemakers and nonconformists, this place would be overflowing with tens of thousands.'

'I see your point,' Harrison said. 'But what's the theory?'

'The theory is that they're watching us. They've put all their bad eggs in one basket and they're seeing what makes us tick. They're so close to snuffing out all opposition, but they won't rest until the job is complete. We're guinea pigs in a great big cage. We're the last of the rebels and nonconformists and they want to make sure none will take our place. I think it was Sun Tzu who said "Know your enemy."'

'I don't like that one,' Harrison said. He shook himself off as if the idea had given him the creeps. 'But I can see the logic.'

'The third theory,' Gavin said, lifting a third finger, 'is that they're doing it to mess with us. You know George Orwell wrote *Nineteen-Eighty-Four* here, don't you?'

'Yeah, I've seen the house he used to stay in, up at Barnhill. I cycled there in my first month. It's remote, even by Jura's standards.'

'Aye, well the theory is that it's no coincidence they chose here. *Nineteen-Eighty-Four* was one of the first books to be banned, but people like your grandfather were pretty successful in spreading it around. The surname of his pseudonym, Smith, came from the main character, of course.

'And it's a big reason why Jura became a place of refuge for rebels and nonconformists. It was symbolic. Sunnyvale twisted that on its head by making it an island prison – the smart-arses are mocking us. They always liked to portray us as loonies and conspiracy theorists. Keeping us here, of all places, is a way of toying with us. Like a cat pawing at a mouse instead of just finishing it off. It's also why some people think the year 2084 was chosen to become Year One in the Sunnyvale Era. That's the theory anyway.'

'Which do you reckon is true?' Harrison asked.

'You want my depressing take on things? Gavin replied, with a sigh. 'I think it's a mixture of all three. I reckon they're simultaneously mocking us, monitoring us and sparing us. They could be listening to this conversation now, for all we know. Never underestimate Sunnyvale.'

Harrison took a long sip of his whisky and stared into the empty fireplace. 'Trust me, I don't.'

28

Harrison's week followed a familiar pattern: early starts, midday finishes and post-work booze sessions. Nearly all of his modest old money wages were being spent in the bar at his accommodation, but he saw no point in prudence. He could barely look ahead to the next month on Jura, let alone the rest of his life.

He came to the last portion of his four-day shift, and for the fourth afternoon in a row he handed a letter over to the wiry, elderly man. They exchanged the usual pleasantries, but Harrison's deep-seated curiosity was rising to the surface again.

'How long have you lived here?' he said.

'Nearly fifty years,' the old man replied. 'My wife was from here.'

'And you decided to stay after Sunnyvale turned it into an open prison?'

'Where else would I go?' he said simply.

Harrison was reminded of the conversation he'd had in the pub with Stan, back in York. Some people were just not designed for introspection.

'It must have changed the island a lot though?'

'Aye, it's much busier than it was. Back then there were only a couple of hundred of us. We really need to build more houses, but it's slow progress with the lack of labourers and raw materials.'

'How else has it changed?'

'We can't use cars anymore. If we could, I'd at least see my daughter more than I do now. We've gone backwards. I know that's the whole point of this place now, but it's bloody silly.'

'Did all of your neighbours leave?'

'Aye, just about. Only a few of us stayed. Everyone on Islay buggered off too, it's just deserted now. Such a waste. Now we're an overcrowded island full of hippies and loafers.'

'Why do you think Sunnyvale has done this?'

The old man shrugged his shoulders, like he was Stan's long-lost brother.

'It's a mug's game trying to work out what them lot are thinking,' he said. 'You'll only torture yourself. We're just specks of dust to them.'

Harrison laughed loudly. 'You have a way with words for someone who doesn't want to reflect too much.'

The old man chuckled lightly in return.

'Well, it is sad. A young man like you should be out in the world, not cooped up for the rest of his life. What the hell has gone wrong with the world? If I looked too closely at everything, I think I'd go mad.'

*

Harrison stayed off the drink before his second lesson with Bonnie. He was determined to show off his progress, as each night after his boozing he had been putting in time with the old guitar from the lobby.

It was late August, and the weather was still perfect for working in the back garden. Bonnie was wearing denim shorts and a vest top, with her link-chain necklace, and Harrison was in plain shorts and T-shirt. He had arrived on Jura with only the clothes on his back, and over the last year he had mustered together a second-hand wardrobe from hand-me-downs and cheap purchases from a monthly market.

'Is there a story behind the necklace?' Harrison said, after their hour-long lesson had finished.

Bonnie looked down and held the pendant, a yellow guitar

pick, between her finger and thumb.

'My mum gave it to me when I was very young,' she said. 'Not long before she died. She said she knew I'd inherited the musical gene from her, and she wanted me to take my talent as far as I could. She also wrote down a quotation for me to keep forever. It's from a French writer called Victor Hugo. "Music expresses that which cannot be said and on which it is impossible to be silent."'

'Your mum sounds like a very wise lady,' Harrison said.

'She was,' Bonnie said, and then she went quiet.

'Sadly I don't have that musical gene,' Harrison said, lightening the mood. 'But with some practice I can at least get a bit better.'

'Your enthusiasm has been great so far,' she said.

'Is that a diplomatic way of saying I'm rubbish?' he laughed.

'Not at all,' she said. 'Granted, you may not have the most natural talent in the world. But hard work will always produce results. My dad says this all the time.'

Right on cue, Gavin came out the back door with a bottle of beer in his hand

'Good lass, Bonnie,' he said warmly, in his thick accent. 'Your dad always knows best, keep spreading the word. I've cooked some salmon and taties if you fancy it, Harrison? You're more than welcome to stay for tea with us.'

Harrison accepted politely and caught an instinctive smile on Bonnie's face when he did so.

*

Harrison joined Gavin, Bonnie and her two brothers at the dining room table. The room was cosy and compact, and the salmon looked deliciously fresh.

'You were great again last night,' he said. 'I reckon the audience had doubled from the week before.'

'Aye,' Callum said. 'There ain't much to do around here, so a bit of music can liven things up.'

'They first started playing together when the boys were knee-high,' Gavin said. 'I'd try to give them a mini football or rugby ball, but they loved their little toy instruments. And they followed their sister everywhere. So it's music, rather than sport, in this household.'

'It sounds like everyone needs it,' Harrison said. 'They were bouncing last night.'

'We play some songs that are banned on the mainland,' Bonnie said mischievously. 'I think people like that.'

'Who's the youngest of the three?' Harrison said. 'You two look the same age,' he added, looking at Callum and Phil.

'I'm fifteen,' Callum said. 'And he's fourteen.'

'That means you're still at school, right? I remember being told it's compulsory till sixteen.'

'Aye, I'm soon starting my final year,' Callum said. 'But I'm in the same class as Phil. There are less than fifty of us in the whole school, so it's a mishmash of ages and abilities.'

'You'd like it at the school,' Gavin said to Harrison. 'You have a sensible head on your shoulders. I've noticed already. You could add it to your rotation, you know? Try it out.'

'I might do.'

'The school is great,' Bonnie said. 'They have this huge library. It was like my portal to the rest of the world. I'm working there as the school librarian now just so I can keep making the most of it.'

'I'd love to see it,' Harrison said.

'We can go after we've finished eating,' she replied. 'I have the keys.'

*

The school was the most impressive building on the island – aside, perhaps, from the whisky distillery. It was on the main road, looking out to sea, just a short walk from Bonnie's house.

'My dad remembers it as a squat, outdated building from the nineteen-seventies,' Bonnie said, as she unlocked the gate with a clunky, brass key from a bundle. 'But the councillors made it their first priority to upgrade it when Jura was sealed off. They were determined to keep education alive, even if everything else was crumbling.'

'That's admirable,' Harrison said. The brick building had two floors, and a large outhouse to its side. Bonnie headed straight for it.

'I could show you inside the main school,' she said. 'But it's fairly typical to ones you've seen before, I imagine. The real star here is the library.'

She selected a smaller key from the bundle and unlocked the door, before stepping aside with her arm outstretched.

'Please go ahead,' she said. 'Welcome to the building which shaped, and saved, my childhood.'

Harrison smiled and walked through the door, as an automatic light clicked on above him. The smell of old books was overwhelming. The row upon row of wooden shelves reminded Harrison of Sunnyvale's HQ, with its endless columns of MDF storage units.

'I just love that smell,' Harrison said, as Bonnie joined him. 'I associate it with learning and whisky and music, as well as books. It's a smell I didn't even know existed a few years ago.'

'Isn't it perfect?' she said. 'I can safely say that I've spent more time in this library than anyone else.'

She walked over to a stout, wooden desk and knocked on its surface.

'This is ours,' she said. 'Dad made it out of a tree that fell down during a storm. It's where I sit when I need to do paperwork.' She continued walking around the perimeter.

'This corner here is for the very young ones who are just starting to read.' There was a yellow carpet, with various cuddly toys on it, and a small bookshelf with children's books.

'Further round here we have our chill-out zone.' There were beanbags and magazines and mini board games. 'You may think it sounds uncool, but the younger teenagers actually love it.'

Bonnie then pointed to the row upon row of wooden shelves. 'Each shelf stores a different genre of book. Fiction, non-fiction, biography and so on. My pet project at the moment is categorising everything according to the Dewey Decimal System. Have you heard of it?'

'No,' Harrison replied.

'Maybe, if you're lucky, I'll show you some day.' She stopped in front of a colourful display on the wall. 'This is quotation corner,' she said. 'I encourage them to write down anything they find particularly interesting or inspirational when they're reading. I then put some of those snippets up here.'

There were about twenty quotes on the wall, written on coloured card with neat handwriting. Harrison absorbed them all, including:

'I have always imagined that paradise will be some sort of library.' Jorge Luis Borges.

'The reward for conformity is that everyone likes you except yourself.' Rita Mae Brown.

'Give me liberty, or give me death.' Patrick Henry.

'These are great,' Harrison said emphatically. 'They're just like the quotes my grandad would underline.'

'Yeah, the children love spotting a good one and then seeing it up there. There's a healthy competition about it.'

'How did you get all these books? This just wouldn't be allowed on the mainland.'

'A lot of them are left over from before the island was sealed off,' she said. 'Then when rumours spread that it was going to be closed off, there was a big effort to stock up on as many classics as possible. My dad was involved in some of the logistics, once he'd decided he was going to stay.'

'I'm amazed they got away with it,' Harrison said.

'Well it was in the early days when it all sounded pretty chaotic. Sunnyvale were powerful but they were focused more on the big cities, I think. Even with their resources, they wouldn't have been tracking every boat that came and left. My dad and the others hid all the books until the coast was clear, literally. And then they built this library to store them.'

'Are you glad that your parents decided to keep you here?'

'Yes and no,' she replied thoughtfully. 'I know it must have been a horrible decision for them. There was no right answer. From what I hear about the mainland, I have a lot more freedom here. And I'm safe. But I often dream about travelling. I have these long, vivid dreams where I'm sailing around the Horn of Africa, or I'm traipsing through the Amazon, or I'm hitchhiking on Route 66.

'All these books helped keep me sane, but they also fuelled my imagination. My brothers aren't really into reading, and they seem to cope with it much better. They accept the mundane reality better than I do.'

'At least it allows you to momentarily escape, even if only in your mind,' Harrison said. 'The mainland is just as much of a prison as here, though. Trust me.'

Bonnie stepped closer to Harrison. Her dark hair was in pigtails, just like when he she had woken him by the tree.

'And what are the girls like on the mainland?' she said.

Harrison found himself blushing a little.

'Can I be honest?' he said.

'I wouldn't expect anything less.'

'Well, I never met anyone as beautiful as you. Or as soulful. When I watch you sing it's like I forget about all the darkness in the world, and all the stuff I've been through. There's something so innocent and pure about you, like you haven't been tainted by Sunnyvale. It's like I've gone back in time and found a woman from another age.'

'A woman from another age?' she said, laughing lightly. 'I kind of like that. As if I'm some timeless Tolkien character, like Galadriel.'

'If you say so,' Harrison smiled. 'And who could I be from your literary world?'

'Hmm. You can be a bit cheeky, like a grown-up version of Tom Sawyer. But then you also have this serious side, like when you talk to my dad, as if you're some suitor from a Jane Austen story. Your face hardens and you try to act all proper. But then there are also times when you walk around a bit like a caveman. Like Tarzan.'

'So I'm Tom Sawyer mixed with Tarzan mixed with a Jane Austen gentleman?' Harrison said, shaking his head with laughter. 'You weren't lying about your imagination. It's off the charts.'

'I've often imagined something else,' she said quietly. And then she leaned in to kiss him, her hands clasping around his waist, and his back pressing against one of the library's large bookshelves.

29

The following months were as close to contentment Harrison had come in a long time. He spent most evenings with Bonnie, after she had finished her shift in the school's library, and he was coming to appreciate the simplicity of his life on Jura.

They climbed the island's 'paps' (the huge hills that dominated the landscape); they visited the famous Corryvreckan whirlpool (where George Orwell once had to be rescued after nearly drowning); he watched every one of her weekly performances at the pier; and they spent many hours walking on the rocks, the seaweed and the sand at the seafront.

As well as showing him how to play the guitar, she also taught him how to kayak in the sea. She had been adept in the water since she was a toddler – it was one of the perks of island life – and it gave her a unique sense of freedom and escapism.

She quickly passed this enthusiasm on to Harrison, who would paddle alongside her several times a week up and down the coastline. Sometimes they shared a tandem kayak, and other times they went individually. It was a hobby Harrison had never expected to grow so passionate about. He quickly took pride in how far he could push himself (sometimes they would spend all afternoon out on the water) and he enjoyed the aesthetic benefits to his shoulder and arm muscles.

He finished his time as a postie and – as Gavin had recommended – he started helping out the teachers at the school. He shared his experiences on the mainland with the intrigued children, and he emphasised how lucky they were to enjoy such a well-stocked library.

'Make the most of it!' he regularly implored.

Through the autumn and the winter he lived in a state of

relative ease, and he had even curbed his drinking. He still liked a beer and whisky, but only as an occasional treat, and he had reverted to the mindset of just taking each day at a time. Jura was, he sometimes dared to think, starting to feel something like home.

*

Spring arrived, and daylight started to stretch late into the evening. It felt like the island was coming out of hibernation. It was Year 2 of the Sunnyvale Era on the mainland, which meant it was 2085 according to the old calendar. On Jura, it may as well have been 1585. Life adjusted to the seasons, like some medieval village, and the warmth of the sun was greeted like a gift from the Gods after a hard winter.

Harrison was eating with Bonnie, Gavin and the brothers at their terraced house. It was a typical Jura meal: venison, potatoes and vegetables. Harrison still lived in the old hotel, but Gavin insisted he stay for food at least a couple of times a week.

'I've been thinking,' Gavin said, as he cut up a piece of venison. 'And I reckon you should join me at the next council meeting, Harrison. It's something you should be looking to get involved with one day.'

'Sure,' Harrison replied. 'Sounds interesting.'

*

The meeting was held in the parish church the following week, just a short stroll from Gavin's front door. It was a solid, simple masonry building, with the walls faced in white stone render, and there was a solitary bench at its front.

'I'm not especially religious,' Gavin said, as they entered the church through its side door. 'But on the island we make a point of respecting people's beliefs. I quite like the fact we have our meetings in this church. Christianity has a long tradition here.'

Harrison had never been inside an active church before (Sunnyvale's control room had been thoroughly stripped and remodelled) so he had nothing to compare it with. There were long wooden benches facing a raised platform or podium, behind which there was a wooden cross on the wall. Gavin leant in and explained about the pews, the pulpit and the historical meaning of the cross. Harrison had briefly flicked through a version of the Bible in Pop's haven, but it wasn't a story he was especially familiar with.

An elderly man, dressed in a suit, stood up to the pulpit and raised his hand. The twenty or so assembled council members – all sat in the first couple of rows – abruptly ended their conversations and looked to the front. Most of them were men of at least sixty, though there were three or four younger men (around Gavin's age) and a few women. Harrison was comfortably the youngest face in the room.

'That's Peter Cunningham,' Gavin whispered. 'He's the chairman of the council.'

'Good evening everybody,' Peter said. He was tall, upright and bald, and he had a Scottish accent as thick as Gavin's.

'Welcome to the latest full council meeting. As always, we'll work through the agenda before opening the floor to general comments at the end.'

Harrison noticed a middle-aged lady, wearing tortoiseshell glasses, sat at the very end of the first pew. She was taking notes, and Gavin caught him glancing at her.

'She takes the minutes,' he said. 'She's Peter's wife. They like to think of themselves as Jura's power couple, I think.'

'Firstly,' Peter said loudly. 'We've come through the worst of the winter. We sadly lost over a dozen of our eldest inhabitants – some from natural causes, some not helped by the cold. It's a miracle we didn't lose more in the tents and shelters. It illustrates more than ever the need for us to build more homes as quickly as possible. I'll pass over to Adam for an update on that front. As ever, the raw materials and labour are the problem.'

*

Harrison listened intently for a couple of hours as the meeting progressed. He began to appreciate the efforts these councillors were putting in to keep the island going. It was an uphill battle: they faced the elements, a lack of critical resources, and uncertainty over migration numbers (newcomers could suddenly be shipped here at any point, or they could go months with nothing).

As well as dropping off people, Sunnyvale would occasionally send shipments of food and other essential materials. But these were sporadic and inconsistent, like a prisoner receiving tasteless gruel at an unspecified point in the day.

The council also faced apathy. A lot of people struggled when they got here, even if they had been so-called Luddites or rebels before their capture. They didn't want to work. What was the point? Harrison hadn't really thought about it before, but he learned that the suicide rate was high. He thanked his blessings that he had managed to get into a reasonable routine, especially since he had met Bonnie.

The meeting came to a close and they confirmed the date of their next one the following month. The hubbub of chatter restarted and a tray of soft drinks and modest snacks appeared at the back of the room.

'Help yourself, Harrison,' Gavin said. 'And then I'll

introduce you to a few people.'

Harrison got himself a plate and was soon shaking hands with Peter Cunningham.

'This is Harrison Snow,' Gavin said in introduction. 'He's been seeing Bonnie for a while, so I should dislike him, but he's a decent young man. He's been on the island over eighteen months.'

'Pleasure to meet you, Harrison,' Peter said. 'How have you adjusted to life here?'

'I've just about managed. I'm working in the school at the moment. Before that I did all sorts. I was lucky to get a room in the old hotel when I first arrived, so I can't complain.'

'Aye, it was tough out in the shelters this winter,' Peter replied. 'We do our best to help, but there's only so much we can do as a council. As you probably saw tonight, we have to make do with very little.'

'I definitely have a newfound respect for what you do,' Harrison said. 'And I'm very grateful for it.'

'You'll never guess who he's related to,' Gavin said. 'Guy Smith. You must remember him?'

Peter's eyes flashed for a moment, and Harrison couldn't quite work out whether it was with surprise, or intrigue, or something else.

'You don't say?' Peter said. 'I haven't heard that name in donkey's years. He must have been your grandfather, I presume?'

'Yeah,' Harrison said. 'Did you ever deal with him directly?'

'I never met him in person, no. But we communicated with him. He was a brave man. Is he still alive?'

'No. He died a couple of years ago. He was ninety.'

'Shame,' Peter said diplomatically. 'Anyway, it was nice to meet you Harrison. I must glad-hand a little with the others before the night is up.'

He buttoned up his suit jacket and ambled over to another councillor, who shook his hand warmly.

'He seemed a bit off about my grandad,' Harrison said to Gavin. 'Or am I just making that up?'

'I don't know,' Gavin said. 'Peter can be hard to read sometimes. But he's devoted his life to Jura and the council. He's been chairman for as long as I can remember.'

He put his arm around Harrison's shoulder in a fatherly manner. 'I had another motive for bringing you tonight, laddie,' he said. 'You're the perfect cover for having a few beers. Bonnie and the lads will think we're still at the meeting. Let's head to the bar at the old hotel.'

'If you insist,' Harrison laughed.

30

Harrison sat in his familiar stool and ordered his familiar drink. The landlord gave him a quiet nod.

'This one's on me,' Gavin said. 'To celebrate your first council meeting. Hopefully the first of many.' He slapped him on his back warmly.

'Why are you so excited about me joining you tonight?' Harrison said.

'Ah, it's just nice to see some young blood. I feel so bloody old and stale on this island sometimes. And those meetings don't help. Everybody means well but it's like a funeral parlour.

'I'm looking forward to you stirring the pot, that's all. Truth be told, I'm thinking of stepping down and recommending you take my place.'

'Why?' Harrison said. He hadn't expected this. 'What have I done to deserve it? I wouldn't know what I'm doing. I'm not qualified.'

'None of us are, laddie. We're all winging it.'

'I'm too young,' Harrison said.

'The others are too old,' Gavin replied. 'You don't have to decide now, but have a think about it.'

Harrison sat silently for a few moments. 'I know why you're doing this,' he said. 'You want me to start thinking long-term, don't you? You're worried I'm gonna break Bonnie's heart.'

Gavin laughed generously. 'You're nobody's fool, are you? There are two types of people who live here: those who can adapt, and those who can't. We try to keep things positive, but as you heard tonight there are a lot of people who struggle.

'You're a good kid. Bonnie thinks the world of you, and so do I. But sometimes I can sense the restlessness in you. It's only natural, I'm not criticising. I'm just trying to help you make peace with your situation. Being a proactive member of the council could help with that. It's all about setting long-term goals – envisioning life here in ten years, twenty years, thirty years.'

Harrison muttered platitudes but the colour had drained from his face. He was definitely content in the moment. He had adapted to island life better than many others: he enjoyed his current job, he adored Bonnie, and he felt relatively free from Sunnyvale's clutches. But Gavin's words were echoing in his head. Ten years? Twenty years? Thirty years? *Forever?*

He threw the whisky down this throat and excused himself to the toilet.

*

Instead of going to the bathroom, he walked outside for a burst of fresh air. He had felt suddenly claustrophobic in the bar, and he needed the view out to sea.

The water's calmness was normally comforting, but now it seemed only to serve as some kind of moat trapping him in. He was marooned. He was *imprisoned*. He was shocked at himself for being so rattled by a few sensible words from Gavin, but the weight of the reality was sitting on his chest.

As he tried to control his breaths, he spotted a bushy white cat in the distance, before it disappeared behind a thick-trunked tree. He had only seen it for a second or two, but it was enough to unbottle another flood of emotions and memories. *Aslan.* What had happened to Pop's cat? He had grown quite fond of him in the time he lived at the bungalow, and he had no idea of his fate.

Would his mum have spared the poor creature? Would he

have found another happy home? Or would he have been left to fend for himself on the streets? Despite the ruthlessness Sunnyvale had shown towards many humans, the thought of any callous act to a helpless cat angered him more.

He thought of the night when Aslan had brought a mouse into the bedroom, scaring him and Amberley, and of the very first time he had met the cat shortly after Pop's death. Without him he would never have discovered the haven.

This, in turn, led him to reflect on his brief but intense time with Amberley. Surely she couldn't have been the one who ratted him out? The Great Liberator had just suggested that to mess with his head, right? It could have been all of them. Or none of them. Or some of them. He couldn't trust anyone on the mainland.

But he could trust Bonnie. She was unaffected. Untainted. She was the best thing to happen to him, and he had to make it work. Could he really settle here *forever*, though? Every autumn, winter, spring and summer? Every sunset, every storm, every sleep? Every single second?

Only one thing was certain: he needed another drink.

*

Harrison and Gavin stumbled through the doorway of the terraced house, giggling and shushing one another. It was dark outside, and the street was still.

Bonnie heard the commotion and walked into the hallway in her nightie.

'The boys have school in the morning,' she said. She meant to admonish them but she couldn't help but find the scene quite comical. Gavin was struggling to untie his shoelaces, and Harrison was grinning gormlessly in her direction.

'I can smell the booze from here,' she said. 'Must have

been a long council meeting.'

'Aye,' Gavin replied, still giggling. 'It's been a tough night's work. But somebody has to do it.'

'Come on, you oafs,' she said. 'I'll get you a glass of water and then it's time for bed.'

Two minutes later, Gavin was snoring loudly on the sofa. He was fully clothed and still had one of his shoes on. Harrison was in bed with Bonnie. The room was swirling.

'Bonnie,' he whispered drunkenly.

'I'm not doing anything,' she said. 'You're too drunk and I'm up early for work. So are you.'

'Bonnie,' he whispered again.

'What?'

'I want you to run away with me. Let's get off this island. Together.' And then his head slumped on the pillow and he started to snore just as loudly as Gavin.

*

The following afternoon, Harrison was finishing his shift at the school. He walked from the classroom to the library to return a few books, where he found Bonnie slumped in one of the beanbags. She was looking listlessly out of the window, where summer was slowly becoming autumn.

'Remind me not to drink again on a weeknight,' Harrison said lightly. 'I know I should take responsibility but it was your dad's fault.' He laughed quietly but received no response.

'Are you alright?' he said.

She sighed wistfully. 'You came into my life like a whirlwind, Harrison,' she said. 'Like a prince from all the fairytales I'd read. Like a suitor from a mysterious, exotic land. But that doesn't give you the right to mess with my head.'

'What do you mean?' he said. 'Is this because I had a few

beers with your dad? It's no big deal. I thought you liked how well we got on? I couldn't say no when he insisted.'

The library was empty, apart from the two of them and the thousands of books.

'It's not that,' she said. 'It's something you said when you got back. Do you remember?'

'Ah, don't test me,' Harrison replied. 'I remember coming back, yeah. Your dad couldn't get his shoes off. I dunno what I said though.'

'You said that you wanted to run away with me. That we should get off this island. Together.'

Harrison bowed his head. 'I don't remember saying that,' he said. 'It must have been the booze talking.'

'They say a drunk mind speaks a sober heart,' she said.

'Or maybe a drunken idiot is just a drunken idiot,' he retorted.

Bonnie played with one of her pigtails and continued to stare out the window.

'It's perfectly normal for you to question things, Harrison. I have done every single day of my life. After reading *Robinson Crusoe* as a child, I dreamt of being rescued by some majestic ship. I even had an imaginary friend called Friday.'

'I'm sorry,' Harrison said.

She averted her gaze from the window and looked up at him. He was stood awkwardly by her beanbag.

'Don't be,' she said. 'We have a lot to discuss if we're going to make this happen.'

31

Harrison's first reaction was to treat her words like a joke, but then he saw the determined look in her eyes. He knew that look well; it was when Bonnie was no longer playing around.

'You can't be serious?' he said.

'Why not? For twenty years I've hidden away. I'm like Anne Frank in her attic, just with nicer scenery. I didn't sleep a wink last night after what you said. It got my imagination going.'

'Imagination is one thing, reality is another,' Harrison said.

'That's precisely my point,' she said. 'I've only ever lived in a world of imagination. I *want* the reality.'

'The reality is very dangerous,' he said.

'I know. Of course I know. I know a few other things too. I've read enough adventure books to know how your story would end. You're a man-of-action. You'd eventually grow restless here, probably after we've got married and had a few kids. You'd either drink yourself to death, or launch some valiant-but-stupid escape attempt. I'd be the stick-in-the-mud, the boring, homely island wife. You'd love me but you'd never fully settle. It would be unspoken torture for both of us.'

Harrison's silence was damning.

'That doesn't have to be our narrative,' she said. 'We can take control. We can take a chance.'

'You really mean this, don't you?'

'I do,' she said.

'What about your family? Where would we even go?'

'Somewhere. Anywhere. I don't care. I love my dad and my brothers but I'm an adult now. I can make my own choices.'

Harrison started to pace up and down the room. Bonnie continued to sit serenely in the beanbag.

'This is insane,' he said. 'The last time I rocked the boat I was caught before I could even blink. And look where that got me.'

'But if you had your time again, you'd do the same thing, wouldn't you?' she said. 'What alternative did you have?'

'This isn't the same,' he said. 'We have a life here. We can read widely, we can work honestly, we can talk freely. I sometimes struggle to picture the long-term future, but what we have right now is good. Why would we throw that away?'

'Because we're still prisoners,' she said. 'Whichever way you try to explain it, or justify it, or quantify it. We're prisoners. It's the principle.'

'Is it worth risking everything for a principle?' he said.

'I can think of no greater reason. Have you ever read about Phillis Wheatley? She was sold into slavery as a child. But her talent for poetry couldn't be stopped. We have one of her collections in this library.

'She wrote: "In every human Beast, God has implanted a Principle, which we call Love of Freedom; it is impatient of Oppressions, and pants for Deliverance."'

'That's a nice addition to quotation corner,' Harrison said. 'But what we're discussing here is different.'

'The principle underlying it is consistent,' she said. 'I am impatient of this oppression. I pant for deliverance. I'm surprised you need persuading – you've already been down this path before.'

'Which is why I'm wary now,' he said. 'What did Kipling say? "The burnt Fool's bandaged finger goes wabbling back to the Fire."'

'Another one for quotation corner,' Bonnie smiled. 'You're just as bad as me.'

'Why now?' Harrison said. 'What's changed?'

'I suppose I've always hoped, deep down, that I would be

brave enough to say it. I probably never would have if you didn't say it for me last night.'

'The mainland is as much of a prison as here,' he said. 'In fact, it's worse. Swapping a safe prison for a dangerous prison isn't exactly freedom.'

'I know,' she said. 'But it's about the journey. It's about the principle. It's about our free will.'

'I can't believe we're having this conversation,' Harrison said.

'You started it,' she said jokingly. 'If only you'd come home and whispered sweet nothings into my ear instead.'

'Never underestimate Sunnyvale,' he said. 'Your dad warned me of that. They could be listening to us right now.'

'Never underestimate Bonnie,' she replied. 'You remember how I told you this library was specially built around the time the island became exiled? Well, my dad secretly installed signal-blockers into the installation. We're safe in here.'

'Impressive,' Harrison said.

'It's another reason I come here so often,' she said. 'It's the only place I feel truly unwatched. It's my haven.'

Harrison smiled broadly. 'I know exactly how you feel. But what now? Shall I summon our private jet and have us transported to the mainland?'

'Don't be facetious,' she said. 'I don't have any substantial plans. How could I? I've never even been on the mainland. It's just an idea for now. An aspiration.'

'There's no life for us there,' he said. 'That's exactly what the Great Liberator said to me. I'd be spotted by a Stinger within five seconds and sent back here. Or worse.'

'There must be ways around it. Your grandad survived till he was ninety, right? And so did that woman you mentioned.'

'They were spared because they were old and harmless. And, for all I know, Tessa was one of them anyway. It's hard to explain unless you've been there. Sunnyvale control *everything*. It's all-consuming, all-encompassing. It's relentless.'

'There must be a way,' she said emphatically. 'Didn't your grandad work for some underground resistance? Can't we get that going again?'

'So easy to say, so difficult to do,' Harrison replied. 'We wouldn't know where to start. I'm sorry to be the killjoy, but I just can't see how we could make it work.'

Bonnie stared silently out of the window.

'Let's get through this year and see how we feel next spring,' he said. 'If you still feel the same, I promise I'll reconsider.'

*

The year passed and the fire in Bonnie still burnt brightly. It was a strange role reversal for Harrison to be the sensible one – he was used to being gung-ho – and he sometimes felt a lot older than his early twenties.

He and Bonnie had gone round in circles with the same discussions, and his conclusion was unchanged. He knew that she was right in principle – he understood the yearning more than anyone – but what could they actually do? What tangible, practical steps could they make? He exhausted himself trying to find loopholes and rabbit-out-the-hat solutions, but none were forthcoming.

They continued in their routine and – as planned – Harrison took Gavin's place as a councillor. He was the youngest one by far, and he was absorbing as much as he could in the meetings. As always, they faced an uphill battle.

Generally, his relationship with Bonnie was strong, but they also both felt a hollowness and helplessness. He was growing sick of being the wet blanket constantly putting out her fire. It had, at times, been a fractious winter.

32

It was a bright March morning when their lives took a dramatic twist. Bonnie was in the library with the youngest class of students, when one of her colleagues took her to one side.

She was informed that there had been some sort of accident at the building site where they were (slowly) constructing new homes. Both of her younger brothers – who were there on work experience – had fallen from a great height. The scaffolding they were stood on had collapsed. They had died instantly. There was nothing anybody could do.

She took the news calmly, not wanting to break down in front of the children. Only after she had been excused to go home did she collapse into a heap on the sofa. She wept and howled at the injustice of the universe, her chest heaving with sobbing breaths and her heart broken beyond repair.

*

Harrison heard the news later that day, after he had returned from a cycling trip up to the northern part of the island. He rushed first to the building site, where a group of fellow councillors had congregated around a hazard sign and an orange cone. They were deep in intense discussion. He quickly learned that the bodies had already been taken away, and so he cycled as swiftly as he could to see Bonnie.

As he arrived at the front door, he heard stumbling footsteps approaching from down the street. Gavin was teetering towards him with a near-empty bottle of whisky in his hand. His cheeks were red and blotchy, his nostrils were covered in snot, and his eyes were bloodshot and glazed over.

'I can't believe they're dead,' he cried quietly when he saw Harrison. 'My wee boys. Dead.' He took a huge, final swig from the whisky bottle and then dropped it to the floor. It smashed into pieces.

'I had to identify their bodies. No father should ever have to do that, laddie.' Harrison helped him inside and closed the door behind them.

*

The funeral was a week later. There was a respectful turn-out from the island's inhabitants, including the boys' classmates from school, and Peter Cunningham gave a short speech. It had been a battle to keep Gavin sober for the event, and his eyes were now permanently bloodshot.

Bonnie wore a black dress and carried herself with dignity. She was distraught, but she was determined to give the boys a proper farewell. She had organised the funeral – busying herself with the logistics had given her some form of focus to help distract from the sorrow.

The boys were buried, the ceremony was over, and the crowd had dispersed. Harrison walked with Bonnie back to the library, which she had been using as a base for all her planning. She took off her black, veiled hat and sighed deeply.

'And so begins the rest of our lives,' she said mournfully. Harrison helped her onto a chair and pulled one up next to her.

'You've been amazing this week,' he said. 'I don't know how you did it.'

'It was all a front. If I ever stopped to think too much I would break down.'

Gavin entered the room, ashen-faced, and kissed Bonnie on the cheek before settling into a chair.

'Bless you, Bonnie,' he said. 'Thank you for everything.'

She returned a weak smile. 'You know the worst thing about them dying?' she said reflectively. 'They never saw anything but this island. They lived their whole lives as prisoners.'

'Ah, they were happy lads, Bonnie,' Gavin said.

'I refuse to let that happen to me,' she continued. 'And I won't keep kicking the can down the road. Tomorrow is guaranteed for nobody. I want to *do* something.'

'Where's this coming from?' Gavin said. 'It must be the grief talking. I get it.'

'Dad, I've thought this my whole life. I told Harrison last year. I've tried to put it to the back of my mind, I've tried to suppress it. But I think about it every second of every day. And when I go to sleep, I dream about it.

'The boys' blood is on Sunnyvale's hands. I spoke to the construction workers and the reason the scaffolding collapsed is because of the shoddy materials we have. It was all rusty and rickety. We just don't have the resources to do these things safely. We're trying to function as some mini society but it doesn't work. It's pathetic. Everyone here is supposed to be some kind of rebel or nonconformist, and yet we all just accept our miserable fate. Enough is enough.'

Harrison leant forward in his seat. 'I agree,' he said. 'Enough is enough. I've tried to rationalise it and be grateful for what we have. I've tried to quash my natural instincts, even when my soul was screaming at me to do something. But Callum and Phil dying was a turning point for me. I want to fight back. Bonnie is right.'

Gavin looked momentarily stunned, but then he nodded his head in grim acceptance.

'I've lost my wife and my two boys. I couldn't cope with losing you as well. But I am also sick of being passive, of stumbling around like a wretched drunk.'

'It's reached the point where I'm going to do something either way,' Bonnie said. 'Whether you support me or not.' She looked at him with her determined eyes.

'Aye, well I know that look when I see it. Resistance is futile at this point. Count me in, you two. Let's give these bastards a bloody nose.'

'The problem,' Harrison said, 'is working out a first step. What can we actually do? It's tormented me for months.'

'Have you thought of harnessing the power of the council?' Gavin said. 'Take the issue to the people. As Bonnie said, this is supposed to be an island full of rebels. We can't be the only ones who have reached the end of our tether.'

'I never thought of that,' Harrison said. 'I'd always pictured it as a solo thing. That's not a bad idea.'

'Aye, make sure the next full council meeting is hosted in this library so we can talk freely. We'll have a much better chance with their help than if we act alone. We can plan it properly. And we can get a few allies on board, at the very least.'

33

A fortnight later, Harrison, Gavin and Bonnie had the platform they wanted. Harrison had managed to persuade his fellow councillors that the church should occasionally be swapped for the library as a meeting venue, just to keep things fresh. They brought across dozens of chairs from the main school, and Bonnie's stout desk would act as the pulpit.

It was a cool evening, and the sun was setting on the horizon when the meeting started. They sat through the usual formalities, led by Peter Cunningham, until they reached 'any other business' on the agenda. Harrison stood up and cleared his throat. He was wearing a smart pinstripe suit, and his wavy hair was swept neatly to one side.

'If I may have the floor for a few moments,' he said. 'I have something very serious to discuss. All I ask is that you allow me to make my statement in full before interjecting.'

The atmosphere had been stale, but the assembled councillors now realised that this would not be a typical meeting. Peter's wife even looked up from her meticulous note taking.

'I'd like to say, first of all, that I am speaking for myself, as well as on behalf of my girlfriend, Bonnie, and her father, Gavin, the former councillor. They are both in attendance this evening.' They were sat behind the councillors at the back of the room.

'They are, of course, related to the two young men who died recently. And their tragic death has prompted us to suggest some changes about the way the council, and this island, operates.

'We greatly admire the efforts of the councillors. It is not an easy job and we are grateful for your work. But we think a shift in attitude is needed. We are all too passive, too accepting and too meek. We are too defeatist. We believe it's time we started thinking of ways to fight back against the tyranny of Sunnyvale.'

An audible gasp went around the room, and Peter's wife stopped making notes altogether.

'Hold on, young man,' Peter Cunningham said loudly.

'As I said at the start, please let me finish before you interject,' Harrison said firmly.

'We are not naive,' he continued. 'I have felt the wrath of Sunnyvale, like everyone else on this island. But we shouldn't have to live like this. We don't have enough warm places for people to sleep. We lack the resources to build and improve and expand. We rely on occasional shipments from an organisation and entity that despise us. We are living in purgatory, in no-man's land. Any so-called freedom we have is an illusion, and it could be snatched from us at any point.

'At the moment, we are a thousand beaten individuals. Our spirits have been sapped. But we have the foundation, here, for a new resistance movement. We can start fighting back. Together. At the very least, we have to try.

'I know all the doubts you are already dying to voice. *What do you mean by resistance? In what form will it take? How can you be so stupid?* Our initial proposal is simple. We want the council's backing to help transport myself, Gavin and Bonnie back to the mainland. Gavin has a few contacts he thinks would take us in.

'We would lie low for a while, and then we would start distributing some of the banned books from this library. We would start organising underground meetings. We would look to build a network of resistors, just like there was a few decades ago.

'And then we would look to help more people escape from the island. It would have to be gradual, of course. And we know Jura is being monitored. But, after years of inactivity, I'm confident that Sunnyvale will be a tad complacent about us. They think they have us beaten. The Great Liberator himself told me that they "leave them to it" here.

'We realise the plan is modest, and somewhat sketchy. But great oaks from little acorns grow. We seek your support. This library has signal-blockers, so all relevant discussions would have to be kept between these walls.'

The councillors looked at the ceiling, and at each other, with confusion at this revelation. And then Peter Cunningham stood up and took his position at the desk pulpit. He started to clap sarcastically.

'Bravo, young man. Bravo,' he said. 'That was quite the speech. Top marks for effort. Unfortunately, I'm going to have to keep this discussion very brief. Your plans put everyone on this island in severe danger, and it is my duty as chairman to nip them in the bud.

'We sympathise with your recent loss. Clearly, your brains are still affected by the fog of grief. Please feel free to take a leave of absence from the next few meetings, and we look forward to welcoming you back when you are at full health.'

Harrison, who was still standing, chuckled with contempt. 'Do the other councillors not even get a say?' he said.

A white-haired man to Harrison's left stood up.

'I echo Mr Cunningham's views,' he said. 'Patience is our greatest asset. Untimely and rash actions will only worsen our situation. We have to play the long game. It may not be our generation which benefits, but we have to trust that the tide will eventually turn. Everything we've built for nearly twenty years should not be jeopardised by an impatient and impetuous young man.'

'Here, here,' a couple of voices murmured in agreement.

A middle-aged lady, wearing thick-rimmed spectacles, then stood up.

'I also concur,' she said. 'Just waking up tomorrow is an achievement for us. Every day of survival is a victory. That's how we should see it. It's not perfect, but it's survival. Years ago, many people would go their whole lives without leaving their little village. This is no different, we just need to alter our perspective.'

'Just as I expressed a moment ago,' Harrison said. 'It's all too compliant. All too defensive. All too *grateful*. And, dare I say, all a little chummy. You all have nice houses here, don't you? Why rock the boat?'

'Stop talking, laddie, before you get yourself suspended,' Cunningham said.

'Does even one person here agree with us?' Harrison implored. 'Or will you all tootle into line and follow Mr Chairman?'

A small, unassuming man sat on the edge of proceedings started to tentatively raise his hand, but he quickly dropped it when Cunningham fixed him with a glare.

'So be it,' Harrison said. 'But I encourage you all to look at the display on the wall over there. It's called quotation corner, and they've all been chosen by the children. Cast your eyes to the second quotation down, in the middle panel. For those who can't see, I'll read it out for you.

'It says: "The reward for conformity is that everyone likes you except yourself."'

34

'It was worth a try,' Gavin said, later that evening. The councillors were long gone, and moonlight was filtering through the window as they stacked the chairs and gave the room a quick tidy.

'Couldn't we try going to the people directly?' Harrison said. 'Who cares what these stuffy old councillors think?'

'It's too risky,' Gavin replied. 'We were able to control this meeting by having it here, with the signal-blockers. I don't see how we could get the message out there to everyone without arousing suspicion.'

'I just can't shake the feeling that we're missing a trick,' Harrison said. 'Of the thousand people here, surely at least a hundred or two would be on board. That would be a great start.'

'I know,' Gavin said thoughtfully. 'But our first priority has to be making a move without being detected. We can rally more people down the line. For now, the focus should be on us. We have to be selfish, at least initially.'

'When do we make this move, then?' Harrison said.

'Let's give ourselves some time to regroup,' Gavin said. 'I still think our plan is solid. We take a fishing boat at dawn and follow one of the usual fishing routes. We keep up the appearance until anyone watching loses interest. It's just another boring day on Jura. Then, in the late morning, we bolt across to Tayvallich.

'It's about an hour-long dash, north-east from here. It's easy to navigate because we'll be going up Loch Sween, which is flanked on either side by land. Once we get to Tayvallich, I have a reliable contact at the pub there. Our families go way back. I'd bet my life on him still being there.

'We'll get him to drive us up into the highlands. He has an old Range Rover and his own stash of petrol. There, I have another old contact. We'll stay for at least a few weeks in a little ramshackle farmhouse he has on his land. It's completely off the grid. And then we can plan our next move. It's not perfect but it's our best shot, given the circumstances.

'It would have been handy to have the councillors on board,' he added. 'As they may have had their own contacts and ideas. And they could have engineered some kind of distraction to help with our getaway. A fire, or something. Anything that would have consumed the attention of any man, or machine, watching us. But I'm not surprised it came to nothing.'

'Why haven't people tried escaping before?' Harrison said.

'They have,' Gavin replied. 'In the first few years, there were a handful of attempts. They all ended in failure. Bad weather, misfortune or Sunnyvale snuffing them out. You made a good point in the meeting, though. It's been a bloody long time since anyone tried. Our best hope is that they're a bit complacent.'

'It all sounds good to me,' Harrison said.

'Give me a week or two to finish working on the fishing boat,' Gavin said. 'I want to make sure it's the best-running boat on the island. We can't afford being ruined by a dodgy engine. And I've already started moving a handful of the books. I reckon we can take enough to fit in a suitcase. Other than that, we'll be travelling as lightly as possible.

'Until then, we have to keep up appearances. Go about your day-to-day business as usual. Bonnie, you have your school trip tomorrow, right? The outdoor survival course thing for the kids? You should go as planned. Pretend everything is normal.'

Bonnie was looking longingly out the window, the moonlight illuminating the soft, feminine features of her face. The light revealed a flicker of a smile.

'It feels good to be doing something proactive for once,' she said. 'Even if we didn't get the answer we wanted from the council. I feel alive. Truly alive.'

*

That night, Harrison was sleeping as well as he had done in months. Any nerves were outweighed by excitement and pride at finally doing something positive. He had yo-yoed between so many contrasting emotions since his arrival on Jura. He had felt trapped, claustrophobic and confused; and then he had forced himself, against his nature, to be sensible and accept his fate. It was psychologically exhausting.

But now his direction was clear. The competing voices on his shoulder were silenced. He just had a week or two to go before he would finally be fighting back. He was in a deep sleep in his room at the old hotel, dreaming of the Scottish highlands – the nature, the openness, the freedom – when he was forcefully awoken by a thumping hand on his shoulder.

'Harrison, Harrison, wake up!'

He opened his eyes, startled, to see the barrel-chested figure of Gavin looming over him. He grabbed Harrison by his shoulder and hauled him upright.

'What the hell?' Harrison protested. He looked at his bedside clock and saw that it was just after five o'clock. He was now stood half-naked, face-to-face with Gavin, whose eyes were wide with intensity.

'Listen to me, laddie. Just listen. I did some digging last night after our meeting. Something didn't quite feel right. I knew Peter Cunningham was a spineless, conservative old sod, but he shut us down even quicker than I expected. It got me thinking.'

'What are you on about, Gavin? Have you been drinking?'

'Just listen,' he half-whispered and half-growled. 'It niggled me so badly that I couldn't sleep. So, I thought "Fuck it". I broke into his house an hour ago to look at the council's budgetary accounts. He still keeps paper versions of everything. They all looked in order. So then I had a root around everything else in his office. He had a little compartment under one of the drawers which he must have thought was secret. This is where I found this.'

He shoved a picture in Harrison's hand. It was several decades old, judging by the full head of hair on Peter Cunningham's head. He was at some kind of formal event, perhaps a graduation. He had his arm around the shoulder of another young man, who was smiling directly at the camera. They looked like friends, at ease in one another's company.

'Don't you recognise him?' Gavin said in an exasperated tone.

'Well, yeah. That's Peter Cunningham.'

'No, no, the other one.'

Harrison did recognise the other man from somewhere, but he was too disoriented to work it out.

'Who is it, Gavin? What is all this about?'

'That's a young version of Bill Davis. Bill bloody Davis. He was the CEO of Sunnyvale until a few years ago. Before that new guy came in and changed the title to Great Liberator.'

'So Peter Cunningham was pals with the man who became the CEO of Sunnyvale?' Harrison said, with a dry mouth.

'Yep,' Gavin replied. 'And he cared enough to keep a dusty old photograph of him all these years. The man is a mole. A plant. A puppet. He has to be.'

'How long have you known Peter?' Harrison said.

'That's the first question I asked myself. And I do remember that he moved here shortly before the island became exiled. We just thought it was bad luck at the time, but now it all makes sense. What do I always say? Never underestimate

Sunnyvale. And yet that's exactly what I've done.'

Harrison swore under his breath.

'He'll have reported last night's meeting,' Gavin continued. 'I'm sure of it.'

'Where's Bonnie?' Harrison said.

'She's already gone to that school trip to the west part of the island. She went straight there from the library last night to help set things up with a colleague. She doesn't know any of this.'

'We have to get her. We have to go,' Harrison said urgently.

'I know,' Gavin replied. 'But there isn't time. That's why I came straight here. I'll go west to find Bonnie and bring her back, but it might be too late. The odds are against us. You need to go ahead, alone.'

'I'm not leaving her behind,' Harrison said.

'We have no choice, laddie. It's now or never. Grab a kayak and head for Tayvallich. Take a map and compass and head north-east – once you get into Loch Sween it's easy. When you get there, head straight to the pub near the pier and ask for Tommy. Tell him that I sent you. You'll be safe with him. Bonnie and I will come by boat as quickly as we can. We'll be right behind you. We might even be able to pick you up on the way if I find her quickly.'

'I'm not leaving her,' Harrison repeated emphatically. 'Either we all go or none of us do.'

'Listen to me, laddie. It's blown, it's over. This isn't some old war film where we all die on the hill together. You have to go *now*. There's nothing chivalrous about staying behind and getting caught too. It's time to throw caution to the wind, just go.'

'Why don't you go now and I'll find Bonnie?' Harrison said.

'That isn't an option,' he replied. 'Not after I lost my wife and the boys. I'd rather die. But one of us needs to go on. We can't all wait around like lemons for Sunnyvale to close in. It could take hours to find her – all I know is that she's somewhere inland from the west coast. Every second we natter here is a second wasted.'

'This is wrong,' Harrison said.

'We have to hedge our bets,' Gavin replied firmly. 'I'm making this decision for you, Harrison. You can't see the wood for the trees. You have to go. Get your essential equipment together. There's a kayak out front, you should be in the water in two minutes. It has to be done, laddie.'

35

Harrison slapped himself in the face to make sure it wasn't a bad dream. He sat in a red, single man kayak (it was the same one he had often used when out with Bonnie) and pushed himself off into the water, with just a small rucksack for company. The first rays of dawn were breaking through, but the island was perfectly quiet and the sea was calm.

Gavin had gone off in his fishing boat, sailing around to the western part of the island where he would pull into port and search for Bonnie. With some luck, it would be a quick job. But there was no guarantee.

Harrison tried to block the chaos from his mind and focus on his task. Gavin was right – he had to go on ahead in case the other two were caught. It was a brutal decision, but it was the right one. He moved the paddle rhythmically through the water, just as Bonnie had taught him, and was soon a good distance from land.

He resisted the temptation to turn around and take a look at the island where he had lived for two-and-a-half years. If he had, he would have been awestruck by its beauty: the dark, sloping paps overlooking the little gathering of civilisation at Craighouse shore. Regardless of the circumstances, he was grateful to have experienced living in such a beguiling place.

He paddled and paddled, and his arms and shoulders were soon starting to ache. He was constantly navigating with the map and compass (a skill which would have been completely beyond him before his time on the island) easing into a north-easterly direction.

He passed lumps of uninhabited, rocky land, and forced himself not to think about the perils of a wrong turn. The vastness of the ocean was just waiting to swallow him up if he erred. Mercifully, it remained calm and steady.

The furthest he had ever done in a kayak in one day was about twenty kilometres, and he knew this would be a longer journey than that. He would have to draw on every reserve of strength and fortitude to make it. Despite the danger and the pressure, he was surprisingly calm. His breathing was steady, and he tried to zone out into a state of relaxed, but total, concentration.

As he paddled and swept and edged his way forward, some ancient instinct forced him to look back. He swivelled his neck. Jura was now just a distant speck, and thick, black smoke was billowing high into the air, far above its imposing paps.

Fire. A distraction, perhaps. Just as Gavin had mentioned. But why would he start one now? Did it mean he was on his way with Bonnie, and he needed the cover? Or that they'd already been caught, and it was his last-ditch attempt to buy Harrison some time? He couldn't work out which was most likely. The possibilities tormented him, but he forced himself to banish all speculation from his mind. He just had to keep going.

He had brought a large bottle of water and a bunch of bananas with him, which he would have to ration throughout the journey. It was going to be a marathon.

*

The hours slowly ticked by, and Harrison was being pushed to his mental and physical limits. His upper body muscles were burning with fatigue. The weather was in his favour – it was a warmer-than-average March day – but there had been no sign of Gavin's fishing boat. He refused to dwell on what this might mean.

He was dreading some hint that Sunnyvale were onto him.

It was, he had always thought, the biggest flaw of Gavin's initial plan. Surely they couldn't just sail straight to the mainland in a fishing boat without being seen? He knew as well as anybody the fearsome technology that Sunnyvale possessed. But he took hope from the fact that he had got this far. The fire may have been a sufficient distraction – he could imagine an office full of Sunnyvale employees watching the scenes through some satellite drone, and failing to notice this tiny red speck moving north-eastward.

He managed to bring the kayak to a halt at the tip of a big lump of rock. According to his map, this was just about at the entranceway of Loch Sween. As Gavin had described, this was flanked on both sides by the mainland, and it would be much easier to navigate from here. There was still a considerable distance to go, but he just had to continue north to Tayvallich. The most perilous part of the journey was over.

He hauled himself and the kayak onto the rock's surface, and flopped down. He lay, spread-eagled, and allowed himself to close his eyes. He could scarcely lift his arms above his head. *Ten minutes*, he said to himself. Ten minutes, and then back to it.

*

The rest was both helpful and unhelpful. It gave him a fresh burst of mental energy, but his sore muscles had seized up. It took an almighty effort to shuffle back into the water. Once he was paddling again, though, his brain and his body fell into sync, and he was on his way.

The land flanking the loch was his first view of the mainland since he had been exiled. It was an exhilarating feeling, but he knew it would all count for nothing unless he could be taken in at the pub in Tayvallich. With each stroke, he was closer to his goal, but it was all so tenuous.

His arms and shoulders were burning again, and he started to rally himself under his breath.

'Come on,' he said. 'Cowards die many times before their deaths. The valiant never taste of death but once.'

Then, a few minutes later, he recited the verse from the Robert Frost poem:

> *I shall be telling this with a sigh*
> *Somewhere ages and ages hence:*
> *Two roads diverged in a wood, and I—*
> *I took the one less traveled by,*
> *And that has made all the difference.*

He laughed to himself as he remembered the absurdity of Pop's plans for Operation Neo, realising that he was now doing something similar. If anything, this plan was even more brazen. He was well aware that some (including the Great Liberator) would call it stupid.

But on he went, pushing through the sapping fatigue with nothing but willpower. He was so exhausted that he was now experiencing something close to euphoria.

His mind flashed back to when he had first heard of Pop's death, as a floppy-haired, spoiled layabout. He had come so far since then. He recalled his first meeting with Bonnie – when he had woken to an angel – and their subsequent guitar lessons. He pictured her dark hair, in pigtails, and her determined eyes, and the yellow guitar pick she wore as a necklace.

She was a free spirit, like him, and the thought of her powered him on towards Tayvallich. According to his map, he was very nearly there.

36

There was a large enclave of water to Harrison's left, in the distance, which looked like it may serve as Tayvallich's port. There were fishing boats of all shapes and sizes, and a smattering of activity on the small pier. It was very picturesque. It was now the late afternoon, and Harrison had, quite literally, been kayaking all day. The euphoria had given way to severe pain and discomfort. He desperately needed some food and at least twelve hours of sleep.

He angled the kayak towards the port, which was about a kilometre away. He hoped for a final burst of energy, but the well was completely dry. His body had been pushed further than ever before, and it was now starting to shut down.

He was close, so close.

Suddenly, a familiar sound filled the sky. In Harrison's dehydrated and confused state, he wasn't sure whether he was imagining it. But then it grew louder. It was an ominous buzzing sound.

A Stinger emerged from nowhere – it was a slight speck in the distance and then, within seconds, it was hovering directly above him. It was quickly followed by another, and then another, and then a huge swarm of them flew noisily towards Harrison, who sat helplessly in his kayak. There were dozens, and then there were hundreds, until it seemed the whole sky was blotted out by these ugly machines.

Harrison held both arms out by his side.

'Is that all you've got?' he shouted belligerently.

He reached into his rucksack and took out an empty banana skin, which he promptly threw high at the Stingers. It stuck to the surface of one of them. Then he did the same with his water bottle, which bounced harmlessly off.

He screamed in anger and frustration, and some confrontational instinct urged him to stand up in his kayak to throw the rucksack itself at the Stingers.

His mind was clouded with fury and fatigue. He clumsily attempted to haul himself to his feet when suddenly, violently, the kayak capsized. Harrison was swept underwater in an instant. His mouth was open as he fell below the surface, and he swallowed a lungful of ice-cold sea water.

He was struggling with all his might, but the paddle leash had caught on one of his trainers and was trapping him underwater. It was viciously cold, and Harrison's brain was flooded with panic. He wriggled and wrestled with all his might, but he couldn't free himself. The more he strained, the more water he swallowed. With frightening speed, the last remnants of fight were draining from his exhausted body.

A couple of old fishermen by the pier had watched the swarm of Stingers arrive and had seen the bizarre commotion, and they rushed to untie the ropes tethering their boat to shore. Their progress was agonisingly slow. It took them more than five minutes to release the boat and to navigate it into the right spot so they could reach him, about a kilometre from land.

One of them jumped into the water and lifted Harrison's head above the surface. He then unhooked the foot from the paddle leash and swam them both towards the boat, where his colleague helped haul the freezing-cold body aboard.

They cleared some space on the floor of the boat, kicking aside fishing nets and boxes, and immediately began pumping Harrison's chest. Sea water spewed from his mouth, and the second fisherman vigorously applied CPR. The Stingers still hovered overhead.

Pump. Pump. Pump. He crudely applied as much force as he could in hope of a reaction – occasionally trying mouth-to-mouth resuscitation – as the other fisherman radioed for professional help. He pumped valiantly for five minutes, ten minutes, fifteen minutes. Sweat poured from his furrowed brow, and his chest heaved with exertion, as he worked maniacally to somehow save this poor young man.

But his brave efforts were futile. The body was cold, pale and lifeless. Harrison Snow was dead.

37

One week later

It was a drab and drizzly day in York. Alexa Snow was sat in her spectacular office, her appearance immaculately groomed and manicured. She was conversing with her husband, Elliot Patrick, who was standing by her side in jeans and a Sunnyvale T-shirt.

Beyond the office's high walls, the worker bees were grafting as diligently as ever. She was still running a tight ship, and the pace of Sunnyvale's production and distribution was uniformly relentless.

They were a couple who were always in control. Unruffled. Unflustered. Unflappable. But they both received the shock of their lives when a figure knocked on the office door and entered the room. They couldn't believe it was him.

*

The Great Liberator stepped into the old Chapter House and offered a warm greeting. His steps echoed on the tiled floor, and he took a seat opposite Alexa's desk. The muscle-bound aide kept watch from the door. Alexa and Elliot were uncharacteristically speechless.

'I hope you don't mind me dropping in like this,' he said in his friendly, avuncular manner. He was wearing blue jeans, a black jumper and loafers (as well as his ever-present beret).

'I was on vacation in London with my family, and I thought we could incorporate a visit to York. I liked it here a couple of years ago, but I didn't get chance to see too much. I was off and away as soon as I'd finished my speech.'

'Of course we don't mind,' Alexa stuttered. 'It's a pleasure to host you, sir. Any time. Would you like a drink?'

'No, thank you. I must confess I also have an ulterior motive for coming here,' he said. 'I have some news to pass on to you, Alexa.'

He leant forward in his chair and fiddled with his black beret. He fixed her with his piercing green eyes.

'I'm sorry to tell you that Harrison is dead. He got close to a native family on Jura and they concocted some hare-brained plot to escape. He attempted to kayak all the way to the mainland, but he came into some difficulty and drowned.'

Alexa closed her eyes and remained perfectly still for over half a minute. Then she took a deep breath.

'I gave him every opportunity,' she said. 'I couldn't have done any more.'

The Great Liberator nodded dolefully.

'It doesn't surprise me,' Elliot chipped in. 'Once a problem, always a problem. What happened to the other escapees?'

'They never made it off the island,' the Great Liberator said. 'They were apprehended before they could set off. One of them started a fire, though, which is why Harrison was able to get away. We fell for the distraction like amateurs. Even our most advanced technology was drawn towards it.

'Harrison was actually very close to making it to the mainland. We'd have caught up with him eventually, but it's rather embarrassing that this has happened. It led to some heated discussions about our island experiment.'

'What were the conclusions?' Elliot said.

'It's time to shut it down,' the Great Liberator replied. 'I was never a huge fan of the concept anyway. It was conceived, of course, by my predecessor. Put all our bad eggs in one basket. Contain them, observe them. Learn what we can to improve our effectiveness in stamping out all opposition.

'But it has long outserved its purpose. Truth be told, it was surprising how compliant these supposed rebels were. Most of them just wanted a quiet life. It's probably why we grew so complacent about attempted escapes.

'Anyway, it's time to shut it down, like some maladaptive computer programme. It's not worth the time and hassle anymore. Harrison has done us a favour, in that sense.'

'They'll all be liquidated?' Elliot said.

'Correct,' the Great Liberator replied simply.

'What happened to Harrison's body?' Alexa said.

'We cremated it.'

She closed her eyes again and took another deep breath.

'For what it's worth,' the Great Liberator said. 'I found him to be an engaging and articulate young man. He could have gone far with us. But he chose the wrong road.'

The room was silent for several moments. Drizzle continued to drum lightly on the office's stained-glass windows.

'Thank you for letting me know to my face,' Alexa said.

'I have one more thing to add,' he said. 'And then I really must get back to my family.'

He leant back in his chair and crossed his legs.

'This job is deceptively draining. I envisaged doing it for many years, but I'm already starting to miss the golf course. And my wife is sick of me never being home.

'As such, I'm planning to step down at the end of next year. I've successfully overseen the beginning of the Sunnyvale Era, but it's time for some new blood to drive us forward.'

He prodded his sleek, horn-rimmed spectacles, sitting atop his small, feminine nose.

'Elliot, I'm going to be recommending that you succeed

me as the Great Liberator.'

Elliot Patrick's thin eyes narrowed, and an ambitious smile spread across his face.

'It would be an honour, sir,' he replied, in his nasally voice.

Printed in Great Britain
by Amazon